IN STRICT CONFIDENCE

DWAYNE JOSEPH

bgp
BROWN GIRLS PUBLISHING

Houston, Texas • Washington, DC

This book is a work of fiction. Names, characters, places and incidents are products of the author's imagination or are used fictitiously. Any resemblance to actual events or locales or persons, living, dead, or somewhere in between, is entirely coincidental

Brown Girls Publishing, LLC
www.browngirlspublishing.com

First Brown Girls Publishing, LLC trade printing February 2014
ISBN: 978-1-6251736-8-3

Cover and Interior design by: Jessica Tilles/TWA Solutions.com

Manufactured and Printed in the United States of America

For the fans. For letting me know my hard work was appreciated.

ACKNOWLEDGMENTS

Mystery suspense. This is a love of mine. I love the complexities of the tales. I love the drama that unfolds. More than anything I have written in the past, this novel that you are holding is by far the most special to me. I was twenty-two years old when this tale popped into my head. At thirty-nine now it is truly an incredible accomplishment for me. I've never done as much research on a novel as I had to do for this one. From talking to police officers, to sitting with two thick books on police procedures and forensics, to sitting in the Barnes and Nobles café with a book on trauma and psychiatry…this book made me work and I'm glad it did! It was challenging and I enjoyed stepping up to the plate and making it happen.

Readers…wow….can't believe it's been over two years since I've written anything. I can't thank you enough for continuing to let me know that you all were still out there still believing in my work.

My sincerest appreciations: Lord…what You mean to me is almost hard to put into words. There is but one way and that is your way. Thank you for the fires you've taken me through. Thank you for constantly being there. To my wife, Wendy…what can I say but I love you. You have my back like no other. To my kids, Tati, Nati, X…I love you guys and I'm so proud of everything you do. My family…I miss and love you guys. To my Chi-town family… Levid, D (Team Leiva), Cris, Tino, Pep, Lisa, Lissy, Rebecca, Cookie and all of the kids… Have I ever not known you guys! Love you for real! My friends…Chris, Lisa, Gregg, Kristie, Brian, Micah, Tiffany, Tho, Sathy, Long Le(man you let me borrow your science fiction book back when we were teenagers and from there a love of books spawned. Writing came after that) Thank you guys for being the best.

To the book clubs…. I'm back!

A special shout to my peeps, Peron Long, Anna J, La Jill Hunt, Eric Pete…keep doing great things!

Lastly to Victoria Christopher Murray and ReShonda Tate Billingsley… I thank you two from the bottom of my heart for helping me to fall in love with writing again. Thank you both for believing in this book and believing that it could have an audience. Thank you also for believing in my talent. I am so ready to do this! Finally no Dwayne Joseph book would be complete without a shout out to my New York Giants… it will always and forever be about Big Blue!

Much love to all….now get to reading!
Dwayne Joseph

Dsjose24@yahoo.com
www.facebook.com/Dwayne.S.Joseph

Prologue

Chris Kline's eyes fluttered open and he saw only darkness. He was lying on a cold, hard ground—concrete, he thought, naked—no wait, not naked. He still had his boxer briefs on. He sat up and as he did, a wave of unsteadiness came over him. *Whoa.* He shook his head, trying to clear cobwebs, and when his equilibrium settled enough, he tried to stand, but couldn't because of a manacle fastened around his right ankle. He shivered.

Where am I?

What's going on?

Think, Chris. Think!

Chris trembled again. He wrapped his arms around himself and tried to focus in on the darkness around him, trying to make out something, anything. A window, a door. But he could see nothing but darkness.

He shivered again. He was cold. So, so cold. Where were his clothes? Where was he? Where was his…

A breathe of air caught in his throat. In the confusion he'd forgotten all about his little brother, Chad. Where was he? They were together, weren't they?

Think, Chris. Think!

Where were they last?

Chris shook again and blinked his eyes and tried to remember the last thing he could. School. No—after school. He and Chad walking home. It was cold and windy. A typical late October afternoon. They were hurrying, trying to get home to watch *Legend of Korra* on Disney XD, when something happened.

What?

Think, Chris.

Crisp air. No one around. Everyone inside but them. But soon they were going to be inside, too. They just had two more blocks to go.

But then…

Think!

But then…a car pulled up at the curb beside them. It was a black car, kind of like the ones the cops on the TV shows drove. Chad hadn't noticed the car. He'd been too into his Nintendo DS, playing Mario Go Kart. Had he not been playing, he still wouldn't have noticed anything. He never paid attention to his surroundings. Not the way Chris always did.

Chris saw the car slow down, saw the driver's side window go down. He put his hand on his brother's shoulder. Was about to tell him to run when the driver called Chris' name.

Then what happened?

Chris shivered again. God it was so freaking cold. The air, the ground. What the hell had happened to his clothes? How did he get that way? And where the hell was Chad?

Think!

The window to the black car went down. The driver called his name. Then said Chad's name. Then stuck his hand out and showed them a badge, and said that something had happened to their parents. That they'd been in an accident, and that he was the police officer who'd been sent to get them, to take them to the hospital to see their mom and dad.

Chris thought about not going with him, but Chad began to cry for his mommy and daddy. God he was such a baby sometimes.

The police officer smiled and reassured Chad that his mommy and daddy were okay, and said that the sooner they got in, the sooner they'd see them. Chris looked at the officer. He had straight, dark eyes. Eyes that he didn't trust. Eyes that seemed to hide something. Chris loved cop dramas on TV and he'd seen a lot of episodes with kids getting into cars with cops who had suspicious, dark eyes. Nine times out of ten, the kids were never heard from again.

He was about to ask what hospital his parents were in, but before he could, Chad ran to the cop's car, pulled the passenger door open, and got in. Chris called out his brother's name, went to the car and opened the door. He was about to yank him out of the car, but as he reached for his brother's collar, something hot, searing and electric jolted through his body. Seconds later, he fell into the car, unable to move, unable to scream. His eyes felt heavy as his vision became blurred. He tried to keep them open, but they felt as though lead weights had been tied to them, and so slowly they closed, and as they did, he saw the cop lean toward Chad. Seconds later, Chad slumped over on to his side.

Chris' eyes closed after that.

Then, they opened to darkness and his clothes were gone. And his brother…

Chris heard whimpering suddenly. It sounded like someone crying. Whoever it was…they were close. Very close. A few feet away. Across from him somewhere.

Chris tried to peer into the darkness to see who it was that had been whimpering. Their voice…it sounded familiar. "Chad…is that you?"

The voice whimpered again, then said faintly, "Ch…Chris?"

Chris' heart beat heavily. "Chad! Are you hurt?"

"I…I can't get up, Chris. There's a chain around my ankle."

"I know," Chris said. "There's one around mine, too."

"I'm cold. I have no clothes on. I…I can't see."

Chris grabbed the manacle and tried to force it down from around his ankle to no avail.

"I'm scared, Chris," Chad said, his voice beginning to crack.

Chris exhaled. He was scared too. Deathly afraid. "Everything's going to be alright," he said, trying to believe his own words.

"I…I want Mommy and Daddy," Chad said, beginning to sob.

Chris squirmed. Tried to get his ankle free again, then tried to stand. He needed to get over to his little brother. "Calm down, Chad," he said trying like hell to do that very thing. "Just calm down."

"Where are we, Chris? Where's Mommy and Daddy?"

Chris grabbed the chain and pulled on it.

Chad began to cry harder, louder. "Chris…help me!"

Shut up, Chad! This is all your fault. If only you hadn't gotten into the damn car. Chris wanted to yell that and more. But his brother was scared, terrified. He couldn't lose it.

He fought with the manacle again, felt his bare skin burn as he squirmed on the concrete.

Chad continued to cry. Continued to call for help. To say how scared he was.

Chris shook his head. He should have dragged his brother by the hand and made them run the minute the car's windows began to slide down. Chris tried to pry his ankle free again, and when he once again got nowhere, he did the only thing he could. He screamed for help.

Gwenn was determined. She was going to hit fifteen miles. She had wanted to ride earlier in the day, but she had to work overtime to take care of an issue with a client's network. Riding at night was something she didn't enjoy doing, but the iron-woman marathon was four months away and work had been getting in the way lately. So she had no choice but to ride. At least there were light posts along the path.

Gwenn pumped her legs. She was sweating profusely and breathing hard and she loved it. She was going to finish this time! She wasn't going to give in to the fatigue and the cramping. She was going to show her ex - the asshole that he was - that he was wrong. She could see things through to the end.

She worked her legs. Right. Left. Right. Left. She was in a zone, seeing nothing but the finish line, the cold air feeling like a summer breeze across her face. Fifteen miles today. Sixteen by the end of the week. Next week she would hit twenty.

Right leg.

Left leg.

Ignore the dips and bends along the trail. Ignore the small twigs and fallen leaves.

Ignore the…

Gwenn was falling suddenly. Head first, her arms flailed out in front of her. She had hit something.

She fell hard, her bike missing her by inches. She cringed as she felt a sting in her elbow and her knee. *Thank God* for helmets, she thought.

She frowned and rolled over, hoping that despite the pain, she would be okay to continue on. She hoped her bike would be, too.

"Dammit," she whispered.

She looked around. Fortunately, no one had seen her tumble. She frowned again and put her palms down flat on the hard grass. She had fallen just off to the side of the bike trail. She was preparing to push herself up when her fingers touched something cold, fleshy. "Just great," she said. She must have landed by a dead animal.

She made a face and looked to see what it was that her fingers had touched. No smell. *At least it wasn't a skunk*, she thought.

And then she screamed.

Beside her, half of his face shrouded in darkness, the other half lit by the light posts, his eyes lifeless, was a little boy with a light-blue pacifier in his mouth.

Chapter 1

Cigarette smoke drifted in movie-like slow motion. Thick. Like gaseous dirty cotton. It wafted around the lacquered bookshelf consumed by Freud, Nitschke and other prominent psychiatric minds. It hovered over the maple desk systematically littered with folders, loose papers, pens and pencils. It sighed within the creases and folds of the expensive beige leather loveseat and chaise lounge.

With the light being supplied by only a small desk lamp sitting toward the edge of the desk, the room was unnervingly dark, ominous. It made the smoke appear more noxious.

Allen Kline sat behind his desk, his face illuminated by the dull glow of the lamp, but at that particular moment, he wasn't really sitting there at all.

He was somewhere far away, wearing a white linen top, with beige linen pants, barefoot, sitting on a checkered blanket with his wife, a picnic basket beside them, in a field of green grass littered with dandelions. Sweet scents of jasmine and summertime floated around them. In this place, blue jays and red cardinals fluttered around and sang sweet melodies that tickled the caverns in his ears from trees full with green leaves and strong branches. In this paradise, the sky was sea-blue, the clouds flawless white, and Allen could breathe in and out and swallow the serenity of it all without gagging or coughing.

He felt compelled to do so, and he did. He took a deep breath and let the clean air sit inside of his lungs. He leaned back. Lay his head on his wife's lap. Looked up into her small, beautiful blue eyes and smiled at her.

She smiled back, then leaned down and kissed him softly on his lips. Allen mmmm'd. He loved her kisses. Adored the feel of her lips. They'd been what had sealed the deal for him. Her lips. He'd never felt lips as soft as hers before, and he'd never missed a pair of lips the way he had when she'd stepped back after their first kiss.

His wife pulled back and smiled her sweet smile at him and then looked to her right and watched their sons toss a football back and forth. He turned his head, too to stare at them. Ten and thirteen, they were typical boys. He watched them play catch for a minute or two with a wide smile spread across his face, and then turned, stretched out his arms and looked up at the pristine blue sky, and let the sun's rays wash over him.

This, he thought with a satisfied exhale, was nirvana. He took another deep inhale through his nostrils, but instead of the breathing in clean, pure air, he began to gasp.

Something was wrong.

The serenity…it was disappearing. The peace, once calm and still, was now dancing on the very edge of his fingertips.

Nirvana was drifting away.

Allen begged it not to go. Begged for its company to remain. He tried to breathe the air in again, but this time the flavor was bitter and dry. He gagged as his linen top disappeared suddenly and became a wool turtleneck. His beige linen pants became black cotton slacks. His feet, no longer bare, were covered by black shoes made by Sketchers.

Blue sky turned grey. Green and yellows leaves swirled together to become a putrid mustard tone. His wife screamed. He looked to her. Watched helplessly as her long, brown hair fell to the ground, while her eyes hollowed out, and her beautiful lips disappeared as her skin shriveled.

Allen reached for her as she screamed out again. He reached and grabbed not shriveled skin, but bones. He called out her name. Held onto her bones tightly, prayed for the horror, the hell he was experiencing to change, to go away. But it didn't. With a final cry, his wife's bones became dust and sifted down through his arms. Allen screamed as the once calm wind whipped up into a frenzied tornado and carried her ashes away. He cried as his sons disappeared into the tornado's funnel as well, leaving him alone with the birds' blissful compositions from the trees, which had become distorted notes of fear, as reality punched him viciously in his mouth.

Heaven was gone.

Allen sat stone-still and breathed slowly, doing the best he could to keep his composure.

"I…I see you're smoking now, Patrick."

Sitting in a chair on the opposite side of the desk, Patrick, took a long drag on his cigarette, held smoke in his lungs for a moment, and then blew out a long stream of cancerous air. "Yes. I am," he said, his tone matter of fact.

"You never have before."

Another deep pull and then release. "It's something new I've picked up."

Allen fought the urge to cough. "Something new. Any particular reason?"

Patrick shook his Yankee baseball cap covered head. "No. I just decided to do it."

"People often smoke to relieve tension or to ease stress. Are you stressed? Is what you do getting to you?"

The corner of Patrick's mouth rose up into a smug smile. "Not at all, Allen. Do you think it should?"

Allen swallowed nicotine-laced saliva. "You kill adolescent boys, Patrick. Don't you think it should get to you?"

Patrick flashed his smile again and sat still. Despite the jet-black aviator shades that concealed his eyes, Allen could tell Patrick was staring at him. Seconds went by without a response, and then Patrick said, "What I do is necessary, Allen. I've told you that before."

"Yes you have expressed that to me, but you've never told me how your killing is necessary."

Patrick straightened himself in the chair, took a long drag on his cigarette again, held it, and then instead of blowing the smoke up into the air, he leaned forward and blew a stream directly into Allen's face.

Allen tried not to, but he couldn't help it; he gagged and coughed.

Patrick chuckled. "Don't you like the smoke, Allen?"

Allen coughed several times and when his fit passed, he shook his head and said, "No. I don't."

"Why not?"

"I don't like the smell or the taste it leaves in my mouth."

"I look pretty sophisticated with this cigarette, don't you think?"

"Not particularly. It's hard to find anything appealing or sophisticated about something that could...kill you."

"I guess I'm not very interesting to you then, because I could kill you, too. Isn't that right? As a matter of fact, I could kill you two times, couldn't I?"

Fear gripped Allen's throat as he sat stone still, while his heart hammered and a chill originating from the base of his spine, crept up his back.

He could die two times.

Allen's heartbeat pounded at the inside of his chest. Sweat trickled down from his temples. It ran down the middle of his back and chest, and pooled at his armpits, despite the Degree antiperspirant he'd caked on that morning.

"Couldn't I, Allen?"

Allen swallowed saliva that hadn't formed and gave a slight nod. "Yes..." he paused, looked at Patrick intently and then continued. "Yes... you could."

Patrick smiled. It was evil and filled with absolute truth. "Yes I could," he said smoothly. He took another pull on his cigarette and let the smoke sift around in his lung cavity before blowing it out. "Tell me, Allen...do you think about that every day?"

Allen took a short, shallow breath. "Is that what you want me to do? Think about it every day?"

"Do you?"

Allen stared at the man, whose face he'd never fully seen, and said very honestly, "Yes. I do."

Patrick flashed a smile again. Brad Pitt in the most devilish fashion.

"You like that, don't you?" Allen asked. "I'm afraid. Very afraid, and that pleases you."

Patrick took another drag on his cancer stick, exhaled and said, "Of course I do, Allen. I guess that makes me narcissistic, huh?"

"Do you think you are?"

"I love myself. I love to be in control."

"You enjoy manipulating others," Allen chimed in.

Another smile. "Yes. I do. I guess I must be narcissistic then. Is that your diagnosis, doc?"

"I would say that you are."

"You know me well, Allen."

"I…I don't think so."

Patrick took another drag, blew it out into Allen's face. "Oh sure you do, Allen. I'd say you know me very well."

Allen watched him closely. There'd been something in his voice… something telling, as though his words had meant much more. "What makes you say that?"

"You know I'm a man of my word, Allen. No one else knows that when I say I will do something, I will do it without hesitation, without remorse. If I say that I'll kill your two boys, you know that I'll do it without so much as breaking a sweat. Right, Allen? Don't you know that about me?"

A shiver came over Allen as he thought about how different his life had been just one week ago. He'd been a psychiatrist with a thriving private practice. His latest self-help book had cracked the top ten on the New York Times bestseller list, and was in its' fourth printing. His oldest son told him that he wanted to follow in his footsteps, while his youngest son confessed that he wanted to be the next Eli Manning. One week ago, life for Allen Kline was perfect, or as perfect as it could possibly be. And then, Patrick walked into his life and snatched that perfection away with a photograph and a promise.

Allen nodded slowly. "Yes," he said his tone thick with dread. "I do know that about you."

Patrick took another long pull and blew it out slowly. "See, Allen. No one knows me like you do."

"Why? Why are you doing this to me, Patrick?" Allen asked, tears welling in his eyes and threatening to fall. "What have I ever done to you?"

"You've done enough, Allen. You've done enough."

Allen shook his head. "I…I haven't done anything."

"Oh, yes you have."

"Tell me," Allen begged. "Tell me what I've done."

"Not now, Allen. Not yet."

Allen's bottom lip quivered. "Pl... Please, Patrick. Please…please let my boys go. I…I promise, I'll make amends for whatever it is that I've done."

Patrick took a drag on his cigarette, exhaled. "I don't believe you, Allen."

"I…I promise I will," Allen insisted.

Patrick took another long pull on his cigarette. Through clenched teeth he said, "You're a fucking liar, Allen."

Allen shook his head. "I…I'm not lying. I swear to you. I'll make amends. Just let my boys go. Please!"

"Stop begging, Allen. It's fucking pathetic."

"I…I just want you to let my sons go."

"Stop begging," Patrick ordered again, his tone acerbic. "Stop begging or you will never see your sons again. Do you understand?"

Allen trembled as another chill came over him. He nodded slowly and with barely a voice, said, "Y…yes."

Patrick smiled, took another angry pull on his cigarette, leaned forward in his chair, exhaled a cloud of smoke and pointed a gloved index finger at the psychiatrist. "If your sons die, Allen, it will be your fault. Do you get that?"

Allen nodded again. "Y…yes."

"Good." Patrick inhaled on his cigarette, outed it on the desktop as he blew out a plume of smoke, and then put the butt into his mouth and swallowed. For several long, tense silence seconds, he sat staring at Allen through his shades. Allen wanted to cry, to scream for help, but he knew his screaming would go unheard, and so he sat motionless, silent.

"I killed another boy, Allen," Patrick said, his tone suddenly calm. "I made him do horrible, indecent things to me and then I strangled him and stared at him and watched him die, just like I did with the others." He paused to let his words sink in and then continued. "Don't you want to ask me why I do it, Allen?"

Allen took a short, cautious breath. He didn't want to ask at all, but he had to. It was part of the game Patrick demanded that he play. "Why…why do you do it?" he asked, his voice weak, faltering.

"I do it because I can," Patrick said, sitting back in his seat. "I do it because they deserve it."

"Why? What…what have these boys done?"

Without warning, Patrick sprang forward from the chair and slammed his hand down on the desktop. "They're guilty, Allen! They're all fucking guilty!"

"Guilty of what?"

"Of being weak little fucks!"

"Weak? How?"

Patrick rose from his chair suddenly, and Allen instinctively shrank back against the leather in his.

Patrick looked down at him and smiled. "Our session's over Allen."

"Over? But…but you haven't explained. How are the boys weak? What have they done?"

Looking down on him, Patrick shook his head. "Some other time, Allen. I have things to do." He smiled his cold smile and then turned and headed for the door.

"Are…are you going to kill again?" Allen asked, not wanting the answer he'd already known was coming.

His back to the psychologist, Patrick answered, "Of course I am."

"When…when will you stop? How many more guilty boys are out there?"

Patrick placed his gloved hand around the doorknob of the door and then turned slightly and looked at Allen over his shoulder. "Oh there are plenty of guilty boys, Allen. But if I were you, I wouldn't worry about that right now." Nothing else needing to be said, Patrick pulled open the door and walked out as soundlessly as he'd come in.

In his chair, Allen Kline slumped forward, rested his elbows on his knees and buried his face in his hands, and cried hard tears for several seconds before he screamed out, slammed both of his fists down on his desktop and then violently swept the papers, folders, pens and pencils from atop it. He yelled out again and then lashed out on the lamp, sending it crashing to the ground, too, leaving him in total darkness.

Another child was going to die and for the sake of his boys, he would do nothing to prevent it from happening.

"God forgive me," he whispered. "God forgive me."

Chapter 2

Ben McCallum stood stoically in front of his window and watched, without any real focus, the everyday commotion occurring along Rivers Street. It was chilly—about forty degrees. People hustled down the block, their coats zipped up to their necks and their hands clamped down on top of their heads, determined to keep the wind from taking their hats away.

Ben sighed.

He wasn't ready. It was too soon. His wounds were still fresh. Blood was still flowing from them.

He wasn't ready, but he'd insisted that he was, not because he wanted to, but rather because he'd had to. He was needed. Not necessarily wanted, but needed.

He sighed again and removed a cigarette from a half-empty pack sitting in his breast pocket. He lit it, took a long, slow, deep inhale and let the smoke sit in his lungs. He'd quit smoking six months ago. Cold turkey. It was a promise he'd made, and it had been an easy one to fulfill and keep because of who he'd made the promise to.

But things were different now.

He blew out a stream of smoke and felt a little more of his soul sigh away with the cancerous air. He took another puff. Soon he would have no more soul left, and then his transformation to becoming the walking dead would be complete. Only then could he hope to feel no more pain. Only then could he pray that the nightmares would leave him alone. He was anxious for that day to come. He was tired of hurting. Tired of remembering. Tired of forcing himself to move on.

Tired.

He took another pull on his Newport, held it in for a brief second, and then let it out. As he did, he caught a quick glimpse of himself in the glass of the window. Eyes, burdened with heavy bags. Cheeks sunken in. A five o'clock shadow now at seven o'clock. Hair in need of a trim. Shoulders sagging. A shell of the man that he used to be. That's who stood before him in the dirty glass. A shell. Someone he was recognizing less and less.

He took a final pull on the cigarette and then outed it on the windowsill. He pulled another one from the pack, lit it, and repeated the process of killing himself slowly all over again. He'd gone from quitting to smoking two packs a day. Maybe someday he'd find the will and desire to quit again, although he highly doubted it.

Ben frowned at the man in the mirror, turned and walked out of the small sitting room he had been standing in and went into his living room. There, waiting for him, scattered across his coffee table, was a stack of papers he wanted to shred into tiny pieces. He shook his head. Six months ago, he'd been able to make and keep his promises. Six months ago, the papers unmercifully waiting for him had been non-existent. Six months ago.

Things were just too goddamned different now. Too goddamned unfair.

He walked over to his couch and sat down heavily, sighing along with the cushion. He set his cigarette in the ashtray and picked up a pen manufactured by Bic with black ink to make everything official. He gripped the pen tightly in his hand, feeling as though he'd break it in half, and looked over at one of the small windows. Somewhere out there in the unforgiving cold was a murderer.

His son's murderer.

Ben clenched his jaws. It shouldn't have happened. His son should have never died. He was a cop, goddammit. He put his neck on the line every single day, trying to protect the innocent, trying to bring injustice to those who'd been wronged. He was a fucking hero without the super powers. His son shouldn't be dead!

Ben tossed the pen angrily across the room, clamped his hand over his forehead and squeezed his temples with his thumb and index finger. "I failed you, Mikey," he whispered. "Goddammit…I failed you."

He applied pressure on his temples as he squeezed his eyes shut tightly as tears welled and threatened to fall. He couldn't cry. He wouldn't. Not anymore. He clenched down on his jaws hard and flared his nostrils as he took a deep breath. If Dr. Rose could only see him now. After all of the sessions and extra hours of overtime. After all of the talking, the analyzing, the insisting that he hadn't been responsible for his son's death. That he hadn't been neglectful. After all of the progress he'd supposedly made… she'd be thoroughly disappointed to see him now. Maybe even disgusted.

He exhaled and grabbed his cigarette, now burned down a third of the way, took a drag on it, and frowned as he blew out a long stream. Fuck Rose, he thought. Fuck the degrees on her wall, fuck her psychoanalytical babble. She didn't know shit. She didn't understand and couldn't comprehend what it was like to lose the very person, above all others that he was supposed to keep safe.

Ben took another hard pull and clenched and unclenched his fists. Unfair, he thought. Life was just goddamned unfair. "Fuck you, Rose. I don't give a shit if there was no way of knowing anything would happen. My son is dead because I wasn't there to keep him safe. Write that down in your goddamned notebook and frame it."

He took another drag on his Newport and then smashed it down into the ashtray. He looked to the stack of papers again. Papers he wanted to rip up more than anything. He exhaled a long frustrated breath, and as he did, his cell phone rang. He picked it up and looked at the ID. His partner Vance. The black Riggs to his white Murtaugh. He answered. "Yeah?"

"I just got a call. A woman riding along the bike trail at Hyde's Park ran over the body of a boy with a pacifier in his mouth. So far, no ID found."

Ben took a breath. Hyde's Park. It used to be one of Mikey's favorite places to go. Used to be. Ben exhaled. "Was she the only witness?"

"According to the primary on the scene…yeah."

Ben frowned. "Okay. I'll meet you there."

Ben was about to end the call when Vance called out. "Ben?"

"Yeah?"

"Listen…you don't have to come if you don't want to. I know that Stubbs says he needs you on the case—and I won't say he's wrong, but I know what you're going through. Believe me…I understand if this is just too much for you to deal with."

"I'm fine, Vance."

"Okay, but I'm just saying, whether Stubbs says he needs you or not—"

"Stubbs wants me back to work, Vance. This is a difficult case."

"It's close to home, Ben."

"I know how close it is," Ben said, his tone sharp. He understood Vance's apprehension. This was a frustrating, stressful case, and he was right—it was very, very close to home. He and Vance had been partners now for six years, and in that time, they'd face a lot together. Ben trusted Vance with his life, and prior to what happened to Mikey, Ben knew that Vance never gave a second thought to putting his life in Ben's hands. But Mikey's death had changed a lot and things were different now. Irreversibly so. Vance was worried about his focus, his ability to do his job. The apprehension was warranted, but it still bothered Ben because he never did anything half-assed. Vance knew that.

"Vance…Mikey's been dead for five months. I've learned to accept it and I'm moving on. You don't have to worry about me keeping it together, and you don't have to worry about me having your back."

Vance sighed and after a short second or two of silence, said "I'll meet you over there."

Ben ended the call and hung his head low. His Captain, Micah Stubblefield, a large man they all called Stubbs, had stopped by his apartment earlier in the week to talk to him. Due to the recession, they'd been forced to make budget cuts and had to let a few officers go. As a result, they were shorthanded. Ben had been taking an extended leave of absence—possibly a year, to get his head together to deal with the loss of his son as well as the breakup of his marriage. He'd tried the bottle, but he'd never been a drinker, and drugs were out of the question, so he settled on depression instead.

But then Stubbs called.

A sick sonofabitch was making little boys jerk him off before he strangled them to death and left baby-blue pacifiers in their mouths. Three boys had been killed prior to Stubbs calling on Ben. One was a random homicide. Two, done the same way meant you either had a copycat or a possible serial killer on your hands. Three sealed the deal. Stubbs, who Ben had known since he'd graduated from the academy, didn't want to bring him back yet, but the mayor was on his ass, demanding that the psycho be found yesterday, and the media were making people in the city feel more and more unsafe with each passing day.

Vance had been doing all he could to find the killer, but he needed his partner, just as Ben would have needed him. Like Michael Jordan and Scottie Pippen, they were a formidable team. And Stubbs needed his best team on the case. He was sorry about the tragedy Ben had to endure, but he'd shown little remorse when he'd told Ben his sabbatical had been cut short.

Ben dragged his hands down over his face and rose from the couch and clipped his cell phone to his waist. He took a long glance at the paperwork sitting on the coffee table waiting for him. He wanted to gather them, hold them loosely in one hand, and set them aflame with his cigarette lighter in the other. He took a breath, dragged his hand down his face again as he exhaled, and then went into his bathroom to shave.

When he was finished, he hurried into his small foyer by the door, grabbed his .40 caliber semi-automatic from a small desk, slipped it into its holster, and then grabbed his keys and his black overcoat and raced out the door.

This would be his first official day back on the job. Ben had insisted that he was fine, that he was ready. It was all bullshit.

CHAPTER 3

Vance raised his eyebrows and frowned as he closed his cell and slid it into his coat pocket.

He'd tried.

It wasn't that he didn't want his partner with him, because he truly did. He trusted no other person, save for his father, more than he did Ben McCallum. He wasn't only his partner; he was also his best friend. A man who'd put his life on the line for him before. A man for whom, Vance had done the same. Theirs was a partnership that clicked from the time Vance, a junior detective with the force, had been paired with Ben, who was ten years his senior. While their personalities were different—Ben being very level-headed and a stickler for rules and procedures, and Vance being more of a hothead who liked to make his own set of rules—both men were passionate and driven when it came to their jobs. More importantly, they both loved being cops and they believed in what they did. The badge meant something to them. The hours necessary to solve a case never mattered because neither man liked to fail, and so not getting the job done was simply an option that didn't exist. Both of their personal lives had suffered in different ways because of their determination.

Very different ways.

Vance often butted heads with his fellow officers because at times he found their work ethics lacking and misguided. That had never been the case with Ben. The fact of the matter was, from day one, Vance had been forced to up his game to Ben's level. That's why, in as subtle a manner as he could, he'd tried to get Ben to stay behind.

His partner, the man he knew and trusted more than anyone, hadn't been the man he'd talked to on the phone. He hadn't been the man he'd seen just three days before in Stubbs' office when Stubbs informed him that Ben was back early from his sabbatical. The Ben he knew, despite looking the same, was still missing.

Vance had tried to talk to Stubbs in private after their meeting. He'd tried to tell the head of the homicide division that despite having been cleared by the staff psychologist, Lisa Rose, Ben wasn't ready to come back. But Stubbs was under a tremendous amount of pressure. It was an election year, and the mayor was sitting on his shoulders with the weight of a five-hundred pound barbell. The mayor's popularity had already suffered because of budget cuts he'd had to implement. Now, a serial killer was loose, and if he had any shot at being re-elected, he had to have the killer found and stopped quickly. So he needed the best people on the case, and the best people were Ben and Vance.

Vance expressed his concerns to Stubbs. He tried to make him change his mind about putting Ben on a case like this. But as the mayor wanted and demanded results, no one's head was safe from being on the chopping block, and therefore, Vance's concerns were heard and ignored. Ben was back on. End of discussion.

Vance wanted to be happy to have his partner back at his side, because he'd missed him. For six months he'd been a ying without the yang, and he'd been looking forward to feeling whole again. But not for a case like this.

Vance shook his head and tightened his grip around his steering wheel. There was nothing he could do about it now. Ben, for better or worse, was back. He could only hope that when the time came, he wouldn't have to worry about his back being had.

Chapter 4

Ben sat in his car, his window cracked open slightly and tried to breathe as evenly and as deeply as he could. He was trying to calm the thunderous beating of his heart, and failing miserably at it. He was on edge and riddled with anxiety. It was a similar feeling to his first-ever day on the job. But he'd been just a rookie, green with inexperience. His heart hadn't been shattered. His spirit hadn't been broken by a loss he wanted so badly to turn back the clock on.

He took a breath and released it slowly as he looked three hundred yards down the block to where he needed to be. He could have backed out. Vance had given him the opportunity. His partner would have understood, because he, more than anyone, understood just how broken he was. He could have remained on the couch and probably should have, but he hadn't out of duty, pride, or maybe just plain stupidity.

He flexed his hands as they were sweating beneath the black leather over them. Sweating and tingling with a sensation that somehow felt... familiar. He took a deep breath again and let it out, his warm, cigarette-laced breath fogging the glass. "This is it," he murmured as he watched nosey bystanders and heartless, story-hungry reporters jockeying for position to get the bird's eye view of the tragedy that had taken place. Bystanders he could deal with, but reporters... In his opinion, they were heartless bastards who could give a rat's ass about the victims or the victim's families. He twisted the corner of his mouth into a snarl. He hated them. Hated their insensitivity, their I-don't-give-a-shit, if-it's-news-it's news philosophy. He hadn't been a fan of them before, but he'd tolerated them.

But after Mikey's death…

Ben sighed and hoped he could do what he needed to do without hitting one of them in the mouth. He opened his door and stepped out into the blustery wind that seemed to pick up just to make a point.

Seconds later, he was forcing his way past reporters, leaving "No comments," behind. After signing in the logbook at the entrance of the crime scene, which the primary officer had secured with yellow tape, Ben left the melee of onlookers and reporters behind and walked down a short hill to where Vance stood watching as the crime scene investigator took photographs of the body.

Ben paused at the bottom of the hill as his heart began to race. Not ready. He wasn't ready for this. He turned around. He needed to get away. He couldn't do it, couldn't handle it.

"Ben?"

Air escaped from his lungs as he silently cried out. He turned back around. Vance was staring at him, his eyes scrutinizing.

"You all right?" Vance asked, the tone in his voice filled with the knowing that his partner wasn't all right at all.

Ben clenched his jaws. He wanted to say no. To scream it. Hell, to just scream, period. He wasn't all right. He was in pain, going crazy, on the verge of snapping. But he couldn't say that. He nodded. Said, "Yeah. I was just taking a look at the area." He slid on a pair of latex gloves and willed himself to step forward. "So what do we have?"

Vance turned back to the body. "Nude. No ID or clothing. Bruises on his neck. Looks like some dried semen could be on the inside of the hands and in-between the fingers. The pacifier's glued to the mouth, so we won't know until Reds looks the body over to see if any traces will be in his mouth or not. Hopefully, his pattern will be the same and there won't be any."

"Where's Reds?"

"He got stuck behind a two-car pileup."

Ben nodded, then clenched his jaws and stared at the corpse. He didn't know the boy's age, but he was young. Just like Mikey had been. An image of his son ran through his mind. An image he wanted to pound away from his mind. His son beaten, bloodied and nearly unrecognizable. Ben's throat constricted, threatened to close up on him. He forced saliva down and wiped his brow with the back of his hand.

"You sure you're all right?" Vance asked again, his eyes on him intensely.

Ben frowned. "Not really," he said, answering honestly. "But how could I be? I'm looking at the body of what's probably a ten-year-old boy."

"I hear you. But are you all right?"

Ben nodded. "I'm fine."

"Okay."

"Where's the biker?"

Vance motioned with his head to the right. Sitting in the back of the primary's squad car. Woman seems pretty shaken."

"It's not every day you run over a dead body," Ben said.

"Yeah."

Ben sighed. He wanted a cigarette. Needed one. Needed the fix. His nerves were fried and the sight of the body was getting to him more than he'd expected it to. "We'll need to run a check through the missing person database, although I'm pretty sure that's not going to provide us with anything."

"Yeah."

"Anything else found on or around the body?" Ben asked.

"I did a spiral search, but didn't see anything besides shoe and bike tire prints."

"Any sign of a struggle?"

"Doesn't look like it, but Reds will be able to confirm that."

Ben looked around, staring into the shadows amongst the trees and bushes. No witnesses, he thought. Great. "Well, let's go and talk to the biker, then see if we can find any witnesses. We'll come back to speak to Reds when he gets here."

Twenty minutes later, after speaking with the very shaken bike rider, Vance and Ben went back to the scene to meet with the Medical Examiner,

Jim Red, or Reds as everyone called him. A former star lineman for his junior college's football team, Reds was a burly, light-skinned black man with light freckles sprinkled across his cheeks and nose, and carrot-colored hair, which had earned him his moniker. Despite his size, Reds was a pleasant man who loved to laugh and was forever smiling. But smiles had been in short supply since the case started.

"Hey, Reds," Vance said, approaching him, with Ben a step behind. "Where's Birch?"

Reds, who was kneeling beside the victim's body, shook his head and looked up at Vance with a frown. "Birch is at a bachelor party," he said, his voice solemn. He looked back down to the body. "This kid is no more than ten years old," he said, his voice low, his tone flat. "My son is ten. This could be my son. All of these boys could have been my fuckin' son."

The corners of Vance's mouth dropped. Until recently, he'd had no children to call his own, so he didn't know what it felt like from the father's perspective. But his new relationship had changed his perspective, and the thought of this happening made him sick to his stomach.

He took a glance in Ben's direction. He had to give it up to his partner. He could see the pain in his eyes, but he was holding it together and doing his job. He didn't know, if put in his position, whether he could have done the same. At least not on this case.

Reds looked over to Ben. "Hey, Ben. I know this can't be easy for you."

"I'm fine," Ben insisted, trying to keep the irritation out of his voice.

Reds nodded, gave Ben a raised eyebrow that said, *'Yeah…whatever,'* and then turned back to the body. "Well, guys, I won't have all of the details until I process the body, but I can say, based on the petechial hemorrhages in the eyes, the bruising on the neck, the swollen face, and the fact that the Adam's has been damaged, I'm ninety-nine-point-nine percent sure that this little guy died just like the others. I'll have my one-hundred percent confirmation after I do the autopsy."

"Was there any damage to the rectal area?" Vance asked.

Reds shook his head. "No."

Vance nodded. "But that is dried semen on his hands, right?"

"I'll confirm it later, but based on the patches of residue and the musky smell, I'd say it is."

Ben ground his teeth together. This case was just too damned close. "What about the time of death?" he asked.

"I'd say he's been dead for at least six hours, so that puts the time at noon. Oh…and he didn't die here.

"He didn't?" Vance said.

Reds shook his head. "No. The lividity is along his entire lower surface. The back of his head, shoulder blades, buttocks and calves are surrounded by lividity, which means he was lying face up on a hard ground. Concrete most likely. Definitely not grass. Plus, judging by the body temperature, I'd say he's only been out here for maybe an hour at the most."

"Damn," Vance whispered. "How the hell could nobody have seen anything?"

Reds shrugged his shoulder. "People keep to their own business these days. You know how it is."

"Fuck," Vance said. "God fucking dammit."

"Well, like I said, I'll be able to give you more details tomorrow. We can pray that I get lucky and find something to help nail this sick fuck, but honestly, I doubt that's going to happen. Whoever this bastard is, he's very, very careful."

"Yeah," Vance said. "But he'll slip. They all do."

"We can hope. All right guys. I'm going to get the body zipped up and have it transported, and them I'm going to go home and hug my son. What time is the meeting tomorrow?"

Vance frowned. "Nine o'clock."

Reds nodded. "Okay. I'll see you guys then."

Ben and Vance nodded, thanked Reds, and then walked away as he gave them both a dismissive wave and put his focus back on the body.

Stopping at the bottom of the short hill, Vance said, "You know the media's going to want details."

Ben frowned and thought about his son again. He'd been a boy with big dreams and big goals. He wanted to be a baseball player like Derek

Jeter, or a basketball star like Lebron James. His death had been tragic on so many levels. He hadn't been just a story. He hadn't simply been breaking news for the evening. He'd been a strong, young, energetic, loving boy and son, with what was supposed to have been a very long life ahead of him. "To hell with what they want. I'm going home," he said. "You can deal with them if you want to."

"I don't want to, but the mayor and the public's on edge, and the last thing we need is for the press to give out any half-assed information."

Ben shrugged. "You're the lead on the case. And you're prettier on camera than I am."

"Gee… thanks."

"Hey…you're the one that used to model."

"A long time ago, Ben. That was a long time ago."

"Like I said, you're prettier than I am. Anyway…you know how I feel about the media."

Vance nodded. Ben was right…Vance knew all too well how he felt. "Okay. I'll take care of them. You'll be there in the morning…nine o'clock, right?"

Ben took a look down at the deceased body of a boy who'd lost his life far too soon. Just like Mikey, he thought again. "Yeah," he said, pulling off his gloves and removing his pack of cigarettes from the inside pocket of his black trench coat. He shook one out, lit it with his lighter, and took a pull on it. "I'll be there."

"I thought you quit."

Ben took another pull, then held the Newport and looked at it. "That was a lifetime ago," he said evenly.

"Yo…are you're sure you're okay with this?" Vance asked, his voice heavy with concern.

Ben blew out a stream of smoke, then took another drag, held the smoke in for a few moments and watched it drift away as he exhaled. "I got your back, Vance," he said. "I got your back."

"It's not only about you having my back, Ben."

Ben blew out another plume of smoke and looked at his partner. "Isn't it?" he said with an eyebrow raised.

Vance shook his head. "You know it's not."

Ben took another drag, and then looked toward the throng of reporters and people gathered. "Go handle the media, Pretty Rickey. I'll see you in the morning."

Vance clenched his jaw. "Ben..."

"I'm fine, Vance," Ben said, walking up the hill. "I'm just fine."

Vance shook his head and frowned. He wanted to call out to his partner, his friend, but remained quiet. He'd pushed enough. He turned and watched as Reds and his team zipped the body up inside of a heavy, plastic-coated body bag to transport it to the morgue for examination.

He sighed as they carried the body to an ambulance, and then turned and looked up toward the top of the hill overlooking the bike trail. The circus was up there waiting for sound bites. Dealing with them had always been Ben's job because he was the senior officer, and because of the way he handled the spotlight. He had a stern, unflappable demeanor, and always seemed to be all-knowing, even when he knew nothing. Vance usually stood in the background and observed as Ben gave the media just enough, but never anything more.

But that had been the old Ben.

He sighed again. The old Ben wouldn't have left. Vance being the lead wouldn't have mattered to him. He would have stepped in front of the microphones and fielded questions without hesitation.

The old Ben.

Vance frowned. Seeing the dead boy's body couldn't have been easy for him. Although no homicide was a good one, Vance still wished the killer, the press had so tactfully dubbed *The Pacifier*, had chosen older victims. Ben claimed to be fine, but Vance knew that was bullshit. The young bodies were hard enough for him to look at. He couldn't imagine being in Ben's shoes. He had looked into his son's vacant eyes. He had felt his cold, clammy skin. There was no way he could be "fine" looking at the dead bodies of these boys, without it having a profoundly adverse effect on him.

Vance took a breath and released it slowly. He wasn't one to pray on a regular basis, although he did believe in God, but he said a quick prayer for his friend's sanity, and for the hope that Ben would somehow be able to climb out of the depths of hell that Vance was sure his friend was living in. After making the sign of the cross, Vance took a final glance at the crime scene, and then trudged up the hill to answer questions he couldn't really answer.

Chapter 5

"I see you," Patrick whispered. "I see you, *Detective.*" He said the last word contemptuously with a snarl.

Detective.

"You think you're somebody special with your badge and gun, don't you? You think you're important. But you're not, *Detective.* You're just a joke. A pathetic, piece of shit, weak joke and I'm going to teach you one hell of a lesson."

Patrick stared at Ben McCallum through the rear view mirror of his car and took a long pull on his cigarette. It was all working out perfectly. Everything happening just the way he'd planned. Ben was struggling, cracking slowly, surely. It gave Patrick the chills knowing that he was orchestrating the greatest lesson in the history of lessons.

"You should have left well enough alone, *Detective.* You should have left it all the fuck alone. You'll realize that when I'm done with you."

He blew out a stream of smoke. Watched as it sifted over the mirror, and hid Ben from his view momentarily. He took another pull and wished he could end Ben's existence forever at that moment. But he couldn't. He had work to do. More lessons to teach.

To Ben.

To Allen Kline as well.

The good doctor had to be made to understand the cost of his transgressions also.

Their lessons went hand in hand. They both had to see the errors of their ways. And so he would continue on with his work, his lessons, until the time was right to end the class for good.

Patrick blew out another stream of cancerous air, started his car, and drove away, staring at Ben McCallum until he eventually faded away.

Chapter 6

"Where are the boys?"

Allen exhaled while his shoulders sagged as fear and angst pressed down on them, determined to force him to the ground. He'd sat first in his office for over an hour after his latest "session" with Patrick, and then in his car for another forty-five minutes in front of his home with the hopes of avoiding what was happening right now. He hadn't even taken two steps inside when the question was asked.

Where are the boys?

It was a question that plagued his every waking moment and haunted his sleepless nights.

Where were his boys?

He looked at his wife of twenty years and said nothing.

She shook her head. Her eyes were bloodshot red, her skin pale. Her long brown hair was matted and dry. She had on gray sweatpants and a sweatshirt that she was practically disappearing in. Far gone was the vibrant forty-four-year-old who'd looked to be in her mid-thirties. Her once radiant smile was gone, replaced now by a deep frown. Deep but incomparable to the level of the depth of depression she'd fallen into the night Allen told her of their sons' abduction.

"You're...you're home late. That...that means that you...that you saw him again. Where, Allen? Where are my boys?"

Allen looked at his wife, at her now dim, blue eyes, at the tears falling from them. He shook his head. Opened his mouth. Felt his throat tighten.

"Where are they?" she demanded again, her voice shaking but determined.

Allen didn't want to answer her. He didn't want to hear the sound of his own voice as he closed the door behind him and gave her the only answer he could give. "I…I don't know," he said softly.

His wife shook her head again. "No. No." Tears cascaded heavily down her cheeks. "Don't tell me that, Allen. Don't you tell me that."

"I'm sorry, Amanda. Believe me…I wish I could say something else."

Amanda Kline took a labored breath and ran her trembling hands through her hair violently. "We…we have to go to the police," she said. "We…we have to."

Allen frowned and clenched his jaws. "We can't, Amanda."

"No…we can, Allen. We can… and…and we will, dammit."

Allen shook his head as his frown deepened. "No, we won't."

With pleading eyes, Amanda said, "I want my boys back. I want my boys back." She wrapped her arms around herself and leaned back against the wall in their foyer.

"So do I," Allen said solemnly. "So do I."

"Then call the police."

Allen shook his head again and opened his mouth to speak, but before he could, Amanda spoke again.

"How…how can you say that you want our boys back when you won't call the police?"

Amanda," Allen said with a sigh. "You know why."

"He may kill them anyway, Allen! Don't you think our chances are better if we just get the goddamned police involved?"

Allen slammed his hand against the wall. "I don't know, Amanda! I don't know! But I'm not willing to take the chance."

"Not willing? He has our sons!"

"Dammit, Amanda, you've seen the news. You know what he's capable of. He said he would kill them if we go to the police."

"Allen—"

"You haven't seen him," Allen snapped. "You haven't heard the viciousness in his voice. I'm not willing to take the chance that he won't follow through. I can't! Can you?"

Amanda shuddered as she sobbed. "I…I just want my boys back. I want my babies back."

Allen sighed and moved forward and enveloped his wife in his arms. "I do too," he said, his heart wrenching.

Amanda buried her face against his chest and cried hard tears. Allen held her tightly and kissed the top of her head as his own tears fell.

"Why?" she said, turning her head to the side. "Why is this happening to us?"

"I don't know," Allen replied. It was another question he'd been wondering.

Amanda lifted her head and looked up at him. "Do you know him? Do you know this monster?"

Allen shook his head. She'd asked him this before, and his answer had been the same. "No. I don't."

"Then why did he choose you? Why did he take our boys?"

Allen clenched his jaws. Those questions were worth one million dollars.

Why him? Why his boys?

Questions he'd wondered since Patrick's first visit. A visit in which Patrick had walked into Allen's private office, wearing a NY Yankees baseball cap pulled low, concealing his eyes, turned off the overhead lights, leaving Allen's desk lamp as the only light source, and said very calmly: "I have your sons, Allen. Chad and Chris. I have them in a room where no one can hear them scream. They're safe for now, but if you don't listen and do what I tell you to do, I promise they won't be safe for long."

Allen had been sitting behind his desk at the time, going over his notes from his last session with Billy Crenshaw, an eight-year-old boy who'd stopped talking to his mother after his father's death four months prior. Despite the fact that his father had died from natural causes, Billy blamed his mother, and therefore refused to acknowledge her. It was a challenging case, but he was making progress, and he was becoming more and more certain that Billy would be talking to his mother soon.

Allen looked up, his pen in his hand. His sons? Taken? Surely someone had to have been playing a trick. A twisted prank. Cruel even. "Who the hell are you?"

"Change your tone, Allen. Your boys' lives are in my hands."

Allen shook his head. "You're lying. Who set you up to this?"

Patrick stepped forward, reached into the inside pocket of a black trench coat he had on, removed a photograph, and tossed it onto Allen's desk top.

Allen looked down at the photograph, which was face down. "What is this?" he said, looking back up.

"Pick it up, Allen."

"Who are you?"

"Pick it up," Patrick instructed again.

Allen stared at him for a moment, and then picked up the photograph, flipped it over, and his heart dropped into the pit of his stomach. His sons both stripped down to their underwear, lying separately on the ground, a chain around each of their ankles. They looked like they were sleeping, although Allen knew that was hardly the case.

"What…what the hell is this?" Allen demanded, his eyes still on the horrific image.

"No one set me up, Allen. And I don't lie."

Allen looked up. Tried to see into the shadows, tried to get a glimpse of Patrick's eyes as he stood casually in front of him, but as hard as he tried, he could see nothing. The photograph gripped tightly between his fingers, he said, "You're..." He paused, looked down at the photograph again. "This has got to be a joke," he said, his tone begging for that to be the case. "It's nearly ten o'clock. My wife would have called me by now."

The corners of his mouth rising, Patrick said, "Call Amanda, Allen."

Allen looked at him curiously as his heart thudded rapidly. He'd said his wife's name. Who the hell was he? He picked up the phone, and with his hands tingling with nervousness, dialed his home phone number and waited on pins and needles for his wife to answer, which she did on the first ring.

"Allen!" she said, her voice filled with anxiety. "Allen!"

"Amanda…are the boys home? Are they all right?"

On the other end, his wife broke down. "He…he has them, Allen. He told me if…if I called you or anyone that he…he would kill them."

Allen strangled the receiver in his hand as bumps rose along his forearms. He looked up to see Patrick staring at him, his mouth curled into a smile.

"I'll call you back," Allen said into the receiver, and then hung up as his wife screamed his name. "Who…who the hell are you?" he asked Patrick.

Patrick smiled wickedly. "I'm a killer, Allen. A cold, calculated killer, with lessons to teach."

Allen looked down at the photograph of his sons and stared at them for a long, couple of dread-filled seconds, before looking back up. "What do you want? Money? I'll pay whatever you want."

Patrick said, "I don't want your money, Allen. I just want your time. Your time and your undivided attention."

"B…but why? Why me?"

"In due time, Allen. You'll find out in due fucking time."

The sudden use of profanity made bumps rise from Allen's skin. His voice had been calm, but the edge in his tone was violent, bitter, deadly.

"If not money…then what? Stocks? Jewelry?"

"I already told you, Allen. I want your time and attention. I want your confidence. That's what you give your patients isn't it? Time, attention, and confidentiality."

Allen shook his head as confusion had him unsure as to how to respond. "I…I don't understand…"

"I killed a child, Allen. A boy. He was ten just like your youngest son. I had him do horrible things to me, and then I strangled him and left his body to be found." Patrick paused and stared with eyes Allen couldn't see, as Allen sat motionless.

He'd killed a child. A boy. The same age as his youngest son. He'd had him do horrible things.

Allen barely breathed as the pounding of his heartbeat echoed loudly in his ears.

He'd killed a child.

"Why are you telling me this?"

"Because I want you to listen, Allen. To really listen."

"I don't understand."

Patrick smiled. "You will, Allen. Trust me…you will. Now…I'm leaving. But I will be back. After my next kill. And you'll listen again. And you won't say a fucking word to anyone because if you do, I will send you a very different photograph. One that you really don't want to see. Are we on the same page, Allen?"

Allen looked at Patrick, dumbfounded, horrified and understanding all too clearly. "Y…" He paused and took a short breath, his body trembling with each beat of his heart. "Yes," he said finally, his throat dry.

Patrick smiled. It was a calculated, satisfied, malicious grin. "Good. And just so we're clear, if you do get tempted…as quickly as you make your call, your boys would be killed even faster."

His throat closed, Allen could only nod.

Patrick flashed another satisfied grin and then backed up toward the door. Putting his hand behind his back and resting it on the doorknob, he said, "By the way…my name is Patrick," and then he turned the knob, opened the door and walked out.

That was four days ago. And now, two "sessions" later, Allen was holding on to his wife, keeping from her the fact that Patrick told him that his being chosen hadn't been random, that somehow he was to blame for his boys being taken.

Allen looked at his wife, clenched his jaws, and did the only thing he could do. He lied and said, "I don't know."

Chapter 7

Hey Vance!"

Vance Newsome looked down and smiled. "What's up, little man," he said, looking down.

"Ain't nothin'. I've just been here waitin' to teach you a lesson again."

Vance raised the right corner of his mouth. "Is that right?

"You know it!"

Vance nodded. "Well, I hate to break it to you, little man, but you never taught me a lesson in the first place, because I let your scrawny butt win. Now, step out of the way so the soon-to-be champ can show you what a real lesson is!"

Vance chuckled as DaShawn Taylor rolled his eyes and stepped to the side, allowing entrance. "Whatever. You know you can't handle me."

Vance clamped his hand down on top of DaShawn's little head. "Boy, you better go and practice, because you're in trouble. I'm bringing the mean right hooks tonight."

DaShawn slapped Vance's hand from his head, said, "I'm not scared of you! You hit like a girl."

Vance tilted his head back and laughed heartily, the way his father used to. "You're in trouble now," he said.

DaShawn rolled his eyes again, then turned away from the door. "Mom! Vance is here to get beat down!"

Vance shook his head and laughed again as DaShawn ran to his bedroom to prepare for their weekly boxing match on the Wii. He shrugged out of his leather coat and hung it on a coat rack to the side of the door.

"Hey, baby!" DaShawn's mother said, emerging from the kitchen.

Vance looked at her as she approached, and wondered how the hell he'd been so lucky to have ended up with her. She was a stunning, black woman. A queen with almond shaped eyes, a slender nose that buttoned slightly at the tip, full, sensuous lips, and a curvaceous body that showed she wasn't afraid of food or the gym. How her ex could have ever laid on hand on her in a far different manner from the way Vance enjoyed laying his hands on her, he could never understand. She was perfect. A woman to be adored, treasured and respected. And she was his.

Vance looked at the woman he'd fallen in love with at first sight one late summer day as he was in the grocery store looking to restock his refrigerator and freezer with Mountain Dew and Hungry Man frozen dinners and smiled. She was always a much welcomed sight and distraction, but even moreso now with the case that seemed to be going nowhere. "Hey beautiful," he said, welcoming her into his arms.

Holding one another, they kissed deeply for several long seconds until Alyssa Taylor pulled away and looked in the direction of her son's bedroom.

"He's busy practicing for his beatdown. He won't be coming out of his room for a while," Vance said.

Alyssa gave him a smile that made his blood flow. Her smile had grabbed his attention immediately in the frozen food aisle, right after her very round and full behind. "I know, but still…"

Vance pulled her into him again, pressed his lips against hers and kissed her with starved ferocity, to which she willingly responded to, before pulling away and saying, "We could always just go to your room if you're that worried."

Alyssa shook her head and grinned. "You're a naughty boy," she said.

Vance took her hand in his. "Allow me to lead the way and I'll show you how naughty," he said with a slick smile.

Alyssa laughed. "If I didn't have to get back into the kitchen I would take you up on that offer."

Vance groaned and bit playfully on her neck. "Forget the kitchen."

"I can't. I have food on the stove cooking."

"Let it burn," Vance joked.

"And the apartment with it too, huh?" Alyssa said.

Vance kissed, then sucked on her neck, then slid a hand beneath her shirt and bypassed her bra and took her full breast in his hand. "You said work needed to be done in here," he said passing his finger over her nipple, which was quickly becoming engorged.

Alyssa moaned and pressed her hips into him. "You're bad," she said as he ground his crotch against her.

"Very," he agreed.

Alyssa put her hand behind his head and kissed him deeply before pulling away again. "Believe me, baby, if DaShawn weren't here, I would let the place burn down while I let you show me just how bad you can be. But..." she smiled and backed away. "...I need to get into the kitchen."

Vance groaned again and as he did, his stomach rumbled. It hadn't dawned on him until that very moment that he hadn't eaten since the morning, and truthfully, the glazed donut he'd had didn't really count. He said, "Okay. I guess I can go and beat up on the little punk in the meantime. I could stand to let out some aggression right about now anyway."

Alyssa put a hand on his cheek and gave him a loving gaze filled with sympathy. "You didn't have to come over, you know. I would have understood if you needed some time alone."

Vance exhaled as his smile faltered. "I promised DaShawn I'd come over. Besides...I wanted to see you."

"DaShawn's a big boy. He would have been all right."

"I know, but still..."

"Baby...he saw the news this morning. He knows what you're dealing with. He would have been okay."

Vance set his jaw and pulled his lips back against his teeth. "I want to catch this son-of-a-bitch so bad," he said as anger simmered just beneath his surface. "I want to catch him and strangle him the way he strangled those boys."

Alyssa frowned and looked toward her son's bedroom, where he could be heard cheering as he prepared to go one on one with Vance. She shook her head. "How can someone do anything like that to a child?"

Vance wasn't supposed to discuss the details of the case with anyone outside of the team working it, but this case was different, and saying to hell with rules and regulations, he confided in her, knowing that she wouldn't take it anywhere, and quite honestly he needed to, because talking to Alyssa about it helped to relieve the tension that was building up with each passing minute. "There are some sick fucks out in the world," he said, his tone filled with contempt.

Alyssa sighed. "I know. But I just don't see how a human being could look a child in the eye and do those things. Children are innocent. I just... just can't understand it."

Vance clenched one side of his jaw and tugged on a diamond stud in his left ear. "We aren't dealing with a human being," he said, flaring his nostrils. "We're dealing with a monster, so we couldn't possibly understand it."

"And you and Ben still have no leads?"

Vance exhaled. "We don't have shit," he said honestly.

Alyssa wrapped herself up in her arms, then looked back at him. "I...I don't know what I would do if something like that were to happen to DaShawn."

Vance looked at her, his eyes focused and hard. "You don't have to worry about that," he said. "Nothing...and I mean nothing like that will ever happen to him. I promise that."

Alyssa looked toward DaShawn's room again as she ran her hands up and down the back of her arms. "Just knowing that whoever is doing this is somewhere out there...it scares me. I can only imagine how hard it must be for the parents who've lost their sons to this devil already. I truly feel for them."

Vance thought about the boys, the John Doe's. Street kids with no history. They'd been trying diligently to find relatives or friends. They'd searched missing children databases, but thus far had been unsuccessful and that only added to Vance's frustration. He never liked having to deliver news of death to surviving family members, but if there was one thing he vowed to do, it was to make sure that each one of the boys got closure. They deserved that much.

Vance softly took hold of Alyssa by her arms. "Look at me, baby," he said softly.

Alyssa frowned in her son's direction and then turned and met Vance's determined glare.

"Don't be scared, okay," Vance said. "I promise you, nothing's going to happen to DaShawn. Ben and I are going to find the piece of shit, and when we do, he's going to beg us to kill him."

Alyssa nodded and then a frown fell over her face.

"What's wrong?" Vance asked.

Alyssa's frown deepened. "I've been thinking about Ben. I've been wondering how he's handling being back to work."

Vance sighed and cocked his eyebrows. "He's fine. At least that's what he says."

"You obviously feel differently."

Vance took a full breath. "I feel..." Vance paused and exhaled. "I feel sorry for him. It really isn't fair for him to be working this case."

"But you need him," Alyssa said more than asked.

Vance frowned and nodded. "I wish you knew Ben like I do. He was so different before...before Mikey's...death. It would have been one thing had Mikey died of natural causes or in an accident of some kind, but for him to have died the way he did. I mean, shit...his killer has never even been found, and believe me, we've been trying like hell to find the son-of-a-bitch. But whoever did what he did, was..." Vance paused again, closed his eyes slowly, pressed his lips together, and then opened his eyes and said, "Whoever did this was calculated. They knew what to do. They left nothing behind to be found. They made sure there were absolutely no witnesses. There's no doubt in my mind that this was personal. Ben feels the same way, too, and Mikey's death, along with the blame he's carrying around on his shoulders, has really broken him down. Like I said...I wish you got to know him before all of this happened."

He paused as Alyssa put her hand against his cheek. "Oh, baby," she said softly.

"Ben was a hell of a cop before this happened. I mean the knowledge and experience he has…it's immeasurable. Having him on the case really is necessary because he's been down roads like this before. If I were Stubbs and I had the media and the mayor on my ass, I would have put Ben on the case, too."

"Even though you know this could tear him apart more than he's already been?"

Vance sighed. "Yes," he said begrudgingly. And he hated that. A lost son. A marriage broken apart by tragedy. Ben didn't deserve to be working the case. He didn't deserve more pain and sorrow. But there was a killer out there who had to be stopped and as much as he didn't want him to be, Ben was needed.

Alyssa caressed his cheek and then reached up on her toes and kissed him on his lips.

"Ben's lucky to have you as a friend and partner."

Vance frowned. "I wish I could be there for him more as a friend than partner right now."

Alyssa gave him a slight smile. "You will. After you both make the city safe again. And maybe I can be there for him, too."

Vance looked at her and smiled. "Thanks for being my shoulder. I needed it."

Alyssa gave him another kiss. "That's what I'm here for."

"And I appreciate it."

Vance drew her into him and kissed her long, hard and deep. He hadn't been looking for love when he'd met her, but love he had definitely found. He was a lucky man.

Alyssa pulled her head back, smiled, touched his cheek again and then turned and disappeared into the kitchen. Vance smiled again, then pulled his cell phone from his pocket. With the case and the self-exile Ben had been living in since Mikey's death, he hadn't had much of an opportunity to be the friend that he used to be. He found Ben's number and hit the talk button. It rang once and then went to voice mail. He hit the end button and slid the phone back into his pocket. He would catch Ben in the morning. Right now he had a beatdown to administer on the Wii.

He turned to head toward DaShawn's room and as he did, the living room window caught his eye. He stood still for a moment. Somewhere out there was the killer searching for his next victim. "We'll stop you," he said.

They were strong, determined words filled with a doubt and hopelessness he'd never felt before.

Chapter 8

Mikey was screaming.

Calling for his dad.

Ben did a three-hundred and sixty degree turn. He was in the woods somewhere, surrounded by darkness and trees without leaves. "Mikey!"

He squinted his eyes, tried to get a better focus into the blackness around him, lit sparsely by moonlight that bobbed and weaved behind thick, grey clouds. "MIKEY!"

His son screamed out again.

"I'm here Mikey! I'm here. Where are you?" He stepped forward. Slipped on something loose beneath his feet and turned his ankle. "Shit!"

He clenched his jaw and kept himself from going down. He couldn't fall. His son needed him. He moved, despite the pain, limping slightly, determined to find his boy. Determined to save his angel. "Mikey!"

Mikey screamed again. A harder scream this time. One filled with more terror.

Ben's heart hammered beneath his chest as he moved past tree limbs, hanging, reaching for him. He slid on rocks, snapped twigs, labored through patches of mud. He called out again: "Mikey!" He did another three-hundred and sixty degree turn as Mikey called for him. "Where are you?"

Ben gritted his teeth as terror flowed through his veins. His son. He could hear the screams, but he couldn't pinpoint from what direction they were coming from. They seemed close, yet so far at the same time. He dragged his hand down over his face. Clenched his jaw again as tears began to well. "Mikey!"

The naked trees began to swirl around as the ground beneath his feet became unsteady. Despite his fight, tears began to fall from his eyes. He called out to his son again as another cry pierced the darkness and confusion around him. His throat was raw, burning.

Trees spun faster. The ground swooned harder. Unable to keep his footing, he went down to one knee. "Mikey!" he said again. "I'm…I'm trying!"

His chest burned as he took labored breaths. His son was screaming, calling for him. He shook his head. His son needed him. He was supposed to protect him. But he was failing him.

Again.

Ben's eyes snapped open as he sat up in his bed.

"Mikey!" he yelled. "Noo!"

He pressed the palm of his hands against his eyes as his chest rose and fell quickly. "Christ," he whispered. He pulled his hands away, tossed his blanket aside, and swung his legs off of his bed. "Christ."

Beads of sweat trickled down his forehead, while his heart galloped. He wiped sweat away with the back of his hand and took a deep breath, and held it in until he couldn't any longer.

Goddamn dreams, he thought exhaling slowly.

They wouldn't leave him alone.

He took another deep breath, released it, and looked over at the time displayed on his alarm clock. Four in the morning. He shook his head, wiped more sweat away, and wondered if he was ever going to have a full night's sleep again. He frowned and rose from the bed. No, he surmised as he reached for his pack of cigarettes on his dressing table. No. He would never have that luxury ever again. He shook a cigarette loose, set the pack down, grabbed his lighter and set the cancer stick ablaze. Sleepless nights, he thought taking a deep drag. They were forever going to be in his future, because he had nothing else to look forward to.

He blew out a long stream of smoke, left his bedroom and went to the living room. He grabbed the remote and turned on the television, not because he wanted to watch anything in particular, but rather just because he wanted another source of noise beside the faint sound of his son's screams still in his head. Screams he'd never heard but imagined in different lengths, different octaves.

"Goddammit, Mikey. I was supposed to be there. I was supposed to protect you."

He wiped a tear away from his eye, took another pull on his cigarette and sat down on the lone beige couch he owned, as Billy Mays tried to convince him, along with whatever other insomniacs that were wide awake, to purchase a scratch repair kit for the car.

Beep.

Ben looked to the corner of his coffee table. His cell phone, letting him know that he had a message. He frowned. He'd meant to take it in the room with him, but he'd forgotten. Hopefully he hadn't missed a call from Vance. His partner and best friend needed to know that he could be trust on his being there when he needed him. Ben sighed, looked at the phone and saw two missed calls. The first was from Vance. Eight hours ago. The second was from Sarah. He sighed and pressed the button to listen to his voice mail. He had only one message waiting, and it wasn't from Vance.

Ben…it's Sarah. It's been a few days. I was hoping to have the paperwork back by now.

Ben sighed again and looked at the stack of papers still scattered across the table. Divorce papers. The final nail in the coffin.

I…I know it's not easy, Ben, but…it's time to move on.

Time to move on, Ben thought, taking another long pull on the cigarette. He didn't want to fucking move on. He just wanted to move back. Back to a time when everything made sense.

I'm coming over tomorrow morning to pick them up. I'll be there by seven. Please be there.

Ben let out a hard exhale of smoke and tossed his cell to the side. Please be there, the way he hadn't been before when he was needed the most. She hadn't said those words, but Ben knew that's just what she'd meant. He could read between the lines.

He hadn't been there for Mikey.

He hadn't been there for her.

Two reasons why he was where he was now.

He took a final drag on his cigarette, then smashed it down into his ashtray on the corner.

Please be there.

He flattened his lips against the front of his teeth, looked at the papers waiting for his John Hancock, and then leaned forward and grabbed the pen sitting beside them, while a new pitch man on the television tried to convince him to buy the ShamWow.

Past—four months prior

Sarah woke with tears in her eyes. She'd had another torturous nightmare of her, Ben and Mikey walking in the park. The sun was high and blazing brightly in the clear, blue sky. Ben and Sarah were smiling and exchanging loving glances while Mikey ran ahead of them, tossing a baseball into the air and catching it in his glove. People walked around, their mouths wide with smiles. It was a perfect day. One Sarah didn't want to end. But it did, because it wasn't real. The warmth, the joy, the love, the happiness...none of it existed.

Not anymore.

Sarah rolled over onto her side and sobbed softly as tears continued to fall mercilessly. She hated the dreams and wished they would leave her alone, but she knew they wouldn't. They would return the next time sleep fell over her to torture her all over again. Pure hell. Dreams of what used to be, of what would never be again.

Two months ago, her son, her angel was killed violently, without remorse, without an explanation, and worse yet, without a viable suspect. The person had left no trace of their existence behind. It was almost as though they didn't exist. But then, of course they did, because Mikey was gone.

Sarah's body shook as she cried. Why her baby? He hadn't done anything wrong. He was incapable of being anything other than perfect. So why? Who could have done that to him?

Sarah stretched her arm behind her and patted the other side of the bed. Ben's side. As she'd expected it was going to be, it was unoccupied. "Damn you, Ben," she said, sniffling. "God damn you."

She was tired of having to suffer alone. Ever since Mikey had been murdered, that's what she was. Alone. Ben was out, looking for his son's killer. He was determined to find him. He wanted justice, revenge, peace. Sarah understood his wants, his needs and ached for the same thing.

But…

All of her wants, her desires and her needs wouldn't change one very real and painful fact—nothing was going to bring Mikey back. Mikey was gone far too soon and instead of having Ben by her side to grieve with her, or at the very least, to give her the shoulder she desperately needed to cry on, he had all but abandoned her and left her out to tread in the middle of a dark sea of despair and depression.

Sarah looked up through her tears at her alarm clock on her night table. It was two o'clock in the morning. She frowned and reached for her cell phone sitting in front of the clock. Finding Ben's number, she hit the send button, and as it rang, she asked herself why she was bothering to put herself through the agony.

"Yeah," Ben said, answering on the fourth ring.

"Where are you, Ben?"

Ben exhaled heavily into the phone. This was a dance they'd been doing all too frequently lately. "You know where I am, Sarah."

"This isn't going to bring Mikey back," Sarah said, wiping tears away with the back of her hand.

"So what are you saying, Sarah? That I shouldn't try to find the sonofabitch who killed him?"

"No…I'm not saying that, Ben. I want his killer found, too."

"Then why would you say something like that?"

Sarah pulled her cell away from her ear and covered her face with her hand. This wasn't supposed to be happening. They weren't supposed to be arguing. But since Mikey's death, that's all they'd done. Tragedy was supposed to have been pulling them together, but instead it was breaking apart what she'd thought had been a very strong and solid foundation.

She put the phone back to her ear. "Ben…" she said, her throat tight, her voice just above a whisper. "Please…can you just come home?"

"Sarah—"

"Please, Ben," Sarah implored. "I…I need you here."

"Sarah…" Ben said again, his tone heavy with aggravation. "I can't."

"Please, Ben. I'm tired of being alone. Just give me one night. This… this is so hard to deal with."

"Christ, Sarah…I know it's hard."

"Then come home."

"I can't. Shit…I need to find him."

"It's been two months, Ben."

"And so what? I should just give up?"

"I'm not saying that."

"Then what are you saying?"

Sarah let out an exasperated breath. "Ben…I—"

"I need to go, Sarah."

"But Ben…please I—"

Click.

"I need you."

Sarah slammed her phone down on her bed and shed tears of frustration, anger and sadness. Not this way. It wasn't supposed to be this way at all.

"Damn you," she said again. "I need you. Why can't you just be here for me?"

She covered her face with her hand and shed more hard tears. She needed someone to talk to. Someone willing to offer a shoulder. She knew of one person who'd offered to be that someone whenever she needed. A friend. That's all. Nothing more. "Damn you, Ben," she said again.

Sarah picked up her cell phone again, and dialed a phone number that didn't belong to her husband.

Chapter 9

Chris Kline opened his eyes. He'd been dreaming. First about his mother, father and brother. They were somewhere warm and bright. A beach, maybe, or a park. The location didn't really matter. All that did was that they were safe and that they were all happy in the dream. They were all smiling.

Somewhere in the middle of the laughter, the dream changed and he found himself in third period Math class, sitting next to Shelly Hebron, the prettiest girl in the entire school. At least to Chris she was. Shelly had soft, brown eyes, a tiny nose, small perfectly-shaped, naturally pink hued lips, and dimples. Her hair was dark-brown, straight and stopped in the middle of her back. She had curves that no girl her age should have had, and a set of perky breasts that garnered attention. She was the girl that every guy in the school wanted to date. There were even rumblings about a few of the male teachers trying as discreetly as they could to catch her eye.

Shelly Hebron.

The word was she was dating a sophomore in college, some basketball player. A shooting guard. High school guys simply couldn't measure up. But Chris didn't care. Just seeing her sitting beside him in Math each day was enough for him. The dream he'd been having had been just like real life. No talking, and a whole lot of staring. Chris could have looked at her forever—well, for as long as the dream would have allowed. But his admiration had been cut short by the sound of a key sliding into a lock.

Chris blinked as faint light spilled into the dark room as the door was pulled open. Seconds later, the fake cop stepped into the doorway, blocking most of the light, and stood still, staring into the room.

Was this it? Chris wondered. *Had he come to kill them, or by some miracle, to let them go?*

He stared at the fake cop, whose face he couldn't see because of the light being behind him. He wanted to say something, but a knot was caught in his throat. Fear, he knew. His heart beating heavily, he stared, while his captor stood menacingly silent.

After a few long, taut seconds, Chad's tiny voice cut through the silence. "A…are you going to…to kill us?"

Chris looked over in his brother's direction. His scrawny arms were wrapped around skinny legs and his pale skin almost seemed to glow in the faint light. He always hugged his knees to his chest when he was afraid.

"Not yet," the fake cop said. His voice was low and seemed to bounce off of walls in the room. "But I will."

Chris looked away from Chad, who'd begun to cry again, and stared at the fake cop as he began to back out of the room. "You're not going to get away with this," Chris said, doubt hovering behind his words. "Our parents are out there looking for us. So are the police. Someone's going to find us."

The man laughed. "Someone will find you," he said, definitively. "But by the time they do…it will be too late." He backed out of the room.

"Someone's going to find us!" Chris yelled again as his brother's sobbing grew in volume.

His eyes on them, the fake cop closed the door slowly, leaving Chris and Chad in darkness. Chad cried hard and loud. As he did, Chris shivered.

Not yet. But soon they would be dead. Soon. Unless he got them out of there.

Chris swallowed saliva as Chad continued to weep, and looked toward the door. On the other side was freedom, but a chain was keeping him away. He trembled again. Never in his life had he ever felt so afraid.

Not yet.

Not yet.

The fake cop's words continued to bounce of the walls.

Not yet.

Not yet.

Chris bit down on his tongue. It was the only thing he could do to keep the tears, which were threatening to rise and fall, at bay. He couldn't cry. Not now.

Chris bit down on his tongue just a little harder and then wrapped his fingers around the only thing that could ensure that the fake cop's promise would be fulfilled. Somehow, someway, he had to get the chain off. He began to pull on it from the bottom.

Chapter 10

Sarah McCallum looked up at the three-story house she once called home, through the fogged glass of her passenger window and sighed. Six months ago, she thought. Six months ago the house's outward appearance had been different. The crème-colored vinyl siding had been clean and free of mold and dirt. The multi-colored concrete steps leading up to the front door hadn't been cracked and chipped. The small wrought iron gate allowing entrance to the steps had been jet black and without a trace of rust. Curtains lined the windows, not vertical blinds, allowing not a single glimpse inside. Six months ago, no matter the time of day, light seemed to shine down on the five bedroom edifice as though it came from the heavens signifying that it were under a special watch.

Six months ago.

Sarah frowned.

Six months ago, things had been so different.

"Do you want me to find a parking spot and go in with you?"

Sarah turned her head and looked at the male driver of the Lincoln Town car she was a passenger in. Six months ago, he hadn't existed. She shook her head and gave him a half-smile. "No, that's all right. This shouldn't take too long. Besides…it's probably better that I go in alone anyway."

Her companion pressed his lips together firmly. "I guess," he conceded.

Sarah gave another half-smile and then leaned toward him and kissed him softly on his cheek. "Twenty minutes tops," she said, hoping that would be the case.

He nodded and said, "Okay," his tone clearly signifying that he doubted twenty minutes would be all she needed.

Sarah gave him another kiss, this one on his lips, and then opened the car door and stepped out of the warm interior into the crisp, frigid morning air. She lifted the collar of her leather coat around her neck, and hurried across the street to the house that she would never be able to fully turn her back on, no matter how badly she wanted or tried to.

Closing the gate behind her, she ascended the five concrete steps to the front door and pressed on the doorknob. Her heart beat heavily as she shivered from the cold. *Please,* she thought. *Please don't be there.*

The latch on the lock clicked and the door swung open.

Sarah sighed as her very soon-to-be ex-husband stood in the doorway, his expression hard. "Hello, Ben," she said evenly.

Ben looked at her for a lingering second and then said, "Sarah." He stepped to the side. "Come in."

Sarah sighed again. If their meeting didn't require privacy, stepping one foot over the threshold wouldn't have been an option, but as it was, no one needed to be privy to the conversation they were about to have. She stepped past Ben into the foyer that was only slightly warmer than the outside. She turned around in time to see Ben staring out across the street.

"Is *he* coming inside?" he asked, looking at her over his shoulder.

"Like you really want him in here."

Ben shrugged and slammed the door shut. "Just asking."

Sarah sent the corner of her mouth upward, her eyes saying, *Yeah okay.*

Ben shrugged again and then moved past her into a small hallway, and opened a door to an apartment off to the left of a flight of stairs leading upward. Sarah followed behind, but before stepping into the apartment after him, she paused and looked up the stairway.

The home belonged to Ben's parents, who'd inherited it from their parents. Two generations of McCallums had once called the three-story house with mini-apartments on each floor, their home. Ben was the third in line. Mikey was to have been the fourth. Sarah frowned as memories of her son running down the steps from his play area on the third level ran through her mind. God, how he'd loved the house and his numerous rooms and hideaway areas, she thought. Especially in the basement. He'd had many adventures as he entertained himself. Unlike Ben, who always thought there'd been far too much square footage, Mikey adored the house and couldn't wait to make the "castle" his. Like her son, Sarah loved the old home, although the lower level creeped her out. There'd just always been something "medieval" about it. There was a dungeonesque quality to it with its lack of windows that she could just never warm up to, and so she rarely ventured downstairs.

Sarah felt a clutching in her heart as she looked up to the door at the top of the staircase. The bottom level had been Mikey's favorite, but because she didn't want him downstairs, Sarah let him have the third level all to himself. He'd been the only tenth grader who had an apartment for which he didn't have to pay rent, Ben used to say.

Sarah's favorite floor in the home had been the middle floor, because of it abundance of windows and access to the backyard. She let her sight linger on the carpeted stairwell and fought the desire to pray for her son to come running down, and then turned and walked through the door, stepping into a small den, which was thankfully much warmer than the foyer.

She removed her gloves and took a look around. A small desk with a cordless telephone sitting in its base and mail both opened and unopened scattered across it sat against the wall to her left. A leather sofa, with Ben's leather coat thrown across it was against the wall to her right, beside the entrance leading into the living room. A large fish tank—sans water or fish was flush against the wall across the tiny room. Sarah took a few steps into the den and looked into an adjacent sunroom to the left. At one point the sunroom used to hold her plants. It was now completely empty, save for cobwebs in the corners.

"You haven't done much," she said.

"What's there to do?" Ben said, moving from the den to the living room.

Sarah looked at the blinds closed shut over the windows and thought about opening them for a fleeting moment to let the morning light in as she always did when she woke up, but then shook her head and followed him. "You could try to move on," she said staring at his broad back. She didn't mean to, but she found herself remembering how she used to knead the tension from his shoulders and the lower part of his back after long frustrating days. The good days. She quickly shook the memory from her mind.

Standing beside his coffee table in the middle of the room, Ben looked down at the stack of papers sitting in the middle and said, "You mean the way you have?"

Sarah let out a soft breath. "It's called surviving, Ben."

Ben nodded, then picked up the papers, turned and faced her. "So that's what these are? Survival?"

Sarah frowned and kicked herself for ever saying anything. "Ben…" she started with a sigh. "Let's not—"

Ben cut her off. "Because this seems a hell of a lot more like abandonment to me."

Sarah stared at him long and hard. "Abandonment?" she said. "Don't you think you own the title for that?"

"I'd just lost Mikey."

"And so had I, Ben. But at least you hadn't lost me, too," she said, feeling the sting of tears threatening to rise behind her eyes.

Ben clenched his jaws. "So you're punishing me for dealing with the pain differently?"

"Oh, that's such bullshit, Ben and you know it!"

"You made vows to stay with me through thick and thin, Sarah. Through good and bad. Remember?"

"Oh, I remember, Ben. I remember clearly. But you made vows to me, too. And when the bad came, you were nowhere to be found."

"I was trying to deal with the loss of my son, dammit!" Ben yelled, slamming the papers back down onto the tabletop.

"So was I, Ben! So was I! But I was still willing, wanting and trying to be there for you. I didn't abandon you when you were at your lowest point. I didn't leave you alone to suffer as you tried to tread water, fighting for the will to just breathe!"

"Sarah—"

"—Shut up! Just shut up!" Tears were flowing from her eyes now, her body trembling. They'd had this argument before, but never with the papers between them. Without the papers, though slim, a sliver of hope still remained. A chance to reconcile, repair and move on. But with the papers there… a finality existed. What they had was over, represented by signatures on the dotted line. With the papers between them, the words and the pain behind them seemed to hurt even more.

"I needed you, Ben. I needed you so damned bad. You were the only one who understood what I was going through. Yours were the only words I wanted and needed to hear. But *you* left me."

She wiped tears away and squeezed her eyes tightly, trying in vain to quell the flow that couldn't be stopped. "You left me and every single day of loneliness, another piece of me died."

"Sarah—"

"—I was almost gone, Ben. There was almost nothing left. The only reason I'm standing here now is because of Brandon."

"Oh, please…he saw an opportunity and he took advantage of it."

Sarah slit her eyes. "Go to hell!"

"You know I'm right, Sarah. He did like all guys do…he played the friend role and then struck when the time was right."

"And so what, Ben? So what if he did? At least he was willing to be the friend that you couldn't be."

"You don't love him, Sarah, and you know it. You're still in love with me."

Sarah shook her head. "Whatever, Ben. Keep lying to yourself."

"I'm just stating a fact," Ben said. "You can try all you want to deny it, but I see in your eyes that you still love me."

"Ben—"

"These papers can be ripped up," Ben said, pointing down to them. "We don't have to end this. We can try counseling again."

Sarah wiped more tears and shook her head.

"We can make it work," Ben said, his eyes pleading, his voice insistent.

Sarah shook her head again. They'd tried. More importantly, she'd tried. To get him to open up. To get him to lean on her. To get him to fight for their friendship, their marriage. She'd tried until trying left her weak and even more broken inside. She'd tried until she just couldn't try anymore. It didn't matter that there was truth to his words. She had to survive, and surviving meant walking away.

She wiped more tears and took a slow breath. "I…I need to go," she said, the fight in her voice gone.

"Sarah…please," Ben said, the fight still in his, though softer. "This doesn't have to happen."

Sarah stepped toward the table and put her hands up as Ben reached out for her. "Don't, Ben. Just don't."

She grabbed the papers from the table and flipped through them quickly, checking to see that he'd done what she needed him to do. Satisfied, she frowned, said, "Goodbye, Ben," and then turned and walked away as he called her name.

Refusing to stop, she hurried out of the apartment. Standing in the small hallway, just before the foyer, she paused momentarily and looked up to the area Mikey had called his own.

Six months ago, she thought.

Fresh tears fell as she exhaled. She slid back on her gloves, held on tightly to the papers, and walked out of the house, and ran across the street and got into Brandon's car.

"Are you all right?" Brandon asked with concern in his voice.

Keeping her eyes looking forward through the windshield, Sarah said, "Please drive."

Out of the corner of her eye, she saw Brandon look at her for a few seconds before he shook his head, put the car in drive, and press on the gas pedal.

In the side mirror, Sarah watched Ben standing in the window of the sunroom looking after her. *Goodbye*, she thought, as he and the house that she would always be connected to disappeared.

Chapter 11

Patrick watched through fogged glass as Sarah rushed to her car where Brandon was waiting for her, and climbed in. Tears were falling from her eyes and papers were in her hands.

Patrick smiled.

"Your life is falling apart more and more isn't it, Ben?"

He drummed his fingers on the glass of the window.

"I bet you think you've lost it all, don't you? But you haven't. Almost. But not yet. There's still more work that needs to be done. I still have more lessons to teach. More punishments to hand out for you and for Allen. Lessons and punishments for the things you did to me. For the lies Allen told. Your lives are falling apart, but mine was destroyed. Soon yours will be, too."

Patrick drummed his fingers on the glass of the window again and then watched Sarah's car pull away.

Soon, he thought again with a smile. Soon. He just had to be patient. He couldn't rush the inevitable.

Chapter 12

Ben was scowling over a Styrofoam cup of hot coffee. He'd been scowling since Sarah had walked away from him with the divorce papers he knew she didn't want because she still loved him. He'd seen it in her eyes. He'd heard it in her voice. She still loved him no matter how hard she wished she didn't.

But Ben had screwed up. He'd left her alone when she needed him. He hadn't meant to, but what the hell was he supposed to do? He'd lost his son, his mini-me. He was trying to deal with that reality. He was just trying to cope. He never meant to shut her out. He never meant to neglect her. But seeing her pain, being around it had been torture for him. It had been a constant reminder that he was never going to get to see Mikey again. He was never going to get to see his blue eyes light up when he smiled. Was never going to get to watch him ride his skateboard or pop wheelies on his bike. He was never going to get to watch baseball or basketball with him again. He would never see him grow from a boy to a man.

Sarah's tears reminded him of that.

She needed for him to be strong, but in the seconds, minutes, hours, days, weeks and months after Mikey was taken from him, Ben had just been too damned weak.

He took a sip of his black coffee, courtesy of the coffee pot that never seems to get cleaned, as his thoughts moved from Sarah to her new beau, Brandon. Goddamned opportunist. Ben never liked him. Never trusted him and his slick smile, too small eyes, and crisp Italian suit. From the moment Sarah had introduced him as a colleague at her law firm's

Christmas party, Ben had a bad feeling about him. There'd been a wolf's glare in his eyes that only a man could recognize. Brandon was full of shit. A slick-talking, overconfident son-of-a-bitch, who, when given the chance was going to go after his wife. It took Ben all of five minutes to figure that out. But he trusted his wife and knew he had nothing to worry about, because an opportunity for Brandon to slither his way in just wasn't going to happen. He and Sarah were best friends and great lovers. They were made for one another and they were going to be together forever with Mikey standing between them, his hands in theirs.

And then, tragedy struck.

Now Sarah was surviving with Brandon latched on to her arm, while Ben still struggled to walk amongst the living.

Life was just too goddamned unfair.

"You all right?"

Ben looked up. His own cup of coffee in hand, Vance had just walked into the tiny conference room where he'd been sitting alone, waiting for everyone to arrive for their meeting to discuss the case. He was dressed in dark blue jeans, a light grey V-neck top that fit tight to show off his muscular torso. His hair was as curly as always, his goatee faded. He was a pretty boy who could have been making money modeling in magazines or videos, but instead, he'd chosen to live dangerously, working a job with shitty hours, that paid him a meager salary.

Ben took a sip of his bitter coffee. "Sarah came by this morning."

Vance gave him an I-got-you nod and took a chair just to the left of him. "She came to pick up the papers?"

Ben took another sip then ran his tongue along the front of his teeth. "Yup," he said curtly.

Vance nodded again. "So…you okay?"

"Thought I answered that yesterday."

"I'm not talking about the case."

"Neither am I."

Vance drank some of his coffee, which smelled like vanilla, and put his cup down and rest his arms down on the table and intertwined his fingers. "Come on, Ben," he said. "Be straight up with me, man."

Ben exhaled. "Be straight up? Okay…I lost my son and my soon-to-be ex-wife is living with a piece of shit whose ass I'd love to shove my foot up into. But that's just all my fault. I'm up to a pack and a half a day in cigarettes and I'm about to start downing bottles of Johnny Walker. My life is about as shitty as a field filled with cows. But like I said yesterday…I'm fine. I'm here. I'm focused. You don't have to worry about your back."

Vance took a slow sip of his coffee and then looked across at his partner. "How long have we been partners, man? More importantly, how long have we been friends?" Waiting for no answer, he spoke again. "Ben, I wasn't asking if you were all right because I was worried about you having my back. I was asking because of all the people that you haven't pushed away, I'm one of the only ones who know how bad you're hurting inside, whether you show it or not. I know what your marriage meant to you, man. I know that you still love Sarah. I'm your partner and friend. You need to vent—I'm here. You need to drown your sorrows—I'm your designated driver." Vance paused and looked at Ben with a hard, unflinching gaze.

Ben stared back, his gaze not hard, but apologetic. Vance was being what he needed right now, even if he didn't want to admit it. He was being a friend. He gave him a nod and then leaned forward and extended his hand across the table. "Thanks," he said humbly.

Vance took it and gave it a firm squeeze as they shook hands.

"Ummm…do you two need a few more minutes alone? Because I can leave and close the door behind me if you do."

Ben and Vance both looked toward the door. Reds, with a file folder in hand, gave them a smile. "Really, it's no trouble," he added.

Vance shook his head, let go of Ben's hand and said, "You got jokes, huh?"

Reds pulled out a chair off to Vance's left, directly across from Ben. "One of just a few. Jokes are in short supply these days."

"I feel you," Vance said solemnly.

Reds looked across to Ben. "Ben," he said with a nod.

Ben nodded back. "Reds."

"Morning, gentlemen."

Everyone's attention went to the door. Tiana Wilkins had just walked in. She was the resident profiler and all-around breaker of hearts for men everywhere. Tiana was a stunning black woman with skin the color of dark coffee, entrancing and intense brown eyes, and a dangerously curved, yet slender body, topped only by a pair of D-cup breasts that had never gone through the blessings and curse of child birth. When Tiana walked into a room, the eyes of men followed closely behind. Unfortunately for them, they never had a chance with her, as she was one hundred percent lesbian.

Ben said, "Hey, T."

She flashed him a warm smile. "Hey, Ben. I wish the circumstances were different, but it's nice to see you back."

"Thanks."

Tiana went around to his side of the table, gave his shoulder a squeeze, and then took a seat beside him and looked over to Vance. "What's up, pretty boy?"

Vance rolled his eyes. "Whatever, T."

Tiana laughed.

Reds cleared his throat. "What am I…invisible?"

Tiana twisted her full lips and kept her eyes on Vance, who raised both eyebrows at her and shrugged.

Although Reds knew he had no chance in hell at pulling Tiana's sexual preference over in his direction, he still couldn't help but to try with constant futile flirtation.

Tiana looked at him. "Hello, Reds."

"Please," Reds said, adding more baritone to his voice, "call me Jim."

Vance couldn't help it; he broke out in laughter. Ben, too, had been unable to keep his composure.

Tiana shook her head. "You're an idiot, Reds."

"And you don't know what you're missing," Reds said.

Tiana raised one eyebrow and smirked. "I'm an expert profiler remember? And judging by what I see when I look at you, I know I'm not missing much."

Vance dragged a hand down over his face. "Ouch," he said, his hand over his mouth.

His light-colored skin turning red, Reds looked over at Vance. "I think you better get Becks in here to replace Ms. Wilkins because she obviously doesn't know what she's talking about."

Tiana laughed. "Definitely not much at all," she said.

Reds shook his head. "Too much you mean."

"Too much empty space in those briefs of yours."

"Boxers," Reds said. "I'm a real man."

Ben chuckled at the banter. It was much welcomed considering the morning he'd had.

"Okay, okay," Vance said. The lightheartedness was welcome, considering the nature of the case they were on and the lack of ground they'd made on it, but it was now time to get down to business. "Reds... where's Birch?"

"Right here!" Jerry Birch said, appearing in the doorway. He was Red's fellow investigative agent. Young, tall and wiry, Jerry Birch was damn near albino with a mop of red hair and red freckles spread across his nose. He actually looked like Richie Cunningham—the 2011 version. "Sorry," he said, taking a seat beside Reds. "Went to my friend's bachelor party last night. Drank a little too much. Duty called."

"Come on, Birch," Reds said. "Didn't your dad teach you how to be considerate with the conversation in front of the ladies?"

Simultaneously, Birch and Tiana said, "What lady?"

Reds groaned.

Vance said, "Let's get to work. Reds—"

"Is this a private party or can anyone join?"

Vance and everyone in the room looked to the door. Their captain, Stubbs, was standing in the doorway.

"I thought you had a meeting," Vance said.

Stubbs walked into the room. He'd once been a starting center for his college basketball team, but to look at him, you would think it would have been football that he would have played. He was a large man, about 6'6," with dark honey brown skin, broad shoulders, and a stomach that at side view made him look at least four months pregnant. With his stomach, lack of neck, and thick jowl, athletic was the one word that no one would think to associate him with. At least not now.

Stubbs was a good guy, but he lived by the CYA credo, and he'd made it perfectly clear in the past, that when push came to shove, he wouldn't hesitate to throw someone under the bus if it ensured that he would continue on with his ascent up the ladder. He said, "Thankfully, the mayor had to cancel, because I wasn't in the mood to have my ass handed to me this morning." He pulled out a chair at the head of the table and fit his large body into the leather chair. "Looks like you were expecting me," he said to Vance.

Vance shook his head. "I just didn't feel like sitting there."

Stubbs looked at him with a cocked eyebrow. "Rule number one…if you're running the show, you should always look the part."

"I'll remember that," Vance said, clearly not liking the public teaching lesson.

Stubbs gave him a smile, then looked across to Tiana. "Nice to see you, T. How's the Mrs.?"

"Gone," Tiana said with a slight frown. "She got tired of feeling as though I was always trying to get into her head."

"I have a head for you to get into," Reds said.

Tiana flashed him an incendiary glare, and gave him the finger. "In your dreams," she said.

"Every night, T.," Reds countered.

Stubbs chuckled and then settled his eyes on Ben. "Ben."

Ben nodded. "Micah."

Stubbs watched him intensely, his eyes asking him if he could handle this.

Ben stared back, his gaze unflinching, saying that he could.

Stubbs watched him for a second or two longer, before acknowledging Reds and Birch, and then putting his sights back on Vance. "So, what have I missed?"

Vance shook his head. "Nothing. Reds was just about to tell us what he had for us. Reds?"

Reds opened his file folder revealing a stack of papers. He selected photographs from the stack and passed out copies to everyone. Ben didn't want to look, but had to. His stomach twisted at the site of the boy's deceased body.

"Well, like I said in the preliminary look over at the scene, he definitely died from strangulation. The size and location of the bruises around the neck are adult sized, although there's no real definition to them, which indicates that our guy once again wore gloves. The bruises, where the carotid arteries are, are deeper than the other bruises, which means this sicko was facing him. The major bruising's on the side of the trachea, while the smaller ones are on the back of the neck."

"Did the little guy get to put up a fight?" Vance asked.

Reds shook his head. "There weren't any traces of skin under his fingernails and there were no bruises on his hands or forearms or face to indicate he was trying to fight the guy off. Also, just like the others, there were stun gun bruises on his neck."

"What about the semen?" Vance asked.

"On his hands and in between his fingers. Same as the others. The patterns and amounts are all consistent and show that he enjoys having these boys get him off until he ejaculates."

A chill came over Ben and beneath the table, he balled his hand into a tight fist.

"Anything in his mouth?" Vance asked.

"Mercifully, it doesn't look like our guy has escalated to that point yet."

Ben closed his eyes momentarily as his body temperature rose. *Too close to home*, he thought. *Too damned close*. This case was opening doors long closed. Doors that desperately needed to be remain locked shut.

"You okay, Ben?" Stubbs asked looking at him.

Ben opened his eyes. Everyone at the table was fixated on him. He needed to keep it together. He nodded at Stubbs and said, "Yeah. I was just thinking. What about the pacifier?"

"Sold in Giants, Safeways, and other stores all over the place," Birch said. "Nothing unusual about it or the glue he used. Standard issue crazy glue."

"No prints?" Vance asked.

Reds gave him a look as if to say, *'yeah, right'*.

Vance sighed and looked over at his partner. "I checked the missing person's database last night, but didn't find anything confirming his identity. Unless a report's filed, he's going to be another John Doe."

"No trace of his clothing anywhere at the scene?" Ben asked.

"None," Reds said. We canvassed but found nothing useful. We took some shoe and tire impressions but the odds of getting anything out of them are slim to none."

Stubbs let out a heavy breath of air and clamped the back of his hand down on the back of his thick neck and squeezed. "Okay…so our guy likes to stun these boys and then force them to get him off before he strangles them. Tiana…what kind of asshole are we dealing with here?"

Tiana frowned. "One who likes to be in control. Based on the nature of the crime, I'd say he's very angry. He was most likely abused as a child and I'd be willing to bet that he was probably the same age as the victims he's chosen. He may or may not know them, but he knows enough about them to know that they won't be missed. You may want to check with homeless shelters and orphanages around the city."

"We have," Vance said. "But so far, we've got shit."

Tiana arched her eyebrows. "That's not surprising," she said matter-of-factly. "You'll have to broaden your search."

"We're doing that now."

"I hope it produces something, but I have my doubts."

"Why?" Stubbs asked.

T. looked at him. "Whoever he is, he knows what he's doing. He's left bodies to be found, but I think he knows their identities will be unknown, which leaves me to believe that this may be a game or challenge of some kind."

"A challenge?" Ben asked. "A challenge to who?"

Tiana shrugged. "The police department. Someone specific. Although I'd say the chances of it being a more personal challenge toward someone specific is more likely."

"So you're implying that this person is out for revenge?" Stubbs said.

Tiana shrugged. "Possibly. Have any of your collars gotten out of jail recently?"

Vance shook his head. "Not really. Most of the perps we've put away are there to stay for a nice long while."

"You may want to check out relatives, friends, boyfriends, etc. Maybe someone is really, really pissed."

Vance leaned back in his chair. "Shit… that could take months."

Tiana shrugged again. "Better you than me," she said.

Vance let out a breath. "Want to do some research for us?" he said to Tiana.

She laughed. "No thanks, pretty boy. I like my evenings."

"Put Cribbs and Weston on it," Stubbs said. "They're both fresh and eager for something to do. What do you think, Ben?"

Ben nodded. They'd joined the departments as junior detectives a few months before his life had changed. As Stubbs said, they were fresh. The job was still exciting to them. The ground work, which somehow Ben knew would prove fruitless, would be good for them. "Better them than us," he said.

"Okay. I'll talk to them after this," Vance chimed in. "Anyway T., what else can you tell us?"

"Well, I'm pretty sure our guy watches a lot of cop shows or does a lot of research on crime scenes and forensics, because he knows what not to leave behind, which means he understands the importance of being detailed."

"Age?" Vance asked.

"Tough to determine, but I'd almost be willing to bet he's in his mid-thirties. This just doesn't seem like acts committed by someone younger. It's too…calculated to some degree."

"What about race?" Reds asked.

"Well, as seems to be the case with most serial killers, he's probably white, but of course there are exceptions to the rule."

Stubbs cleared his throat. "I'm sure I don't need to remind everyone how high up the shit list this is, but I'm going to anyway. The mayor has a poker about halfway up my ass right now. It's hot and extremely un-fucking comfortable. My ass is sacred to me, people. I know you all are doing your jobs, but just for the sake of my being able to tell the mayor that I pushed my own pokers halfway up, we need to find this motherfucker, and find him now. Again, I know you're doing the best you can, but it had to be said."

Everyone nodded. Vance looked at Tiana. "T.... anything else you can give us?"

Tiana thought about it for a moment. "Only that I feel as though whoever this is...he's cold, calculating, and he's not finished."

Vance clenched his jaw. "Okay, well I guess that means we need to stop him before he does."

Everyone agreed with head nods and tight lips.

"I guess that's about it for now," Vance said. "Reds...let us know if you find anything new. Tiana...if anything comes to mind..."

"I'll give you a call," she said.

"Thanks."

Somber and silently, everyone pushed their chairs back and rose from the table. Tiana gave Ben's shoulder another squeeze, flashed Vance a smile, and then headed for the door.

"Hey, T...I'll walk with you," Reds said, hurrying behind her.

Tiana groaned and kept moving.

When Birch walked out, Stubbs, who had remained seated, looked from Vance to Ben. "Gentlemen...this is getting bad. The media coverage is getting uglier and the mayor is ready to roll heads."

"We're trying to find this psycho, Captain," Vance said, clenching his jaw.

Stubbs put up his hands, his palms facing both men. "Like I said...I know you are. But I just wanted to stress to you two privately that you need to try harder. If what T. says is accurate, and this could possibly be a personal attack of some kind, then this shit could get really ugly. Now I'm really tired of the phone calls and I'm sick of having my ass reamed. Ben...I know you needed more time, but we need you on this. Can you handle it?"

Ben worked his jaw. "I'm fine," he said. He could feel Vance's gaze on him.

Stubbs nodded. "Are you seeing Rose?"

"Have an appointment in about an hour."

"Good. Make sure you don't miss it." Stubbs pushed himself back and rose from the chair. "Vance…you're running the show. Sit here next time." That said, he walked out of the room, leaving the two partners alone.

Vance looked at his partner. "This sucks, man."

Ben said, "Yeah. It does."

"Want to ride back to the park? Check the scene again…see if we get lucky and find someone around that recognizes the kid. I also want to check with the local shelters. See if they have any recent runaways and I want to talk to the rider again to and see if she remembers anything else that she may have been too freaked out to remember yesterday."

"If I didn't have to meet with Rose I would."

"How's that going? Helping at all?"

Ben exhaled. Although the staff psychologist, Lisa Rose, had advised Stubbs that Ben hadn't been ready to get back to work, the chief had still insisted that he be cleared for duty. His insistence had come with a compromise with Rose, so he was still required to have once-a- week sessions with her. Stubbs received weekly updates from Rose. Assurances that with the strains of the case, Ben was still of sound mind and body to do his job. Of course, the requirement by Stubbs was really just bullshit. With the mayor breathing down his back the way he was, Ben knew that sound mind or not, there was no chance he was going to be pulled. "If you call talking about shit I'd much rather keep buried, helping," he said, "then I guess it's helping a lot."

"Just be glad it's only once a week."

"Yeah. Thanks for small favors, huh. Listen…I need a smoke."

"What you need to do is quit."

Ben thought about the promise he'd made to Mikey. "Yeah I do," he said. "But just not today."

"I hear you. Okay…I'm gonna go and give Cribbs and Weston some work to do and then head back to the park. See if I can find anything. I'll hook up with you later."

Ben nodded. "All right."

Vance patted him on his shoulder and then left the room. Ben stood still for a long moment and thought about everything Tiana had said about the possibility of this being a personal vendetta of some kind. His thoughts went to Mikey and the way he'd been taken from him. Nothing physical had been taken the day it happened. Nothing physical had been broken. Just Mikey's life and Ben's heart. A chill came over Ben as he tried not to think about a correlation existing.

Chapter 13

Allen Kline sat behind his desk and let out a slow, anxiety-filled, long breath of air. His elbow was planted firmly on his desktop, his forehead cradled firmly in the palm of his hand. Coffee sat in front of him, steam rising from a mug his sons had given him for Father's Day the year before. On its ceramic side it said, '*World's Greatest Dad.*' Allen watched the steam rise and thought what a lie that was.

World's Greatest Coward was more like it.

That's what he was, wasn't he? His sons were missing and he wouldn't go to the police, no matter how much his wife begged him to. That was cowardice, wasn't it?

Or was it?

A madman, a killer shows up in his office with photographs of his sons being held captive. This killer tells him that he's killed other little boys because they somehow deserved to be killed. He says that they're guilty, and that Allen is guilty, too. That he's a liar. That he's done enough. Then he says that if Allen goes to the police or tells anyone, he'll do to his sons what he does to the boys he kills.

"I killed a child, Allen. A boy. He was ten just like your youngest son. I had him do horrible things to me and then I strangled him and left his body to be found."

A terrifying confession. One that left Allen chilled, almost to the core. But there was more.

"If your sons die, Allen, it will be your fault. Do you get that?"

Those words had done it. They'd reached the recesses of Allen's soul and latched on, making it almost impossible to breathe, think, move. His sons could die and it would be his fault.

If he said something.

So was he a coward or was he being the world's greatest dad as his mug so boldly stated by doing what was necessary to keep them alive? If in fact they were alive.

Allen closed his eyes slowly and squeezed his temples. He took a deep breath and held it in as the October wind blew outside of his window. Howling, mocking. He exhaled. Opened his eyes and watched the steam rise from his mug. He'd had no intention of drinking the coffee. He just needed it there in front of him. He needed some sense of normalcy. It was the only thing helping to keep him sane.

He took another breath and looked over at a dual framed photograph of his boys. Chad had on a t-shirt and shorts and was holding a football in his hand. Chris had on sweats and a t-shirt, a baseball glove and bat in his hands. The picture had been taken a few months earlier at the park. A Saturday.

"My boys," Allen whispered.

Where are you?

What is he doing to you?

What has he already done?

Are you hurt?

Are you still alive?

Allen clenched his jaws and slammed his eyes shut as tears welled. "My boys," he whispered again. "I'm so sorry."

He picked up the photo, held onto it tightly. "I…I want to call the police," he said, tracing a finger over the glass, around the boys' chins. "I…I want to. But…but I can't. I…I don't dare. There may still…still be a chance to see you both again."

A chance.

He looked up to the ceiling, tears trailing from his eyes. "God please forgive me for…for those little boys, but…but I need mine back."

He put the photograph back down gently and took a long, lasting look at his sons. Chris looked like him. He had the same deep-set eyes, the same square jaw. But he didn't have the slightly crooked nose that Allen had. His was straighter, thinner. He was tall like Allen, with a mop of sandy-brown hair, and thin but muscular. Chad did have his hooked nose, but unlike his older brother, he was the spitting image of his mother, with softer lines and a close-cropped head of blonde hair.

"I need you boys back," Allen said, staring at them, at the smile on their faces. "I…I don't want those boys to die, but if…if it means getting you back safely…"

He paused as tears snaked harder, faster. Boys were dying, but dammit, not his boys.

Not his boys.

"Forgive me," he said, tracing his fingers over his sons again. "Please forgive me."

He took another slow, deep breath, held it and then exhaled quickly. He wiped his tears away with his fingertips and then leaned forward and grabbed his mug by the handle. Bringing it to his lips, he thought: *I am not a coward. I am not a murderer. I am the world's greatest dad.*

He took a slow sip of coffee and then reached for his appointment book. He had a ten a.m. coming in that he needed to get ready for. He took another sip and wondered when his next late night appointment from Patrick was going to be.

Chapter 14

Amanda Kline clicked on the talk button on her telephone and held her breath as the dial tone hummed melodically, piercing the silence around her.

Make the call. That's all she had to do. Make the call. Tell the police that the killer they were looking for had taken her sons. Tell them all about his "sessions" with her husband.

Amanda pressed the 9 button as her heart rate quickened.

Make the call. For your sons. To hell with what Allen says.

She pressed the 1 button. Her heartbeat was thunderous now, causing her body to shake.

Make the call. For your sanity, which you are slowly losing. Ignore the apprehension. Ignore the words of warning from Allen. Ignore the possibility that if you do make the call, that your boys could be harmed or worse. If they aren't already. Ignore the feeling of hopelessness. The twist in the pit of your stomach. Don't give in to the doubt, the what ifs swirling around in your mind.

What if Allen is right? What if I make the call and do far more damage? The worst kind of damage. What if following the rules gets me my sons back faster?

What if.

What if.

What if.

The phone in her hand began to shake as her body trembled.

"Make the call," she whispered.

Tears began to fall mercilessly from her eyes. They ran down her cheeks to her chin, and dropped to her lap. "Make…the call," she whispered again, her throat tight.

She took a breath and tried to will her body to stop trembling. That only seemed to make the tremors worse. What ifs continued to sing tumultuously in her head. Fear, doubt, angst assisted with background vocals.

"Pl…please," she begged herself. "Please!"

Tears fell harder as though they were weighted.

"Please," she implored again. "Make…the…call…"

Amanda screamed out and threw the cordless handheld across the room, sending it crashing against the wall. She buried her face in her hands, slumped over sideways on her couch and shattered into more pieces as her boys stared down at her from a photograph perched on the side-table beside her.

Make the call. That's all she had to do. She had tried to get her finger to press down on the 1 button again. Tried to force her way past the trepidation. Tried to do what she swore she was going to do the first chance she'd gotten.

But she couldn't, because as much as she didn't want him to be, Allen was right. She'd seen the news. She knew what Patrick was capable of. She wanted to make the call, but she couldn't. For the sake of her precious angels, she just couldn't.

Amanda cried and begged for God's and her sons' forgiveness.

Chapter 15

Eric Breaden was starving, freezing and tired. He hadn't had a real meal or slept in a warm bed in nearly a year. But that was his choice. The truth was, Eric could have been eating real food or been in his bed snuggled underneath his comforter. He didn't have to be out in the cold, his ears and fingers feeling as though they were being bitten off slowly, in an alley behind a pizza shop, rifling through a dumpster searching for something to eat. He didn't have to think about where he was going to lay his head that night. He could have been home. But no matter how disgusting it was to scour through garbage for food, no matter how bitter the wind, no matter how hard the concrete that he would be sleeping on was, being away from his house was truly the only option he had.

Home was not a place he wanted to be. Home was filled with nightmares and torture, with belts, whips and fists. Home was filled with discipline and punishment handed out in the harshest of ways to ensure that he would grow into being a man and not a "weak-assed pussy."

Eric shivered as he tossed one garbage bag aside and reached for another. The wind blowing was fierce, as though it were angry, as though it were trying to dole out its own form of discipline and punishment. But he would take all that the wind had to offer, because whatever it dished out, was pale in comparison to what his father served at home.

His father.

The reason he ran away from home nearly one year ago. A man who believed that the resolution to everything required blame and the use of a belt, whip, or his hand.

Eric's mother had passed away when he was just five. A heart attack is what the doctors had said. Eric was sure that his father had played a role in his mother's heart going bad well before its' time. Soon after his mother passed, his father packed them up and moved Eric away from the few friends and even fewer family members he had. With no one to reach out to, Eric endured all that his father had to give until finally, at the age of thirteen, he just couldn't endure it any longer.

In the middle of the night, as his father snored from the bedroom, Eric took a Nike bag filled with underwear, socks, t-shirts, sweatpants and sweatshirts, his toothbrush, and a picture of his mother, and left the house he was never going to return to. He also took with him four hundred dollars. It was money he'd periodically and very carefully had stolen from his father and kept hidden behind a loose board in his closet. Two bus tickets and many miles later, Eric ended up in a shelter for runaways, where he remained until one of the employees there, forcefully tried to get special favors in exchange for the cot Eric slept on. Eric could have exposed the employee, but instead chose to just leave and make the streets his permanent home, figuring that it couldn't have been much worse that what he'd already been through.

Eric shivered again. He was rifling through a half empty bag now.

"Do you see anything good?"

He turned and looked over at a thin boy, who'd been standing off to his side. "Give me a chance to go through it. Damn!" he said.

The boy frowned. "I'm starving," he said. He was dressed as Eric had been in black sweatpants, a grey sweatshirt, and a bomber goose-down. Items they'd stolen from the racks of a sidewalk sale just a few weeks prior.

"I'm hungry too, Brian. Shit. Just hold on."

Brian frowned again, pulled his knit hat lower down on his head and nodded.

Eric shook his head. He'd met Brian on the street one night during the summer beneath a small bridge. Brian's story was eerily similar to his own. Death, abuse—sexual, not physical—then escape. Then there was more abuse and another escape. He was younger than Eric—ten years old.

Beneath the bridge, Eric fought off a middle-aged, homeless man who thought Brian had been "sweet" for him again. Brian hadn't left his side since, and Eric didn't mind. The streets were a lonely place to be.

Eric sighed, shook his head and then removed a half-eaten cheesesteak sub, wrapped loosely in foil. Why the person never finished the entire sub, Eric didn't know, nor did he care. It was food.

He turned with it in his hand to see Brian smiling. Eric's plan had been to split the sub in half. He sighed and held out the sandwich. "Here," he said, his stomach rumbling.

Brian took the sub and without hesitation tore away the foil and ate what someone else wouldn't.

Eric smiled. Brian wasn't blood, but he was the closest thing to a brother that he had. As long as he could, he would always watch out for him. He turned and continued searching for food of his own.

Chapter 16

"So, how are you feeling?"

Ben looked at the department appointed psychiatrist, Dr. Lisa Rose, with an impassive glare. She was a tall woman, about 5'9, thin-framed from hours spent in the gym, with a pair of soft, blue eyes, hidden beneath a set of slender wire-rimmed glasses. Her hair was pulled back into a simple ponytail. Her lips were thin, her cheekbones high. She was wearing a pair of loose-fitting, grey slacks, a long-sleeved white blouse that slouched at the neck. Low-heeled black shoes were on her feet. The modest clothing, the glasses, and the ponytail did little to tone down the fact that she was a strikingly attractive woman.

But Ben wasn't paying attention to her beauty as he stared at her. He clenched the right side of his jaw, something he knew Dr. Rose had noticed and had mentally written down, as he knew everything he did and said was being paid close attention to, and said, "I'm fine."

Dr. Rose nodded and very slightly arched an eyebrow. It wasn't supposed to have been noticeable, but from his years on the force, Ben noticed things, too. She shifted in the high-back leather chair she was sitting in, behind her very polished wooden desk. "Fine?" she said, "Is that it?"

Ben clenched the left side of his jaw this time and looked off to the side, his eyes settling on a framed print of a painting done by Salvador Dali, hanging up against a forest-green colored wall. *Apparition of Face and Fruit Dish on a Beach.* An old girlfriend of Ben's used to have the exact same print in her apartment. It was one of three paintings done by Dali hanging in the small office. Ben didn't know the other two. A tan, leather chaise sat just beneath the painting. Ben was sitting in the matching loveseat. Plush, beige carpeting a shade darker than the furniture filled the room. Thick beige drapes were closed, buffering the sound of the activity from the streets outside. Heavy shaded lamps, one on the corner of Rose's desk, the other on a side table off to Ben's right, were on, the illumination from them casting a soft glow.

The colors, style and feel of the office was supposed to help put patients at ease and entice them to open up. Ben had no doubt that its effects worked very well, however it had the opposite effect on him. The colors, the serene design, and Dr. Rose's professionally conservative look just annoyed Ben. He was there to open up and talk about his "feelings" that he didn't want to share with anyone because he had to be. It was like being held in an interrogation room with shackles fastened around his ankles to the legs of a hard, uncomfortable folding chair, with handcuffs clamped around his wrists. A prisoner for one hour each week.

He turned back to her. "That's it," he said evenly.

Dr. Rose looked at him with the expression of a teacher about to scold her student. "Are you still having trouble sleeping at night? Still having nightmares about Mikey?"

Ben took a breath, held it, and then exhaled, the mention of his deceased son's name, stabbing at his heart. It had been a struggle to do it initially, but because he'd really had no choice, Ben finally opened up and told Rose about his fitful nights of sleep he'd had, and the dreams of Mikey. Dreams in which he'd always been unable to locate and help his little boy, who screamed and pleaded for him.

Nightmares of the worst kind.

"I am," he said, his voice tight.

Rose nodded. "Have you tried the sleeping pills I prescribed?"

Ben shook his head. "No." Although the nightmares prevented him from getting a full night's sleep, he refused to take any sort of sleeping aid for two reasons. One was because he didn't like taking pills of any kind. Reason two was because as horrifying as the nightmares were, in them he still had a chance to save Mikey. For months he'd been unsuccessful, but there was still that chance. He felt sleeping pills would eliminate the chance altogether of doing what he couldn't do in the real world, and Ben just couldn't and wouldn't allow that. He might never be successful, but he needed for that hope to remain.

Rose nodded again. "How does it feel being back to work? This case can't be easy for you."

Ben shrugged. "It's just like every other case, I guess."

"You're holding back," Dr. Rose said. "I thought you agreed to stop doing that?"

Ben sighed. "It…it's not easy, but I'm handling it."

"Enough to be able to stay on?"

"There's a psycho…" Ben paused as a sharp pain stabbed at his temples and behind his eyes. He felt warm as his body temperature rose suddenly, as his thoughts became fuzzy.

"Ben?" he heard from somewhere far away. "Ben…are you all right?"

The voice—Dr. Rose's—echoed, as though coming from the end of a long tunnel. Ben shook his head. Or at least thought he did as the sudden cloudiness began to fade.

"Ben?" Rose called again. "Are you all right?"

Ben blinked his eyes rapidly a few times and then nodded slowly. "I…I'm fine," he said. "I just had a dizzy spell."

"Are you sure you're all right?" Rose asked again, her eyes scrutinizing.

"Yeah. I'm fine. Lack of sleep that's all."

Rose closed her eyes a bit. Said, "Okay."

Ben took a breath and let it out easily. "Anyway, like I was saying… there's a psycho out there sexually molesting little boys before he strangles them to death. There are no leads yet, no clues giving us any indication as to who this…this sick bastard is. The worst thing is he's probably going to kill again, and if he hasn't already, then it's just a matter of when. I'm handling the case. It's not easy and of course it brings back memories that I'd buried a long time ago, but we're short on manpower and it's an election year, so whether I can handle it or not doesn't really matter, does it?"

Rose looked at him as he stared at her with a hard, intense glare. "Would you like for me to push again to have you taken off of the case?" she asked.

"Sure," Ben scoffed. "That'll do good for my reputation. Just tell everyone that I'm a wreck, and can't keep my shit together."

Rose closed her eyes a bit and stared at him for a few silent seconds. Ben didn't like the way she was studying him, as though his words were very much the truth, and not just sarcastic rambling.

The psychiatrist licked her lips. To someone else it would have seemed sensual. Ben found it antagonizing.

She said, "What about things with Sarah? Did you sign the papers?"

Ben opened and closed his fist. "Yeah. She came by and picked them up this morning."

"And how did that go?"

"How do you think it went?"

"I'm asking you, Ben. I wasn't there."

Ben clenched, opened and closed his fists again, then flared his nostrils. "It went," he said curtly.

"Did you try to get her to change her mind as we discussed?"

He sighed. He'd resisted opening up to Rose when he first began going to her, but once he had, he eventually found himself expressing to her, the regret he felt over the way he had pushed Sarah away, and the hope he still held onto that he would somehow find a way to convince her to give them another chance. Only Dr. Rose and Vance knew just how heartbroken he was, and only they knew about the papers. "I tried."

"And?"

"And...she said goodbye and left with the papers in her hand."

"Did you talk about the feelings you think she still has for you?"

Ben clenched his jaw again as he went back to the conversation with Sarah he'd had earlier. She still loved him. Her eyes said it. The wavering in her voice reinforced it. She was still in love with him, but she was still trying to survive by running away from the truth. He nodded.

Rose said, "Did she deny it?"

Whatever, Ben. Keep lying to yourself. Sarah's words said with tears in her eyes.

Ben shook his head.

"And how do you feel about that?"

"How do you think I *feel* about it?" he said, his tone biting. "She took divorce papers that she doesn't want and got into a car with an opportunist that she's not in love with all because she's trying to *survive*," he said, making quotation marks with his fingers. "It's bullshit. Complete, fucking bullshit."

Rose watched him as he sat tense, breathing heavily through his nostrils. She was evaluating him, probably assessing that he was unstable and unfit for duty. Ben didn't give a shit. His life was a train wreck and instead of mercifully dying when each baggage car collided into the other, he was left broken, bloodied, his legs useless and stretched out behind, crawling, trying in vain to figure out a way to get to safety.

To hell with what Rose thought of him or his psyche. On or off the case, nothing fucking mattered.

Rose watched him for another few seconds and then adjusted her glasses against the bridge of her nose. "You've been through a lot, Ben and you're still going through a lot as well. Nothing that's happened has been your fault." She was looking at him intensely as she'd said that. "You're not a wreck. You're hurting and while Sarah is doing what she thinks is best to cope, you're trying to find your own way out of the madness. This case, although I didn't think it was a good one for you to be on, the more I think about it, the more I'm beginning to feel that it really may be just the right type of case that you need to be on."

Ben arched an eyebrow.

Rose gave him a warm, compassionate smile. "You'll see what I mean when you put a stop to this madman."

"Don't you mean if?"

Rose shook her head. "When, Ben," she said, her voice strong.

"You seem pretty confident."

"Aren't you confident?" she asked. "Aren't you sure that you will get this case resolved?"

Ben opened and closed his fists again. *When,* he thought as he did so. When he and Vance found the killer. When he would be able to finally save Mikey in his dreams. Rose was confident that when would be answered. Ben wouldn't admit it, but he had his doubts.

"I'm not going to push that you be taken off of the case, Ben," Rose said. "But what I am recommending *again,* is that you do take the sleeping pills. You deserve a full night's sleep whether you want to believe that or not."

Ben bore down on his jaws again and pulled his lips in. "Do I?" he said.

"Yes, you do, Ben. There was nothing you could have done to save Mikey."

"I could have been home," Ben said, feeling the sting of tears behind his eyes. He gritted his teeth and held his fist closed tightly.

"You were doing your job."

Ben frowned. "Not good enough apparently."

"So are you saying that it would have been better had someone else's child died that day instead of yours? That Mikey's life was more valuable?"

Ben shook his head. "I'm not saying that," his tone with an edge.

Rose looked at him over the top of her glasses. "You're not?"

"No," Ben said, his anger rising.

"But you said that you should have been home."

"Yes. I should have."

"Instead of being out doing your duty, working to give victim's families justice?"

"I'm not saying that either."

"So then just what are you saying, Ben? Because if you should have been home, then that means you wouldn't have been out trying to keep another criminal from harming another unsuspecting and undeserving victim. So if you aren't saying that Mikey's life was more valuable, tell me what you are saying."

Ben straightened up in his chair as his heart raced. He wasn't saying that, he thought, as irritation over Rose's accusation made him warm. He shook his head, gave Rose a steely glare. She was putting words in his mouth. Saying things he never said. Things he never…

No.

He hadn't thought those things either.

Not when he'd slammed down on his brakes coming to a screeching stop in front of his house, jumped out of the car, his keys still in the ignition, rushed past neighbors and other nosey onlookers, held his badge up for the primary officer on the scene as he raced by him, and followed the unwanted commotion upstairs to Mikey's play area on the third level of the house.

Those thoughts hadn't run through his mind.

Not when Sarah ran to him as he stepped across the door's threshold, her face maroon red with tears flooding from swollen eyes. Not when Vance tried to keep him from entering the room where Mikey liked to play his Nintendo DS and his Xbox360.

No.

He hadn't wished for it to have been someone else's son as he stared down at a small body lying beneath a white sheet. And when he fought and yelled to be let go of, and ran to the sheet and pulled it away only to look down at the barely recognizable face of his son, those thoughts, wishes, desires, and needs never existed.

That was selfish, wrong.

"So tell me, Ben. What are you saying?" Rose pushed again.

Ben clenched down harder as his eyes welled. He tried to keep them at bay, but the tears just couldn't be contained, and as he shook his head, they fell slowly from his eyes.

Dr. Rose sighed, then rose from her chair, moved from around her desk, approached him, and put a slender hand down gently on his shoulder. Her voice soft, soothing, she said, "There was nothing that you could have done, Ben. Nothing."

No longer able to keep them to a trickle, Ben let the flood gates open and cried freely now as the doctor's words—words he'd heard from everyone—words he'd tried to tell himself—hit him.

There was nothing he could have done.

It had been a day just like any other. Mikey had walked home from school and gone straight upstairs to his play area as he always did. Sarah was at work and wouldn't get home until six. The usual time. Ben was out working on a triple homicide, trying to find the shooter. Neither Ben nor Sarah worried about Mikey because they had taught him well.

Be aware of your surroundings and of those around you.

Go straight home. No hanging out in the street.

Lock the door behind you.

Don't open it for anyone until he called them and got the OK to do it.

It was naive of them, but they weren't worried or concerned in the least about someone getting into their home. The idea of anything happening to their little boy just didn't seem possible.

But something had, and while Ben's tears fell, and while Rose—the only person privy to those tears, squeezed his shoulder, he still fought with the truth; that there just had to have been something that he could have done.

Ben cried for a few more seconds and then took a very long breath and wiped his tears away with the back of his hands, then without a word, he stood up and walked out of Rose's office, leaving her recommendations behind with her. There would be no sleep for him. He didn't deserve it.

Chapter 17

Dr. Lisa Rose frowned as Ben walked out of her office. Pushing him today hadn't been easy or enjoyable, but it had been necessary. He was killing himself slowly, and unless she could find a way to get him to realize that his son's death was not his fault, he was going to continue his spiral downward until he crashed violently. She'd seen in his eyes and body language that he wasn't burying himself with drugs or alcohol, so there was a small victory there, as many of the patients she had who'd dealt with a traumatic loss of some kind, generally did, but she knew something was breaking him into pieces. Something other than the grief. There had been a look in his eyes; a darkness, an anger that seemed to lie beneath the surface of the guilt and pain he was feeling, giving her the feeling that he was suffering far more than he knew or possibly even realized.

He was hurting, but he was also very guarded and trying to peel back his layers to get down to his roots wasn't easy. His tearful outburst had actually surprised her. She had gotten him to open up about his feelings over Mikey's death, and the breakup of his marriage, but never once had he broken down in that manner. It was another small victory in what Lisa knew was going to be a long war. Hopefully, Ben would see the war to the very end and not pull out before he had to. He was a good man, with a good heart, and she felt for him. She felt for his wife also, although she hadn't met her. What they had to endure…

Lisa had no children of her own, but she had a dog. Toby. A German shepherd that she'd rescued from a shelter nearly five years prior. On a whim one day, she'd taken a random trip to an animal shelter, where her eyes settled on the strong, agile, well-muscled dog. Toby seemed like a menacing animal, more long than he was tall, with pointed ears, and a wedge-shaped jaw, with pointed, scary-looking teeth. The average person would have passed on him because of his look, but Lisa didn't see what most saw. She didn't see menace. She saw a gentle soul, whose bark was far worse than its bite. She saw sad eyes. Eyes that almost seemed to hold a lifetime. Eyes that Lisa just simply fell in love with. She left the shelter that day with Toby leading the way by a blue collar she'd purchased. She'd named him Toby after an uncle that she'd lost earlier that year.

Toby couldn't wash dishes or clean his room, but he was truly a child. One who loved to give and receive affection. After a long and grueling day dealing with bottled up emotions, there was just nothing better than arriving home to be greeted by his thick paws, his pointed ears, and excited bark that kept many people away from her door. She hadn't carried him for nine months, or pushed him out of a canal that could open to amazing widths, but Toby was very much her little boy. She didn't know how she would handle losing him. Especially violently.

She sighed again and pressed the rewind button on a microcassette recorder she'd had in her desk drawer. Patients were aware that they were being recorded, but because she kept the recorder out of sight, it became out of mind, therefore any apprehension patients initially felt was gone very quickly.

Lisa leaned back in her chair and hit the stop button when the tape finished rewinding, and then pressed play, and listened very carefully to her conversation with Ben. She'd seen the darkness in his eyes. She now wanted to pay closer attention to where and when it showed up in his voice as well.

Chapter 18

Patrick was smiling.

He was standing at the bottom of a flight of four concrete steps outside of Ben's police station, letting the sting of the late morning October breeze blow over him. A uniformed officer hurried past him and ran up stairs leading into the station. Another moved past him heading in the opposite direction. Both had their coats zipped up, their shoulders up high, their hats pulled down as low as possible in an attempt to keep the cold at bay as much as possible.

Patrick inhaled a deep breath of air through his nostrils. He enjoyed the rush of the cold air as it shocked his lungs. Pussies, he thought, staring at the back of the second officer who'd run past him. He was jumping into the passenger side of a squad car waiting for him at the curb. Patrick turned and looked toward the entrance of the station.

All of them were pussies. Weak, soft, pathetic.

He took another full inhale. The night was going to be cold, ripe. It would be a good night for killing. Allen would like that. So would Ben.

Patrick exhaled, then reached into his jacket pocket and pulled out a pack of Newports. He shook one loose, held it by his lips, then slid the half-full pack back into his pocket, removed a lighter, cupped his hand and lit his cancer stick. He took a long drag on it and then blew out a long stream as another uniformed officer walked past him, giving him a nod as he did. Patrick nodded back and then headed toward his car, laughing as he did.

Indiana - 28 years ago

Ben was smiling. It was the day he'd been looking forward to for weeks. The day his father had promised a surprise. His birthday. His father had said it was going to be something special. Something that would change his life. Ben couldn't wait. He loved his father. His father was a super hero without the super powers, although Ben wondered if he had super strength, the way he saw him work around the house. His father was a tall man, with a barrel for a chest. He had thick arms, big hands, and a smile that put you at ease. Ben wanted to be just like his father when he grew up. A cop with a gleaming badge and a gun.

Smiling.

Ben couldn't stop. Nor could he stop bouncing in his seat. He was sitting in the front today, beside his dad. He usually sat in the back behind him, pretending to drive. But his father had said today was a day of change, and so he was in the front, his hands on both sides of his toy steering wheel, helping to guide his father's station wagon down the dirt road they were on. Ben didn't know where they were going, because his father refused to tell him.

"A surprise," his father had said.

So Ben sat, smiled and eagerly waited as they drove past trees and shrubbery, until they came to a sudden stop in the middle of a clearing.

His father cut the engine and sat still, silent, his hands fingers wrapped around the steering wheel.

Ben looked through his passenger side window. Trees, bushes, grass and an occasional squirrel and bird were all that he saw. He turned and looked up at his father. "Are we here?" His father said nothing and remained still, gripping the steering wheel so hard, Ben saw white around his knuckles.

"Dad? Is this where the surprise is?"

Silence. His father remained quiet, stoic, his eyes staring straight ahead of him, his jaw tight. His silence made Ben's smile drop. Something was wrong. Had he done or said something he shouldn't have on the way? He didn't think he had, but surely he must have because his father rarely got angry. At least not with him. He did get angry at his mother though. Ben always heard him yelling how things were her fault. And how she was a horrible wife. But Ben never really understood what things had been her fault, or what it really meant that she was being a horrible wife. He always thought his mother was pretty special.

Ben looked around at the clearing again and then said, "Dad," before he was suddenly and very violently backhanded in his mouth. The blow had been so sudden and so unexpected that Ben sat dazed and confused as his steering wheel fell to the floor, while tears welled in his eyes.

"Don't you cry, you little pansy!" his father yelled, slapping him hard in the back of his head.

Ben clenched down and tried to keep his tears from falling as blood trickled from his mouth. His father had hit him and yelled at him. He didn't understand it. What had he done? "I…I'm sorry," he stammered.

His father hit him again, this time in his stomach. "Shut up and get out of the car."

Ben bent forward as bile rose in his throat. He squeezed his eyes and begged himself to not throw up.

"Now!" his father yelled again.

Trying his hardest to keep tears from flowing and vomit from rising, Ben opened his door and got out of the car slowly. His father got out and walked around to Ben's side and stood in front of him.

They were completely alone. Ben shivered despite the July heat as his father, who was looking nothing like the man he had known and loved, raised his arm. He cringed as it came down, steeling himself for another blow. But instead of a hit, his father clamped his hand down over his shoulder in the firm, affectionate way he always did, and looked down at him. His eyes, which had been black and beady only seconds ago, were back to being rectangular and kind. His jaw was still strong, but had slackened. He looked very much like the father he knew and not the monster that'd been inside of the car moments before.

"I love you, Benji. You know that, don't you?" His tone was deep, but soft. It was as it always was.

Ben nodded. "I…I know…," he said, his voice low, soft.

His father smiled. "Good." He gave his shoulder a squeeze. "The world can be a cruel place, Benji, and now that you're eight, it's time I teach you a few things about survival. Okay?"

Ben nodded again. "Okay."

"Survival of the fittest, Benji. That's what's important. And only the strong survive. That's why I hit you. To teach you about strength. About how to be strong in the face of adversity. I was a P.O.W. Did you know that?"

Ben shook his head.

"In Vietnam. I was held captive for five months in a cage made of bamboo. I was one of four men in that cage, and during that time we all learned more and more what it meant to be strong, because periodically they would do things to us to try to get us to talk and betray our country. They would punch us, slap us, kick us. They burned us, cut us, stuck us with sharp objects. They shocked us and whipped us. They did other things, too. Horrible things. But you know what?"

Ben shook his head and licked the corner of his mouth gingerly with his tongue.

Using his thumb, his father wiped more blood away, though not nearly as gently. "No matter how much or how hard they hit. No matter how much they shocked, whipped, cut or did other…despicable things to us, we never once betrayed our country. We were soldiers. A family of brothers, despite our different backgrounds and ethnicities, and we never once allowed those Viet-Cong bastards to see us cry, and we never…*never* gave up secrets they demand we give.

"In the face of adversity, we were strong, determined and would die before we gave up any secrets that could bring down our country. We were fit, Benji, and for five months we survived until we were eventually rescued."

Ben looked up at his father. This was the first time he had ever heard of his father's ordeal. He had always respected him, but hearing his words, hearing what he had gone through—he couldn't help but feel a renewed and deeper sense of admiration. His father was tough. Tougher than he could have ever imagined.

"My father taught me how to be strong, Benji. He showed me what it was to be a survivor. When I was eight just like you, he told me of his experiences and then he began giving me lessons. He taught me about honor and about the value of secrets. Can you keep a secret, Benji? If your life depended on it…could you keep them? Would you be strong enough to?"

Ben shrugged. "I…I think so," he said, unsure.

"You can't think, Benji. You have to know. Okay?"

Ben gave a nod. "Okay."

"I'm going to teach you, Benji. Just like my father taught me. I'm going to teach you about strength and about secrets. I'm going to teach you how to survive."

Ben nodded again.

"First thing's first," his father said. "You have to learn about torture. You have to learn how to handle it. You have to learn how to take a hit, how to never show anyone that they or a situation has gotten to you. Second, you are going to learn what it means to keep and protect a secret. Being tough is one thing, but protecting a secret is another. Locking them away where no one can find them—that's the true mark of manhood."

He gave Ben's shoulder another firm squeeze. So firm that it hurt. But after everything his father had just said, Ben wouldn't show it.

"Are you ready to be a man, Benji?"

Ben nodded. "Yes."

His father smiled. "Good. I knew you would be." His father pulled his hand away from his shoulder and put it on his own belt and began to unclasp it. "Get down on your knees," his father said.

Ben looked at him curiously. "What?" he said, and regretted it instantly as his father hit him hard in his stomach, sending him down to the grass on one knee.

"Don't ask a question when I tell you to do something!" his father said, the hard edge back in his voice. "You just do it. Do you understand?"

Fighting tears and struggling to take a breath, Ben shook his head up and down.

"Now…what I'm teaching you now—these lessons—this is just between you and me. This is our secret. Look at me, Benji."

Ben, his stomach turning, squeezed his eyes tightly and quickly wiped at them before lifting his head to see his father undoing the button of his jeans.

"This is our secret, Benji. This isn't for your mother to know. Do you understand?" His father pulled his zipper down. "This is about turning you into a man, Benji. A strong man able to handle anything. Now…come here."

Chapter 19

Vance was back at the park where their last victim had been found. He was still a John Doe, just like the others, and that pissed him off. Someone somewhere had to have been missing their ten-year-old son, brother, nephew, cousin or best friend. So why hadn't anything popped up in the missing's persons database? Why hadn't anyone shown up at the station distraught with tears in their eyes desperately hoping to find their little Johnny's or Jimmy's? Three little boys. Three goddamned John Doe's.

Vance shivered from the cold and the frustration. Could the killer be someone he'd had thrown in jail who had somehow gotten out? Or a relative or friend as Tiana had suggested?

He made his way down the small hill and stood still and looked around at the surrounding area just before the actual crime scene, still roped off by yellow tape. People rode along the commonly used bike bath, while others walked or jogged, either talking to exercise partners, or listening to iPods in their ears. The electric buzz that existed the night before was gone. The tape sectioning off where the boy's body had been found was little more than an area to be avoided in the way you would a mud pile. *The difference between a small town and a city*, he thought, shaking his head. Someone would have seen or noticed something in a small, rural town, but in a big city… In a big city, people adopted a see-no-evil, hear-no-evil mentality. Unless it directly affected them, they went about their business and kept it moving. It made doing his job damn difficult at times.

He showed his badge to a uniformed officer standing watch to make sure no one disturbed the area, and then ducked beneath the tape and approached the area where the boy's body had been placed. Reds and his team had already gathered all of the samples and possible evidence they could, which hadn't been much at all. They had also taken both shoe and bike tire impressions. Vance didn't expect to find anything undiscovered, but miracles happened every day, didn't they? Why not today?

He looked down at the grass and saw nothing significant. He looked around at the mini-forest of trees around him. Reds and his team had scoured those areas, too. Their results had been the same; little to nothing found. Reds may not have been the man when it came to relationships, hence three failed marriages, but he was very much the man when it came to doing his job. He was a perfectionist to the nth degree.

Vance frowned. He'd spoken with the biker who had unluckily discovered the body again, and just as the night before, her story had remained the same. She didn't usually ride at night, but she was working on making her way up to twenty miles to help prepare her for an iron woman marathon she was going to take part in, when she ran over the boy's legs and tumbled to the ground, landing too damn near the boy's body. She was freaked out and hadn't been able to sleep through the night without seeing the boy in her dreams. She wasn't going to give up riding, but she was damn sure going to be switching to a new bike trail and she was definitely not riding after the sun went down.

Vance thanked her again for her time, left a card with her just in case she remembered anything else, and then headed to the park where he'd spoken to random people for information, all in vain, before making his way down the short hill to where he was now, crouched down, staring at brown grass and sparsely leaved trees, with frustration chilling him more than the crisp wind.

He was going to kill again.

Tiana knew it, and so did he.

He worked his jaw and sighed. "Who the fuck are you?" he said to himself. He thought about Tiana's words. Could this really be a game or a personal vendetta? If it was some sort of twisted I've-got-the-bigger-dick type of game, then just what was the ultimate prize? And if it was all about revenge, then who was he out to get payback on? Him? Ben? The entire department? Who the hell could have a hard-on that bad? And why couldn't they just leave behind a note or something to make things just a little easier?

He exhaled and plucked a single blade of grass from the ground. Why the boys? He wondered. He shook his head. Tiana said that the killer was most likely sodomized when he was a child, and Vance was sure that was the case. But so what? Was he supposed to think of this sick fuck as being a victim? Tiana hadn't implied or even suggested that of course, but if given the opportunity, there was a defense lawyer out there who would. He or she would work jurors with a sob story about the psycho being abused and traumatized for life. They would paint a sordid and sad picture and give reasons why, although his crimes were horrifying, he shouldn't be put to death, because deep down, he was really hurting just like the boys he killed. They would argue that seeking the death penalty isn't something God would approve of.

A prosecuting lawyer of course would fight the defense's strategy tooth and nail, doing all they could to show just why the killer deserved to die. They would argue that, victim or not, the killer had the intelligence and cunning to do what he was doing, and because of that, putting him to sleep permanently was justice that each one of the murdered boys deserved.

In the end, the psycho would be found guilty and would either get life in prison, or a death sentence. Either way, he would get a bed, the use of a bathroom, books to read, television to watch, and three meals a day. That was how the system worked.

Vance crumpled up the blade of grass in between his fingers and tossed it aside. "Fuck that," he said. When he found the bastard, he would make sure there'd be no opportunity for the system to come into play at all.

He sighed and stood up. As he did, he noticed something out of the corner of his eyes. A pair of eyes staring back at him from behind a tree several yards away. Vance leaned his head to the side a bit for a better view and the eyes quickly disappeared as someone bolted from the tree.

The killer?

"Hey!" Vance yelled out.

He took off after the set of eyes, which belonged to what appeared to be a boy no more than thirteen or fourteen tops.

Through the sparse trees, over broken twigs and fallen branches, past random bike riders, walkers and joggers, Vance gave chase. The boy was thin, but fast, and knew his way through the park, making quick cuts by sudden paths.

"Stop!" Vance yelled out, his legs pumping, his heart racing. "Stop goddammit!"

There was no slowing down by the teen. He continued to move, continued to make quick rights, quick lefts, doing all he could to get away.

But it was to no avail.

Vance was a former sprinter in high school and college, and although the teen had years on him, he was still too fast. He decreased the distance between he and the teen with each step, until he was close enough to tackle him down to the ground.

Both Vance and the kid grunted as they tumbled on the hard ground. Knowing how to fall, Vance rolled over and within seconds had his knee pressed into the middle of the teen's back, and grabbed hold of his wrist and forearm and twisted his arms back until the kid cried out.

"Ow! Come on….get off of me, man. I didn't do anything!" The teen twisted and squirmed, trying unsuccessfully to free himself.

Vance bent the teen's arm further upward into an uncomfortable, painful position. "Calm the hell down!" he ordered.

The teen continued to fight.

"Unless you want me to drag your ass to the station, I suggest you stop the goddamn struggling," Vance said, his voice very serious.

The teen squirmed for a second or two and then wisely took Vance's advice.

"Shit!" Vance said. He fastened handcuffs around the teen's wrists, patted him down, and satisfied that he'd had nothing on him, stood up, dragging the kid up with him. "What the fuck is your problem?" he said spinning the kid around and staring daggers at him. He should have used softer language, but he was pissed. "What were you doing over there and why the hell did you run?"

The teen looked at him with a defiant scowl, but didn't say anything.

"Answer me here or in an interrogation room," Vance said. "Your choice."

The teen's white face turned blood red. "I didn't do anything," he said.

"And that's why you took off for no reason? Because you didn't do anything? If you ask me, that seems pretty suspicious. Maybe I should just take you in."

The kid's eyes widened. "I didn't do anything," he insisted again.

"You said that already."

"Come on, man. Just let me go."

"After you tell me what you were doing there and why you ran."

The teen frowned then dropped his chin to his chest. "I…I don't like cops, all right?"

Vance nodded. "Had a lot of experience with them?"

The kid didn't reply.

"So what were you doing over there?" Vance asked.

"I…I was just looking."

"Looking at what?"

"At the birds."

"Birds, huh? You see one that scared you and made you run off?"

The kid sucked his teeth. "Like I said… I don't like cops."

Vance stared at him for a long second as people walked by, casting curious glances their way. "What's your name?"

"What do you want to know for? Am I under arrest for something?"

"You just ran away from a crime scene like a bat out of hell. You could be."

The kid frowned again, and then after a second of contemplation, sighed and said, "Eric."

"What's your last name, Eric?"

Eric's forehead knotted up before he said, "I don't have one."

Vance looked down at him. "No last name, huh?"

Eric shook his head. "Nope."

Vance looked Eric over with a scrutinizing glare. He had on a black bomber goose-down jacket zipped up to the neck. A slight tear ran vertically over his right breast, most likely from the fall. Black sweatpants were on his legs. Stains graced his right thigh and the cuff of his left leg. Scuffed white Nike's were on his feet. Vance wouldn't have been surprised if they had holes at the bottom. He might not admit it, but Vance knew looking at him that Eric lived on the street.

Vance closed his eyes a bit. "What were you doing over there, Eric with no last name?"

"Over where?" Eric said.

Vance gave a hard stare. "Don't be a smartass, Eric, or we will be taking a trip. And something tells me that's the last thing you want to do."

Eric looked at Vance, as Vance stared back at him with a glare saying 'try me one more time'.

Eric sighed. "I was just curious. I saw the yellow tape and I wanted to see what was up."

Vance nodded. "Were you over there curious yesterday, too?"

Eric shook his head. "No."

"Where do you live, Eric?" Vance asked, watching him closely.

Eric shrugged. "Around."

"Around where?"

"Just around."

"How old are you?"

"Fourteen."

"Where's your mom?"

"Dead," Eric answered flatly.

Vance nodded. "And your dad?"

Vance watched as Eric tensed up. "He's...he's home."

"And where's home again?"

"Home is... around."

Vance looked at Eric intently as Eric dropped his gaze to the ground. Vance shook his head. He didn't know his story, but it was obvious that whatever it was, it was a sad one.

He sighed. "That yellow tape you saw. Do you know why it's up?"

Eric shook his head. "No."

"The body of a ten-year-old boy was found there yesterday," Vance said, his eyes on Eric. "You know anything about that?"

Eric gnawed on his bottom lip, raised his eyebrows and said, "Nope."

"You don't have any friends that have gone missing or anything, do you?"

Eric shook his head.

Vance nodded. "Curious, huh?"

"Yeah," Eric replied. "I just wanted to see what was up."

Vance sighed and then turned Eric around and removed the handcuffs from his wrists. "So you live around here, huh?" he said.

Rubbing his wrists, Eric said, "Yeah."

"Have any brothers or sisters?"

"Nope."

Vance looked at him for a few seconds. "You need a ride home, Eric?"

Eric shook his head. "I'm good. I don't live far."

"It's cold. I'll give you a ride anyway."

Vance watched as Eric took a tense breath. "For real…it's okay. I can walk. I'm not cold anyway."

Vance looked at him. He wanted to break it to the Eric that he knew he was homeless, and then order him in the car and take him to the nearest shelter, but Vance knew that would just prove to be a waste of time, because the second Vance pulled away, he knew that Eric would bolt right back out onto the street.

Vance frowned and then reached into his pocket and removed his wallet. "Listen," he said, removing a card. "I know you live at home and everything, so you may not be too concerned, but there's some bad things happening to little kids lately. Specifically ten-year-old boys. If you happen to know of anyone who might not have a home like you, give me a call and I'll come and make sure they get somewhere safe." He held out his card. "My cell and office number are listed there. You can call anytime. Deal?"

He watched Eric closely, waiting to see what the teen would do.

Eric looked at him, skepticism in his eyes, for a few short seconds, before he reached out, took the card, shrugged and said, "I don't hang around with any little kids like that, but okay.... Deal."

Vance nodded, and then pulled out three twenties from his wallet. "Hey listen...I see that your jacket got ripped from the fall. This should cover the cost of repair."

Vance watched Eric staring at the money in his hands, a sparkle glittering in his eyes. *Tough kid*, he thought.

Eric reached out and grabbed the money. "Okay...cool."

Vance gave him a nod. "Don't forget...call me if you need or see anything."

Eric nodded. "Okay."

Vance gave Eric a final nod and then turned and headed back toward the crime scene. *Fourteen and homeless*, he thought. It was sad circumstance, but unless the psycho that was out there decided to go after older boys, he was relatively safe. Street kids lived hard, tough lives, but for the most part they knew how to take care of themselves.

Vance paused and took a quick look over his shoulder just in time to see Eric toss the card to the side and pocket the cash before he ran off to wherever it was he called home.

Chapter 20

Eric's heart was hammering. He was certain that he was going to be it for him. He'd all but braced himself to be put into the back of the cop's squad car to be taken to the police station where things would only get worse for him. He was fourteen and homeless and he was going to wind up being placed back in an orphanage somewhere reliving the nightmare he'd run away from. It had been inevitable. Or so he thought, until the cop, who didn't look like a cop at all, but more like an actor playing a cop let him go. He couldn't believe it and momentarily he'd thought it was a joke. That the cop was letting him go only to tackle him down to the ground again just for fun before he took him away. But it hadn't been a joke.

Eric took a deep breath. He was wheezing. The hard running and the fear of being caught had his chest tight. He had asthma and he hated it. He loved sports, but could never play them. That used to piss his father off. He used to call him weak and yell that he was a girl, a pussy because he couldn't run without having an attack. His father was a big, stocky man. A construction worker with calloused hands, who played football and wrestled in high school. It never made sense to him that Eric couldn't follow in his footsteps, and so he pushed him. He made him run, made him wrestle, made him do anything physical until a doctor told him that because of Eric's severe case of asthma, he couldn't participate in any strenuous activity.

Eric's father lay into him that day.

He took another deep breath and held the air in his lungs. He'd figured out over the years how to keep his asthma under control. He'd learned how to expand his lungs with deep breaths. He had an inhaler, but rarely used it.

He exhaled slowly and then took another breath. He felt as though he had pebbles in his chest when he breathed in. He swore under his breath. He'd been stupid for leaning to the side more. He'd seen the cop there crouching, looking around. He should have just stayed hidden behind the tree, but he'd been curious. A body of a little boy had been found in the park. They may not all know one another, but word spread on the streets that the little boy was a street kid. Eric knew the body wouldn't be there, but he wanted to see the area anyway. He wanted to see if there was anything that would possibly give him an indication as to who the kid could have been. Who knew…maybe he did know him? Curiosity almost did him in.

He took another breath. The tightness in his chest was loosening, his lungs expanding.

"Idiot," he said to himself. He should have never gone. He'd come too close to leaving Brian alone, and he'd promised him that he wouldn't do that.

He took another breath and veered right off of the walking path he was on, and then cut through a set of bushes, making sure to avoid thorns, and made his way down a small embankment, leading to the side of a small bridge, with more mud than water beneath it.

"Did you see him?"

Eric sighed as Brian emerged from the shadows beneath the small bridge. Brian wanted to go with him, but Eric didn't give in to him as he had a tendency to do, and insisted that he stay behind. Good thing he had. "I told you there wasn't going to be anything to see," he said, avoiding a mud pile and leaning his back against the slightly molded concrete bridge. He took a breath and held the air in.

Brian frowned. "I guess. I still wanted to come though."

Eric looked over at him as he released his breath slowly. "It was better that you didn't. There were cops around. If they saw you, they would have taken you away."

Brian's eyes widened. "Did they see you?"

Eric thought about telling him the truth, but then shook his head, deciding there really was no need for him to know. "No. I hid."

"See…I could have hidden with you."

"There wouldn't have been enough room behind the tree."

"I'm small though."

Eric sighed and pushed himself away from the cold concrete. "Whatever. Are you hungry?"

Brian nodded. "Starving."

Eric pulled the twenties out of his pocket. "Let's go get some real food," he said, with a smile.

Brian's eyes popped open. "Where did you get that? Did you rob someone?"

Eric shook his head. "I found it on the ground by the tree I was hiding behind."

"Really?"

"Yeah."

"How much is it?"

"Sixty dollars."

Brian's eyes grew wider. "Sixty! And no one missed it?"

Eric shrugged. "I don't know and I don't care. I grabbed it and ran."

"Finders keepers."

"Definitely. Now…do you want McDonald's or Chick-Fil-A?"

"McDonald's! I want a Happy Meal toy."

Eric gave Brian a nod. "Okay. Let's go."

Brian smiled. "Hey…what happened to your jacket?"

Eric looked down at the tear in it, suffered during the fall when he'd been tackled down. *Too close*, he thought. He shrugged. "I don't know. I didn't even see it. It probably got caught on some thorns when I was coming down here."

"Lucky they didn't stick you."

"Yeah. Anyway…come on…let's go eat."

Brian hop-stepped over a few mud puddles and stepped beside Eric. Eric rubbed the top of his head. Brian hated that, and promptly pushed his hand away.

Eric laughed and made his way back up the tiny embankment, with Brian in tow. As they headed back down the main walking path, Brian said, "Eric…who do you think the kid was that they found? Do you think we might know him?"

Eric frowned. "I don't know," he said.

"I heard he was the same age as the other boys they found."

"Their ages were probably a coincidence," Eric said.

Brian thought about that for a second, then said, "I'm ten just like they were."

Eric looked down at him. He was trying to keep the bravado in his tiny voice, but it was obvious to Eric that he was scared. He laid his arm over Brian's shoulders. "Don't worry about the kids or their ages."

"Yeah, but—"

"I've got your back, Brian. Trust me…you have nothing to worry about. Nothing's gonna happen to you."

The corners of Brian's little mouth quivered slightly, before they rose into a smile as he said, "Okay."

Eric nodded then grew silent and continued to lead the way. He looked over his shoulder as the sounds of leaves rustling came from behind them. A jogger—male—was quickly approaching. Eric's heart beat heavily as he tensed up. The jogger got closer. Eric balled his hand into a fist and tried to keep Brian unaware. Coming up beside them, the jogger nodded and then ran on. Brian exhaled the breath he'd been holding and opened his fist as the jogger quickly disappeared down the trail before them.

Brian had been preoccupied with the zipper of his jacket and hadn't noticed a thing.

Eric nudged Brian's shoulder. "Come on," he said. "Let's move faster. I'm starving, too." He increased the pace of his steps, while Brian's steps became a slight jog.

Twenty minutes later they were sitting in McDonald's. Brian had a six-piece chicken mcnugget meal, with small fries, a small coke and an Iron Man II toy. Eric was eating a value mean #1—a Big Mac, super-sized fries, with a large Sprite. He planned to stretch the sixty dollars he had been given as far and long as he could.

He took a sip of his Sprite after a healthy bite of his Big Mac, then looked at Brian, who was making his Iron Man fly from the window ledge beside him to their small square table. Eric smiled and sighed at the same time. Brian was a good kid. Kind with an innocent and gentle heart. It was sad that he'd had to deal with similar bullshit that had him escaping to the streets for safety. Eric had tried more than once to convince Brian to go to a shelter, but if Eric wasn't staying, then Brian wasn't going to either. Eric would have preferred for Brian to be off the streets and out of the cold, but he wasn't willing to sacrifice his freedom for Brian's safety.

Eric took another full bite, stuffed a couple of all-too-salty fries into his mouth, and then took another long swallow of his soda.

That's when he noticed the eyes.

Dark and menacing. They belonged to a tall, thick man with dark hair, wearing a black trench coat over a black sweater, black slacks and black shoes. He was looking in Eric's direction, but his eyes were ominously focused on Brian. He wasn't wearing a uniform, but Eric had had enough experience to know that he was a cop.

Eric frowned. He'd had no intention of leaving the warmth inside to go back to the biting cold outside so soon, but they had no choice. He looked at Brian and said softly through gritted teeth, "Brian…grab your toy and whatever food you want to take. We have to get going."

Brian, who'd had Iron Man doing a flip in the air, looked up at him. "Aww…do we have to?"

Eric nodded. "Yeah. We do."

"But I'm still eating. And it's warm in here."

Eric frowned. "Lower your voice," he said, his voice stern, but quietly forceful. "We have to go now."

"But—"

"There's a cop in here and he's looking this way."

Brian swiveled his head from left to right. "Where? I don't see one?"

"Stop looking around, idiot!" Eric clenched his jaw and forced himself to remember that although the hard life on the streets had forced him to grow up faster, Brian was still just a ten-year-old kid. "Look," he said. "You can stay if you want to." That said, he slid out of his chair and stood up.

Brian was up seconds later, Iron Man in one hand, coke and fries in the other.

"We're going out the back exit. Walk slowly."

"Okay."

Eric took a very subtle glance toward the direction of the man he just knew was a cop. His eyes were buried in a newspaper now, but Eric had the feeling that he'd just looked down. "Let's go."

He led the way, with Brian in tow, taking the exit opposite from where the man in black was. When they got outside he stole a quick glance through the glass doors. The cop was no longer there.

"Shit," he whispered. "Follow me. And stay close."

He quickly ran to the right, heading down the busy block and then dashed across the street as cars just began to move forward as the light changed from red to green. As ordered, Brian was close on his heels. Eric looked over his shoulder. The cop with the chilling eyes was nowhere to be found, but Eric didn't care. He ran down to the end of the block and then made a quick left, ducking into a corner store.

Breathing heavily, he moved down to the end of the chip aisle and looked up at an oval mirror giving an older Middle Eastern man standing behind a counter surrounded by bullet-proof plexi-glass, a view of all of the activity in the small store. Eric stared, looking at the front door in the reflection, waiting to see if they had been followed. Brian stood beside him, bent over, panting, Iron Man still in his hands. Somewhere along the run, the fries and coke had been ditched.

"Is he there?" Brian asked.

Eric continued to stare up at the glass, his heart beating, his palms wet. A minute passed by. Then four before he said, "No."

"Do you think he knows we're here?"

In the mirror, Eric watched as the entrance door opened and two young Latin females—about sixteen—walked inside, all giggles. He shook his head. "I don't think so. If he did, he'd come in because he'd have us trapped. We're good."

"Okay."

"Come on."

Eric went to the door, ignoring the suspicious glare from the store clerk, pushed the door open, took a cautious peek up and down the block, and then looked across the street.

No eyes. No black trench coat.

He turned and looked at Brian, who was closer than white on rice behind him. "I think it's clear. Let's go."

Brian nodded and followed him out of the store Eric looked all around him again, then, satisfied with what he saw, took a deep breath and let it out slowly. He thought about the promise he'd made to Brian back in the park.

"Nothing's gonna happen to you…"

Eric walked, with Brian beside him, and hoped that he was right.

Chapter 21

Patrick watched.

As the two boys finished up their McDonald's, he sat in his car and watched, just as he'd done earlier in the day when they ran down the block, raced across the street and hid in the corner store. The oldest kid, the one who didn't matter, had been so focused on watching people, that he had never even noticed Patrick sitting in his car, double-parked across the street, down a few yards, when they stepped out of the store.

Patrick took a slow, deep drag on his cigarette and let the smoke swirl around his tongue before blowing it out through the crack of his driver's side window. He looked from the oldest boy to the youngest.

"Look at you," he said. "You look so fucking innocent, but I know better. I know what you're capable of. I know what damage you can do. What damage you've probably already done."

He took another pull on his cigarette and blew the smoke out angrily, as his thoughts went back to a moment in time that he could and would never forget.

Twenty-six years ago.

His life had become hell all because of a weak ten-year-old coward. All he'd had to do was keep his mouth shut. All he'd had to do was keep the secret he'd been told to keep. But the little pussy was weak, and instead of staying quiet, he ran his mouth and Patrick's life had been ruined forever, and that set in to motion, a life filled with hatred, disgust and promised revenge.

Everyone had to pay.

The boys who would cause pain, because at some point they would reveal secrets. Allen, who had told lies to wrongfully avert blame. And most importantly, Ben McCallum. He had to pay.

"Twenty-six years," Patrick seethed, blowing out another stream of smoke. "All you had to do was keep your fucking mouth shut, Ben. None of this would be happening now had you done that. Your son would be alive. Your marriage would still be intact. Your life would be normal and I could have dealt with that. But you fucking told."

Patrick pulled on his cigarette again, held the smoke in for a few seconds, enjoying the taste of the nicotine, and then blew it out slowly, his eyes watching the boys through the haze.

Chapter 22

Allen Kline sat in his leather chair, his head pressed back against the head rest. Another grueling day had finally come to an end. Grueling not because of the patients and their issues, which had just become so utterly trivial to him, but grueling because of the mask that he had to wear. He'd been living in hell. Hell that was destroying him from the inside out, and for the sake of his boys' lives, he could say or do nothing.

No. That wasn't entirely true.

He could go to the police. He could tell them what was going on. He could tell them all about Patrick and his visits, his "confessions." He could do that and then pray that the repercussions wouldn't be severe.

He could tell.

Boys were dying. Innocent boys. Innocent like his sons.

He should tell.

It was the right thing to do. He should tell so that other boys' lives would be spared.

Except possibly his own.

Allen closed his eyes, breathed in and out slowly, and then caught the scent of cigarette smoke. His heart dropped into the pit of his stomach as he heard the light-switch for his overhead lights click.

He opened his eyes to darkness. Earlier in the week, frustration had bubbled over and he lashed out and knocked his desk lamp over, causing the bulb to blow. Replacing it had been a low priority.

"Hello, Allen," Patrick said, the tone of his voice even more chilling in the dark.

Allen focused on Patrick's silhouette as he stood in the doorway, a cigarette in his hand. He opened his mouth to speak, but no sound came out as fear had a tight grip on his larynx. He cleared his throat. His heart was beating so heavily, he almost felt out of breath. "Patrick," he finally managed to say.

Patrick stepped into the room and closed the door behind him. "Why isn't your lamp on, Allen?"

Allen swallowed dry saliva and said, "The bulb is blown."

"Do you have more bulbs?"

"I do."

"Where?"

"In my desk drawer."

"So replace it."

Allen opened his bottom drawer, felt around and found the small pack of replacement bulbs. He grabbed one, unscrewed the old bulb and replaced it with the new, then switched the lamp on, setting the corner of his desk ablaze in yellow light, while illumination spread out slightly and cast an eerie glow over the shadows.

Allen could barely breathe as Patrick stepped forward. "That's better," he said. He had on his usual outfit. Black trench coat, with a black sweater beneath, black slacks with black shoes on his feet. As always, black gloves covered his hands, and his black New York Yankees baseball cap was pulled down low over his brow, concealing his eyes.

Black, Allen thought. A cold color void of feeling, void of emotion. The color of death.

"Why didn't you replace it earlier?" Patrick asked, sitting in a chair across from Allen.

"I've been...preoccupied," Allen said. "It slipped my mind."

Patrick stretched his legs and crossed them at the ankles, inhaled on his cigarette, and then blew out a long, thin stream. "You've had a rough week, huh?"

Allen clenched his jaw. He wanted to spring forward out of his chair, reach across the desk and wrap his unsteady hands around Patrick's neck.

He wanted to squeeze and make him tell him where his boys were. But the last time Allen used his hands for anything other than flipping through pages in a book, picking up a pen, or occasionally throwing a ball back and forth with his sons, he had been in seventh grade. He'd had a fight with Tommy Reed. Allen had gotten one punch in—a right hook to Tommy's arm—before Tommy hit him in his eye, his jaw and then stomach, sending him to the ground for a TKO. As badly as Allen wanted to inflict damage, the fact of the matter was, Allen was nowhere close to being a fighter, while Patrick was a cold blooded killer. If he wanted to see his sons again, assuming they were still alive of course, then he had to remain right where he was.

He took barely a breath and said, "It hasn't been the best of weeks."

Patrick pulled in on the cigarette again and blew out another stream. Allen had always hated the stench of smoke, the way it clung to your clothing and hair. He hated it even more now. He cleared his throat and fought to keep from coughing. Patrick had enjoyed enough satisfaction at his expense already.

"Why are you here, Patrick?"

Patrick inhaled, held the smoke in his lungs, released it and said, "Why do you think I'm here, Allen?"

"To tell me that you've let my sons go."

Patrick chuckled. "You wish."

"Yes…I do."

"Wishes only come true in the cartoons, Allen."

"They do in the real world, too."

"Not in my world. And believe me Allen, you are very much in my world."

Allen's heart jackhammered as he found it difficult to take a full breath. "Tell me about your world," he said, his voice even. Patrick had his sons. Somehow he needed to get further into his mind. He needed to know more about what made him tick, what made him do the things he did. Perhaps in doing so he could find the humanity hidden within his dark soul, if any existed. And if he could, maybe—just maybe, there would be a chance to save his boys. The chances, Allen knew, were probably slim, but short of committing suicide by attacking him, it was the only possible chance Allen had.

"My world is a beautiful place, Allen. It's dark, cold and filled with a lot of hatred."

"Hatred for what?

Patrick took a long drag and blew out the smoke hard. "For everything. And everyone."

A tingle came over Allen. This was the furthest he had ever gotten. *Tread lightly*, he thought. The door was finally open—even if just a crack. He had to be careful. He couldn't allow the door to be slammed shut now. His sons depended on him.

Allen took a breath, exhaled very slowly, and said, "What happened to make you hate, Patrick?"

Patrick smoked his cigarette, but didn't reply. He just took smoke in and blew it out rhythmically.

"Did someone do something to you?" Allen pressed very cautiously. "Did something happen when you were younger? Something that made you hate everyone? Made you hate little boys?"

Patrick puffed on his cigarette a few more times and didn't respond.

His inhales, exhales, the humming of his desk lamp, and his own heartbeat were the only things Allen could hear. Had he gone too far? Asked too many questions? His heart thudded, its volume growing. He watched Patrick intensely and he assumed that Patrick was staring back at him. If only he could see his eyes, the mirrors to his soul.

Seconds passed. They seemed like hours.

Finally, Patrick said, """You know the answer to those questions already, Allen."

"I have my opinions…yes."

Patrick shook his head, then outed his cigarette, which he'd smoked almost all the way to the end, and then put the butt into his mouth and swallowed it down. "No," he said, removing a pack from his inside pocket along with a lighter. He shook out a fresh cigarette, put the pack back into his pocket, held the cigarette by his lips and lit it. He took a long pull on it, held it in momentarily, then blew a thick plume. "I didn't say you had an opinion on them. I said that you *know* the answers."

Allen shook his head slightly. "I don't understand."

"You're a liar, Allen," Patrick said, uncrossing his legs. "A fucking liar."

Allen looked at him with a furrowed brow. This was the second time that he'd called him that. "Why do you call me a liar? I've never lied to you."

Patrick took another drag. "Yes…you have."

"Patrick…I promise you…I haven't lied to you. But…but if you feel that I have, then please tell me how."

Silence and the sound of his pulling in and exhaling. Seconds of that. That was Patrick's reply.

"Tell me, Patrick," Allen carefully insisted again.

Patrick sat stone still, the cigarette held in-between his fingers, ashes falling to the beige carpeting. "Twenty-six years ago" Patrick said finally after another pull and exhale of the cancerous smoke. "You lied to a coward. You told him that he hadn't been responsible for things that happened. That he couldn't control the actions of others. But that was bullshit, Allen. It was all bullshit!"

Patrick straightened up in the chair and leaned forward. "You fed him a lie, Allen. You fed him bullshit and that pussy believed it! He believed that he had NOTHING to do with fucking up my world!"

Allen's heart was pounding as its pace increased. *Twenty-six years ago? Who?*

He shook his head slowly. "Who?" he asked. "Who are you talking about?"

"You know, Allen. You fucking know!"

Allen shook his head again. "You're talking about something that occurred twenty-six years ago, Patrick. I've had many patients since then."

Patrick took another hard, angry pull on his cigarette, his hand trembling slightly. He was agitated and Allen feared on the verge of exploding. But Allen couldn't stop. He was so close.

"Tell me," he said again. "Who was the patient?"

Before he realized it was happening, Patrick shot out of the chair, stretched across his desk, and grabbed Allen roughly by his shirt collar with his right hand, while his left held the cigarette inches away from his eye. "All of them you LYING FUCK! You lied to ALL of them!"

He pressed the burning end of the cigarette into Allen's cheek. Allen cried out as his flesh burned.

Patrick shoved him back viciously into his chair. The chair toppled over backward, sending Allen falling hard to the ground, where he hit his head against his bookshelf behind his desk.

"You lied, Allen!" Patrick said, coming around his desk and standing above him. "You fucking lied!"

Allen braced himself for whatever Patrick would do next. His cheek was stinging, burning, and the back of his head was throbbing. He was almost positive that he was bleeding. He looked up as Patrick looked down at him, his eyes still concealed beneath his baseball cap.

"I'm going to kill another boy, Allen," Patrick said, his voice suddenly and eerily calm. "Tonight. I'm going to do it because of the lies you told and because of the way that fucking pussy bought your shit and thought he could just move on as if nothing fucking mattered."

Tears fell slowly from Allen's eyes as the pain from the cigarette burn and the sharp throbbing in the back of his head worsened. "Pl...please," he said softly. "Please don't."

"I have to, Allen. I have to because you have to pay, and he has to pay, too." Without another word, Patrick turned and headed toward the door.

Allen's struggled to take a full breath as anxiety had his chest tight. "Please," he begged again. "You don't have to."

At the door, Patrick turned. "Stop begging, Allen."

Allen knotted his forehead. "My...my sons. What about my sons?" Tears fell hard.

"What about them?" Patrick said, his tone nonchalant.

Allen shivered. "They...they haven't done anything. Please...just let them go."

"I'm not done punishing you yet, Allen," Patrick said simply. And then he opened the door and walked out of the tiny office.

Allen remained on the floor, his tears flowing hard, fast. Patrick's life had somehow been adversely affected and now he was killing innocent little boys. Doing things to them. Unspeakable, horrible things. All because he had done his job twenty-six years ago, his boys were missing.

He slammed his hand down on the carpeting. "LET MY SONS GO!"

He slammed his hand down on the carpeting again, his body shaking as his inconsolable tears fell.

"LET MY SONS GO!"

Chapter 23

The body of a young male was discovered earlier this evening along the bike trail. Because the victim is under age, his identity is being withheld. The cause of death has yet to be determined at this time. Also, before you ask…yes, the victim was discovered with a pacifier in his mouth, but we are not prepared to say that this was the work of the person you all call The Pacifier."

"Detective Newsome…this is the third boy that's been discovered within the past few days, with a pacifier in his mouth. Isn't it fair to say that the killer has struck again?"

"Until the body and evidence found at the scene have been examined, no, it isn't fair to state that."

"Are you saying this could be the work of a copycat?"

"Until we conduct a thorough examination, all possibilities must be assumed."

"Detective Newsome…you've had trouble bringing one killer to justice so far. How is the public supposed to have confidence that you can find two if a copycat exists?"

"We are doing all we can to bring an end to these senseless and horrific acts of violence. We are fathers, mothers, brothers, sisters, uncles, aunts, cousins and grandparents. Although we may not know the victims, we still take these deaths personally. We are here to protect and to serve. The public can be reassured that we are committed to doing just that. Having said that, we do ask that anyone with information in this matter, please come to the police station. They can ask for me directly if they are uncomfortable talking to anyone else. Or if they would prefer to remain anonymous, they can call and leave a message. We are offering a reward of one-hundred thousand dollars for any information leading to an arrest."

"Detective…was the victim strangled to death?"

"As I stated before, no determination has been made as our medical examiners have not had an opportunity to do a full examination, so at this time, we are not prepared to answer that question."

"Are there any bruises around the victim's neck?"

"Again, an examination must be done."

"Bruises can be seen, detective. You have eyes don't you?"

"Without doing a thorough examination, we can't assume that any bruises found had a hand in the victim's death."

"So, you are saying that there were bruises found on the neck, just as there were with the other victims?"

"I didn't say that. You did."

"Why are you so reluctant to give out more information?"

"We give out what's necessary."

"Which hasn't been much. Is this because you don't have much of anything to give? Should the public really have confidence in you, or should they be worried that their sons may be next?"

"First…every person, regardless of what situations may or may not be occurring, should be on guard about anything happening to their children. Secondly…yes, the public should have every bit of confidence that their tax dollars are being put to good use. Third…information is withheld to preserve the nature of the investigation. That's all that we have for you now. Thank you."

Amanda Kline hit the pause button on her remote control and cried softly. This was the seventh time she had watched the news conference. She shouldn't have DVR'd it, because she knew she was going to torture herself. One hour after it aired. At three A.M. while Allen unforgivably slept. First thing in the morning when he left to go and solve other people's goddamn problems. At three-thirty when her sons were supposed to be walking through the door. At seven when they were supposed to be getting ready for bed. And now at ten o'clock, alone, wondering if Allen hadn't come home yet because he was having another "session."

It was self-torture. But she couldn't stop watching.

That monster had her sons and only God knew if they were alive or…

Amanda let the remote fall and hugged her knees to her chest. "Oh God," she whispered, tears falling fast, hard, and heavy. "Oh God."

What if the next live press conference was about one or both of her boys?

What if they were the next victims with pacifiers in their mouths?

What if their necks were the ones with bruises?

Amanda brought her knees closer and rocked herself back and forth. Tears ran down her cheeks and dropped from her chin to the leather of her sofa.

"Not my sons," she said her throat tight. "Not my boys!"

She looked up at the television and through her tears, stared at the lead detective on the case. Vance Newsome. He was trying to stop the monster, but he was frustrated and feeling hopeless. She could see it in his eyes. He was doing everything he could, but nothing was working because that monster wasn't giving them anything.

But she could, couldn't she?

Amanda unclasped her fingers and put her feet down on the hardwood floor. They'd had carpet before, but had the hardwood flooring installed after one-too-many juice spills. She slid forward on the sofa, the flow of tears slowing, her eyes still on Vance Newsome.

She could give him what he needed. The monster. The Pacifier. Couldn't she hand him to the detective on a silver platter?

To save her boys.

Couldn't she give him what he needed?

She picked up the remote and rewound the press conference and then hit the play button.

"...They can ask for me directly if they are uncomfortable talking to anyone else."

Amanda hit the pause button again.

To save her boys...couldn't she?

She stared at Vance Newsome as he stared back at her from the television screen. His message had been to the general public, but his eyes were on her, weren't they?

Chapter 24

Chris Kline refused to give up.

Despite the pain, despite the fear, despite the weakness and numbness, the desire to just lay flat on the cold concrete and give his body and mind a rest, he refused. He wasn't giving in. He just couldn't.

He pulled on the chain. His ankle bone was throbbing and felt as though it could break with the next determined tug. The metal clasp had ripped his skin. He could feel the trickle and could smell the scent of his own blood.

Ignore the pain, he thought. Don't stop. Don't give up. You can't!

His hands were weak, his fingers sore, his callouses raw and on fire, skin ripped there too. *Pull! Pull!*

"Did you get it?"

Chris exhaled heavily and wiped sweat away from his forehead with the back of his hand. "No. And stop asking me. You'll know when I do."

His tone was biting and he knew unnecessary. His little brother was just scared. But he kept on asking, and that frustrated Chris because each and every time he had to say no, that just reminded him that with all of his relentless pulling, he still hadn't gotten anywhere.

"Are we going to die, Chris?"

Chris pulled on the chain. "No," he said, clenching his jaws. "We're not going to die!" He pulled while Chris sobbed. "Shut up!" he snapped. "Stop crying!"

"I…I'm scared. I miss mom and dad."

"We're going to see them again, Chad. I promise."

"When?"

Chris sighed. "Soon. Okay?"

"I…I'm hungry. My stomach hurts."

Chris gritted his teeth and forced his mouth to stay closed. His brother's rambling was only intensifying the level of the frustration and angst he was feeling with each pull, and if he let his mouth fly open, he was sure he was going to hurt his brother's feelings.

He took a deep breath and continued to yank on the chain. *Please*, he thought. *Just give a little. Please.*

He pulled. Clenched through the stinging.

Chad continued to cry. "I'm hungry," he said again. "I feel like I'm going to throw up. Why hasn't he brought us any sandwiches today?"

Chris continued to pull. Continued to fight the expansion of his mouth.

"Chris? Chris!"

"Shut the fuck up, Chad!" Chris yelled. He had tried to ignore, tried to remain quiet, but it was just impossible to do. The tension in his mind and body had just been stretched too thin, and he couldn't fight the urge, the need to explode. "Just shut the fuck up! I'm hungry, too!"

And he was. On three separate occasions since their abduction, the fake cop had brought them peanut butter and jelly sandwiches to eat. He'd also brought them pails to pee in. What did it mean that he hadn't come back? Had something happened to him? An accident? The police? Had they gotten him? If so, what would that mean for him and Chad? Would they be found?

What if something hadn't happened to him? Had he decided to starve them to death or was he going to come back for them? If and when he did, what would happen next? Was he going to let them go? Kill them? Continue to feed them and keep them in the tiny, dark room, with no clothes on their backs?

Chris' head hurt from the lack of sustenance in his system and the stress from the unanswered questions.

"You're not supposed to curse," Chad said. He had stopped crying, but his tone was subdued. Chris's harsh words had hurt.

Chris sighed. He had cursed before around his friends to be cool, but never around Chad. Cursing wasn't something that occurred frequently at home, save for an occasional "Dammit," but outside of the home with his friends and other kids in school, curse words were part of almost every conversation. But unlike his own, Chad's ears were virgin and Chris knew he shouldn't have gone off that way.

He sighed again. "Look…I didn't mean to snap like that, all right? And the curse words slipped out because I'm scared and stressed, and I'm starving, too."

Chad sniffled.

"For real, Chad. I didn't mean it." Chris frowned and wished as he had since they had been taken, that he could throw his arms around his little brother's shoulders. "I miss mom and dad, too, Chad. Just bear with me and try to stay strong, all right? Mom and dad need you to stay strong and so do I."

Chad sniffled again. "O…okay."

Chris smiled and closed his hands around the chain. Somehow… Someway…

He had asked Chad to stay strong, but he had really been asking that of himself. *Stay strong. Keep trying. Don't give up. Fight through the pain, the fear. Pull…pull…harder. Eventually he would feel…*

Something.

Chris' heart beat heavily.

Something had given.

He felt toward the bottom of the chain where it was fastened to a metal plate, which was bolted down into the concrete floor.

Something had given! His heart beat so heavily he could hear it. He felt around with his fingers slowly, searching until he found what he was looking for. A small separation in the link of the chain. He ran his fingertip along the tiny joint and felt it widen as he went along. The gap wasn't wide, but it was wide enough.

Chris took a deep breath as shivers ran along his arms. Something had finally given.

He wrapped his fingers around the chain and pulled with renewed determination. He didn't know if the fake cop had left them there alone to starve, or if he planned on coming back, but either way, he and his brother were going to get out of there.

Chapter 25

Eric had to take a piss, but he didn't want to. Taking a piss meant he had to get up, and getting up meant that he would have to unwrap himself from beneath the wool blanket he had stolen from the Goodwill store, and step back out into the cold—something he really didn't want to do. He groaned and told himself that he could hold it, and tried to go back to sleep. But trying meant lying still, and the longer he lay still, the stronger the pressure on his bladder became.

"Shit."

He sat up and checked on Brian, who was wrapped in his own wool blanket. He was sound asleep. *He should be,* Eric thought. Especially after the way he had stuffed his face at Chick-Fil-A. Who knew a ten-year-old kid could eat two chicken sandwiches, two orders of waffle fries, and gulp down two large lemonades within a span of fifteen minutes? Eric had only had one order of the sandwich and fries with a coke. He felt as though he could have eaten two, maybe even three orders, but he wanted to save as much of the money he had gotten from the cop. He would have kept Brian to only one order also, but the kid was hungry.

Eric groaned again and then worked his way out of the cocoon he had formed. He and Brian were sleeping in a Lincoln Town Car. Its rear end was smashed in. It had no tires. The hood was bent, and its engine was gone. Its passenger door was dented in, but the driver's door was unharmed. The windows were intact, although the rear windshield was spider webbed and would probably shatter if sneezed on just right. The front windshield had a diagonal crack running from the upper left to the bottom right. It was a stylish car that had seen its demise far too soon, and now its final resting place was the junk yard, where it was providing temporary shelter for the night.

They had tried to find shelter in the junkyard before, but they'd never been able to get in because of a pit bull that was usually on the grounds roaming free. But tonight had been their lucky night because the dog had been nowhere to be found, and so they'd scaled the fence and struck gold with the Lincoln. Eric thought about trying to fight the need to step outside again, but couldn't.

He looked over at Brian in the backseat again, and then opened the driver's door, slid past the steering wheel, which had been pushed back slightly from the impact of whatever crash it had gotten into, and got out of the car. Like a slap, the middle-of-the-night breeze hit him in the face. "Shit!" he said again.

His coat still on, he zipped it up and then walked to the front of the car to relieve himself. The wind whipped bitterly again, and for a split second the urge to pee disappeared. But that was only for a second.

His back facing the dented hood, he fumbled with his zipper, with fingers quickly becoming numb from the cold. "Come on," he said, fighting with the zipper. It had been giving him trouble since his tumble after the cop had taken him down. "Come on!"

His fingers stiffening, he bounced on his toes as he continued to struggle with the zipper, which he'd gotten a third of the way down. "Come on…come on!"

As he struggled, the wind kicked up again, almost as though it were having a mocking, laughing fit.

Eric shook his head, continued to fight with the zipper, cursed, bounced and tried like hell to not piss on himself.

With the wind, the frustration and desperation to relieve himself, he never noticed that someone had approached him from behind.

Chapter 26

Patrick drove the knife he'd been wielding deep into the older kid's back. He had been waiting for the right moment to strike, and knew it had come when the kid emerged from the car. He hated using knives. He really wanted to use his hands, but he couldn't risk taking the time to squeeze the life out of him, for fear that the one he wanted would wake up. So the knife it was. It wasn't as thrilling as the squeeze, but it was quieter than his gun.

He drove the knife deeper, and clamped his hand over the kid's mouth to stifle any sound. He had decided the older kid had to die when he had looked at him at McDonald's. "Shhh," he whispered. He pushed the blade in deeper, and when the kid's legs began to give out from beneath him, he let his body fall forward.

Patrick knelt down beside him and listened to the kid's hoarse, labored breathing. "You pissed on yourself," he said, catching a whiff of the strong scent.

He stood up, stepped back to avoid stepping in the kid's urine and looked down at the kid again. He was going to be dead soon. He didn't have to worry about the kid or the knife being found. The kid's death would just be considered a random act of violence, and the knife had no prints.

He looked toward the back of the car and smiled as an intense, erotic, rush came over him. The one he wanted, the one who really needed to be punished was still sleeping.

No one would connect Patrick to the body of a stabbing victim, but they would when they found the boy with the pacifier he had in his pocket.

Chapter 27

Eric had felt pain before. A broken arm. A fractured rib. A severely twisted ankle. A knot the size of a grapefruit on the side of his head. A blackened eye and a busted lip. He'd known pain. Before he ran away from home that had been all he'd known.

But he had learned to deal with it. Learned to take it like a man. He was trying to do that now as he lay face down on the ground covered with limestone pebbles. Trying to take the pain. The sharp, stinging, burning sensation. Trying to deal with the numbness setting in. Numbness that had nothing to do with the cold.

But it was hard. Incredibly hard.

He had been stabbed. On the television and in the movies when someone got stabbed, they always found a way to muster the strength to move, to crawl, to cry out for help. They made it look so easy.

God, that was such bullshit, he thought.

Moving, breathing, talking—none of it was easy to do.

He lay still, listening to the sound of his wheezing as he took short breaths. Listening to the sound of the wind blowing, listening to the sound of pebbles crunching beneath footsteps of the man who had stabbed him. Eric hadn't seen him, but he knew the footsteps belonged to the man from McDonald's. The man with the dark, skeptical eyes. Cop's eyes. He knew it just as surely as he knew now that the he was the one the cop from the park was looking for. The sicko who was murdering ten-year-old boys. He also knew that he was going to take Brian even before he heard the passenger door to the Lincoln creak open.

Eric shivered and tried to move, but the knife was still plunged into his back, and as he did, an electric shock of pain coursed through him. He whimpered as tears fell from the corner his eye, ran across the bridge of his nose, and trickled from the side of his face to the ground.

"B…Br…Bri..an…" he struggled to say.

It was supposed to have been a scream, but he could produce no more than a whisper.

He coughed and prayed to God immediately that he wouldn't cough again, as his body was riddled with intense agony.

"Br..Bri..Bri…an…"

Eric wanted to move. Needed to. He had promised the kid that nothing was going to happen to him. He had to make good on his word. Tears fell harder as he tried to ignore the hurt. They fell faster as the acceptance that the pain was just too severe to reject.

"Br…Bri..Bri..an.."

He laid still, his face on the ground and listened to the slow rush of the wind, and the sound of something crackling just before Brian let out a muffled scream.

All Eric could do was listen, as his heart beat slowly as a prickly sensation came over him. He listened.

Seconds later, the fake cop's footsteps grew closer. Coming back to put him out of his misery faster, Eric thought. He begged for forgiveness for not being able to keep his promise and braced himself for his final moment. But instead of stopping beside him, the footsteps moved past him and continued forward.

"Bri…Bri…an…" he whispered again.

He couldn't move his body, but he could move his pupils, and so he moved them up enough to the see the fake cop walking away with Brian slung over his shoulders.

"N…no…"

Tears fell, the wind blew, and lying in his own piss, Eric wished he would have never thrown the real cop's card away. Of course, it didn't really matter whether he had it or not, he thought, as his eyes closed.

Chapter 28

Ben couldn't stop himself. Enveloped in darkness, he just kept swinging. Right hand. Left hand. Over and over and over. The bones breaking beneath each blow didn't stop him. The blood he was spilling had no effect. Right hand. Left hand. Rage in each blow.

Beneath him, the recipient of each vicious hit lay silently still. Ben stared, tried to make out who the person was that he just couldn't keep himself from pummeling. It was a male, but the victim's face was nothing but a blur. There were no distinct features for Ben to make out who it was, no matter how hard he tried to squint the blur into focus, but for some reason, despite not being able to make out his victim, Ben had the feeling that he knew who it was on an almost intimate level, and for reasons he couldn't comprehend, he hated this person. Hated on a level that made no sense at all. And yet he still hit and hit and hit.

"Hate you," Ben said, his voice laced with rage. "I...hate you!"

He let out an animalistic growl and then wrapped gloved fingers around the blurred victim's throat. The hatred he didn't understand had him breathing heavily as he began to squeeze.

His heart was racing, pounding a thunderous rhythm. Sweat ran down his forehead and trickled into his eyes. He didn't notice the stinging as the darkness around began to pulse blood-red intermittently.

He squeezed. He wanted to end the life of the person he didn't know, yet knew at the same time. He didn't understand it and didn't try to. He just squeezed with death on his mind.

"Die," he said, baring his gums.

He squeezed harder. Tried to make the fingertips on each hand touch.

"Die!"

His nostrils flared, his heart raced. Sweat dripping, he continued to squeeze, determined to snuff out the victim's life.

"Die!" he said yet again. "DIE!!"

He squeezed as the world around him pulsated from black to blood-red in a fashion that matched the frantic beating of his heart. The victim said nothing and made no attempt to free himself from Ben's grasp.

Ben squeezed.

The world pulsed black to blood-red. Black to blood-red.

And then somewhere in between a pulse, his son called out to him.

Ben turned his head and looked over his shoulder. "Mikey?"

"Dad!"

"Mikey!" Ben let go of the blurred victim's neck and searched around for his son as the world around him continued to pulse. "Mikey! Where are you?"

"Dad!" his son yelled.

"Mikey!" Ben spun in circles looking for his boy, not locating him anywhere. But his voice was close. So very close. "Mikey....where are you?"

Ben continued to spin. Mikey called for him again. The darkness and the blood-red continued to flip flop. Ben called his son's name again. He couldn't find him anywhere. "Mikey...where are you?"

"I'm here!" Mikey screamed.

So close. As though he were standing beside, behind, or...

Ben turned slowly, looked down, and shook his head. "N...no..."

The blurred figure was no longer blurred.

"No! No!" Ben said again, his volume rising, becoming a scream.

The blurred figure, who was all too clear now, looked up at him with wide, frightened eyes. Eyes filled with pain and disbelief. Eyes that looked like his only younger.

Ben shook his head harder, then pressed the palms of his hands hard against his temples and applied pressure.

"Why?" Mikey asked, his face bloody. "Why Dad?"

The world pulsed from blood-red to black, blood-red to black rhythmically like a heartbeat.

Tears ran down Ben's face as he screamed. "No!"

And then he sprang up from the couch he'd fallen asleep on, the scream still erupting from his throat. "NO!"

The scream lasted only seconds, but felt like minutes, hours, days, months.

Ben struggled to breathe as his chest tightened up.

The blurred victim. Mikey. Beneath him.

Ben's heart was hammering. His body was covered in a sheen of sweat. His hands were trembling. Mikey.

"Jesus Christ."

He swung his legs off of his couch, leaned forward, rested his elbow on his knees and dropped his chin to his chest. "Jesus Christ," he said again, his throat dry. His hands continued to shake as he forced himself to take a slow breath. "Jesus Christ," he whispered one more time.

He looked at his watch—the digital display showed five a.m. He slumped back against the couch, leaned his head back, and covered his face with his hands. "Mikey," he said. He slammed a closed fist down on the couch. "Fucking nightmares!" He slammed his hand down again. He'd been having the nightmares since Mikey's death. Progressively they had gotten worse, but none had been this bad. None had been this graphic, this violent. His son. He was beating his own son. "Shit."

He ran his hand through his hair and took another full, deep breath, despite the pain in his chest, and clenched his jaws.

Fine.

That's what he told everyone he was.

He was fine. He could handle it.

After all, he was a survivor. He'd overcome sins of his father and found a way to move on. At least he thought he had. He'd followed in his father's footsteps, but not because he emulated him, but rather because protecting people just felt right. After a few years of protecting and serving, he'd somehow convinced a woman who was probably too good for him to fall in love with him, marry him and bear his son. He survived. He lived. And the nightmares from the past had stopped.

But then like a cruel joke, his life crumbled.

His son was murdered, the assailant never found. His marriage unable to withstand the weight of the devastating heartbreak, had fallen apart. And now he was looking for a killer that was doing things to little boys that brought nightmares both old and terrifyingly new.

But he was fine. He was strong, resilient.

He covered his face with his hands again. "Christ," he said as an image of Mikey ran through his mind again. "Christ."

He sat up and looked at his coffee table. Opened files and papers were spread across it. Notes, photographs and other details pertaining to the Pacifier. He had been going over them, looking, trying to find something that he and Vance could have possibly missed, until his eyes demanded that they be allowed to close.

He frowned. Hours of reading and re-reading, of going in-between the lines and staring at photographs he wanted no part of, and still he'd found nothing. He worked his jaw, reached for a cigarette, lit one, and took a long pull, filling his lungs with as much lung-damagingair as he could, before blowing it out in one long stream. He took another pull and then stood up, and after another glance at the paperwork, trudged over to his window and stared out at the pre-sunrise darkness. He was out there somewhere. The psycho, the sick fuck, and he had to be stopped.

Ben looked at his reflection in the cold glass. "You're fine," he said. "You can handle this."

Ben's reflection seemed to look back at him with a devilish, mocking smirk that gave him an uneasy feeling. Ben took a drag and blew smoke into his reflection's face.

"Fine," Ben said again. "Just fucking fine."

As his reflection stared back, its eyes dark, almost narrowed, his cell phone rang. He sighed, and took another drag and then outed his cigarette on his windowsill before moving to his phone. The sun had yet to rise. No good phone calls came before sunrise.

He picked up his cell, took a quick glance at the caller I.D., then answered.

"Yeah."

"We have another body," Vance said.

Ben closed his eyes and exhaled. "Where?"

"65th and Green. Behind the Chuck E. Cheese's."

Ben sighed. Chuck E. Cheese's used to be one of Mikey's favorite places to go. Mikey. The nightmare still had him jittery. "Who discovered the body?"

"Sanitation crew doing their morning pickup. They found him beside the dumpster, pacifier in his mouth."

Ben frowned. "Okay. Who's on the scene?"

"Reds and Birch and the rest of their team. Media, of course."

"Of course," Ben said with an exhale. "Okay...well, I'll be there in about twenty-five minutes."

Ben ended the call and exhaled. "Just fine."

Chapter 29

Ben…before you leave…there's something—" Vance started, but he never got to finish as Ben had already ended the call.

He let out a soft curse and lifted a Ziploc bag he'd been holding in his hand. Inside of the large bag was something that had given him chills. Something that had changed the nature of the investigation completely. A piece of paper, white, with a typed message. It had been discovered beneath the little boy's cold hand.

Vance cursed once again and re-read the words of the message, and as he did, Tiana's words from the meeting came to his mind. That the killer's actions could have possibly been a personal challenge of some kind. That the killer could be out for revenge.

A chill crept up from the base of Vance's spine. "Shit."

Indiana - 27 years ago

Ben was staring out the window, watching the snow fall like rain. The weather man said that a blizzard was coming. That they would be getting anywhere from a foot to a foot and a half of snow. It was going to fall fast and heavy at first, but would lay mainly on the grass and trees during the early part of the day. But when the afternoon came, particularly around one o'clock, it was going to start accumulating on the roads and sidewalks. The weather man suggested that everyone try to get to the grocery stores early for any last minute items they needed, because it was going to be dangerous to be out on the roads after four o'clock.

Ben was thrilled when he saw the report on the television in the morning, but not for the same reasons all of the other kids in the class had been. A large accumulation of snow meant that the roads would be unsafe to travel on, and with them being unsafe, that meant that no one was going to be able to work, and if no one went to work, that meant that everyone would be home, and if everyone was home, then that meant that Ben couldn't receive the secret lessons on strength and manhood that his father liked to teach him.

Ben watched the snowflakes flutter to the ground. *Harder*, he thought. *Fall harder, faster. Stick to the ground now so that she would have to leave work and come home sooner.*

Please.

Ben shivered as the snow fell and fought the urge to cry. *Be a man, he thought. Be a man the way his father demanded he be. Be a man and suck it up.*

After all, that's what he was supposed to do, wasn't he? That's what his father was teaching day after day, week after week. How to be a man. A strong man, able to handle physical and mental torture. A strong man, able to keep secrets because you just never knew when you could wind up in the hands of the enemy.

Secrets and strength.

His father was determined to teach him about those things. Determined to turn his boy into a soldier. Every couple of days since his eighth birthday, when his mother was at work or sometimes while she slept in her bed at night, his father made sure to teach him about manhood. The lessons were harsh and painful, and Ben knew were wrong, but his father had insisted they were necessary.

"You never know when you need to have this type of strength, Benji. You never know when the ultimate test is going to come. When you are going to be called upon to be the ultimate soldier. I know it's hard and it hurts, but it's for your own good."

Ben didn't like the hitting, the touching and the other things his father did to him and made him do, but his father had been a P.O.W., and had survived, and now he was a strong police officer, helping to keep everyone safe, so Ben took the lessons silently. But he hated them. And the more he received them, the less he wanted to be man. He just wanted to be a kid like every other kid in his class. He often wondered if they were getting their own private lessons at home, but whenever he looked into their eyes, he didn't see what he saw in his when he looked at himself in the mirror. A tortured, despondent gaze. Looking at the kids around him, he didn't see hopelessness, he didn't see despair. Instead he saw kids who were carefree and encouraged. Kids who didn't cringe at the sound of opening doors when their mothers weren't around.

Ben watched the snow fall and urged it on, praying for several feet, praying for it to be thick and heavy.

"Ben?"

The sound of his teacher's voice broke his focus. He turned and looked toward the front of the classroom and his heart sank. In the front of the room, standing beside his teacher, Mrs. Dixon, was his father. He was wearing his uniform, his badge gleaming. No one would ever take him for anything but the strong, brave, trustworthy and decent upholder of the law that he appeared to be.

"Ben...your dad is here to take you home early."

His father smiled. Ben had the same charming, though slightly crooked grin.

Ben sighed as his shoulders dropped. He took a quick, lasting glance out of the window and prayed for a miracle. Maybe if he prayed hard enough, his father's cruiser would lose control in the falling snow and they would never make it home.

CHAPTER 30

Come on...just a few more...come on...

Chris pulled on the chain vigorously. He had been doing so since he felt the separation in the link. *Pull*, he thought. *Pull.* His stomach was growling. The fake cop still hadn't returned to feed them. The hunger Chris felt should have made him weak, lethargic, but the opposite had happened. The more his stomach growled, the more determined he became. He pulled and pulled, causing the separation in the link to widen even more.

Almost there. Sweat ran down his forehead. *Almost there.* The callouses on his hand were raw, burning, but he refused to give in to the pain. He had to get out. He had to get Chad out. Chad had become too quiet. The lack of food had gotten to him.

Almost there. He tugged on the chain, harder and harder each time, before pausing to take a breath and give his callouses a break. He reached down, felt by the separation. Was it his imagination, or did it feel wide enough? His heart beat heavily as he finagled it until the chain came free. "Yes!"

He pulled his leg, which was still attached to the manacle and chain, but no longer connected to the metal plate fastened to the concrete. He was free. "I did it, Chad!" he whispered. "I did it!"

He went over to his brother, the chain scraping on the concrete behind him, and grabbed Chad by his shoulders. "I did it," he said shaking him.

Chad, who'd been asleep, said groggily, "You...you did?"

"Yes!"

"Am...am I dreaming?"

Chris laughed. "No you're not dreaming."

"You're free?"

"Yes."

"Are you going to get me out now?"

"Of course!"

Chris moved and grabbed on to the chain connected to Chad's manacle. During the struggle with his own chain, he'd figured out the best way to hold it had been toward the bottom. And unlike with his, he had better leverage with Chad's, so if he did it right, he could possibly get Chad free sooner, without causing him too much pain.

"It might hurt a little," he said to his brother. "You're going to have to be tough and take it, okay?"

"Okay," Chad said, apprehension in his voice.

"I'll try not to let it hurt though," he reassured him.

"Okay, but what if he comes back?"

Chris sighed. That was something he had been thinking about the entire time he'd worked to get himself free. What if the fake cop had come back? If he had before he had gotten his leg free, then his plan was to just lie still as though nothing was going on. But if he came after, then he was just going to have to do whatever it took. The fake cop was big, but David had beaten Goliath, and his friend Mike, who was in the seventh grade and weighed about one-hundred and twenty pounds wet, had beaten up eleventh grader, Jordan Weiss, who was at least seventy pounds heavier. Mike thought he had been fighting for his life. Chris actually would be.

He tightened his aching hands around his brother's chain. "If he comes back," he said, gritting his teeth. "I'll be ready."

He had to be.

He began to pull.

Chapter 31

Sarah McCallum sat on the toilet seat, the lid closed down, and cried softly. In her hand was a devastating reminder of how happiness had been mercilessly snatched away from her. A photograph of she and Ben, with Mikey standing in-between them. Mikey's arms were wrapped around them both. Sarah's and Ben's hands were intertwined across Mikey's midsection. Wide, joyous smiles adorned each one of their faces. The pictures had been taken at Busch Gardens in front of the Curse of the DarKastle right before they'd gotten on.

It had been a perfect day. Eighty-five degrees, low humidity. Bright sun, white clouds in the blue sky. The trip had been a promise Ben had finally kept. Mikey had turned ten that day, and he had wanted nothing more than to go to Busch Gardens and go on as many rides as he could, and eat corndogs and funnel cake all day long. Ben had missed his last two birthdays because of work—tireless searches for bad men doing bad things. Mikey never complained about Ben not being there because in his eyes, his father was a hero. He was out protecting the world. How could he be mad at that? But Ben hated missing those days and so he had promised that no matter the situation, Mikey's tenth birthday would not be missed. For some reason that day was extremely important to Ben, and he wanted it to be the best day Mikey had ever had. So on that day, whatever Mikey wanted, he got.

Tears fell from Sarah's eyes as she leaned forward, her knees on her elbows, her head bowed, the photograph clutched in both hands. Her body shook as she cried softly, trying to keep the noise down as Brandon was sound asleep in the bedroom on the opposite side of the door. She didn't want him to know that she was breaking down because he would want to know why, and although she'd successfully given half-truths in the past, she knew that this time she would tell him the whole truth.

That Ben had been right.

She was still very much in love with him.

Sarah cried and through her tears looked at the family she once had. Life had been a fairytale, only instead of the white picket fence, the additional 1.5 children, and the happy-go-lucky golden retriever, they had an old three-story home with a basement Sarah hated, Ben worked long hours on a dangerous job (one she often worried whether he'd make it home alive from), the additional 1.5 children wasn't possible due to complications from her pregnancy with Mikey, and she was deathly afraid of dogs because of a bite she had received from a neighbor's cocker spaniel when she was five years old. Despite all of that, life had been perfect. But as was the case with all fairy tales, there was always the presence of evil lurking around, and with one wicked, cruel and unsolved spell, Sarah's charmed life crumbled.

Now she was trembling, trying to keep the volume of her grief down as she stared at a son, who was truly an angel now, and a man she was so desperately still in love with, yet running away from because it was just easier to do that. Or so she'd thought until she collected the divorce papers.

Six months.

It was too soon to seek a divorce. She was being unrealistic, irrational. She needed to take more time to heal, to get over the tragedy. She needed to take more time to really think about what she was doing, what she was throwing away.

Things everyone said.

They were right and she knew it. Yet she was still running away as fast as she could. At least she was trying to until Ben made her face the admission she had tried so hard to force from her mind. That no matter how hard he tried to help her move on, no matter how good to her Brandon was, no matter how much he tried to love her, nothing would change the fact that she would never, could never move on and love him the way he wanted her to because her heart would always belong to Ben.

She had divorce papers, signed ready to go, ready to end things.

Tears dropped. Fell on the glossy photograph she'd snuck in to the bathroom. It was always with her. In her purse, in her tri-fold wallet. She wiped the photograph and held it away from where the tears could get to it, and continued to cry, knowing she was never going to do anything with the papers but eventually shred them.

Chapter 32

Déjà vu.

Ben was tired of it. This case. It was harder than he thought it would be. The memories it was bringing up—ones he had buried so long ago—and the memories he was trying like hell to bury. This case was just too fucking hard.

He wanted to quit. He would never tell anyone that, but that's what he wanted to do. Quit. Forget about the Pacifier and forget about the innocent boys who had been killed, and the justice they deserved. Forget about the innocent boys that had yet to be killed. He wanted to say to hell with it and turn in his gun and badge and just go away. Go somewhere where no one knew him, where he knew no one. Maybe then the pain, the nightmares, the memories—maybe then they would leave him alone.

That's all he wanted. To be left completely alone. Dr. Rose had said it wasn't good or productive to shut people out. That as hard as it could be sometimes, he needed to allow his friends to be there for him, that their support would help him move on. But just like everything else she had ever said, that was bullshit. Having people there, letting them in—it didn't help him move past a damn thing. All it did was remind him constantly that his life was in ruins, He had somehow survived a childhood that had finally seemed like someone else's and had become a productive and valued member of society. Life had become something he loved. And then Mikey was taken away, and the concrete, stable ground he had finally been able to walk on, crumbled from beneath his feet, sending him falling down into a bottomless pit of despair. And now to make matters worse, he was working a case that was only increasing the speed of his endless descent.

He took a long, hard pull of his cigarette and let the smoke swirl around his tongue. He wanted to quit so damn bad. It was selfish and morally wrong he knew, but it's what he wanted to do. To hell with anyone that didn't agree with him.

He blew out a long thick trail of smoke and ground his teeth together. He was sitting in his car, his window cracked, looking across at the throng of people standing outside. Some were reporters with microphones and cameras trained on them. Others (the majority) were people there for the spectacle. Like the vultures with the microphones, they didn't give a shit about who had been killed. They just knew that there was a dead body, and Ben knew many of them would have loved a glimpse.

He took another long drag, raised his window, opened the door, got out and exhaled. He wanted to quit, but of course he had no intention of doing that. He was a cop and there was another dead body. He had a job to do. It was that simple. He would deal with the death of his soul later.

He took a final pull and then dropped the almost fully smoked cancer stick to the ground, stepped on it and blew out smoke and then breathed in the crisp morning air. He sighed and looked across the street to where curious bystanders and reporters were all being kept at bay by police barriers and a uniformed officer. He took another breath, wishing it were more nicotine he was dragging in. Through the crowd he saw Vance standing, talking on his cell phone, while Reds, Birch and the rest of their team inspected the latest victim and searched the area for clues Ben knew they wouldn't find.

He thought about how badly he wanted to quit again and then moved. After giving several "No comments," he showed his badge, signed the logbook, took a pair of latex gloves the officer held out for him, and walked over to his partner, who put up his index finger and walked away a few steps to continue with his call.

Ben took a quick glance over to where the young victim lay beside a dumpster. He could only see the body from mid-chest down as Reds' body concealed the upper portion. He was glad for that. He didn't want to see anymore, especially the face. The dream and the violence in it ran through his mind briefly before he forced it away.

As if sensing him there, Reds looked over his shoulder and leveled his eyes on him. There was something in his eyes, Ben thought. He couldn't help but wonder if the Pacifier had escalated in his methods. Ben said, "Reds."

Reds nodded. "Ben." His expression was grim, his eyes almost probing.

Ben worked the right side of his jaw. He didn't like the way Reds was looking at him at all. "What's wrong?" he asked. "Has he escalated?"

Reds looked at him for a second or two, then shook his head. "No. It's the same M.O."

"So what's wrong?"

Reds frowned, and then looked to Ben's right where Vance suddenly appeared.

"Ben," Vance said, his voice low, somber.

Ben turned and looked at his partner. He didn't like the look in his eyes either. It reminded him of the way he had looked at him the day Mikey's body had been discovered.

"What's going on?" Ben asked.

Vance looked at him, his full lips pressed tightly together. "We need to talk," he said after a few seconds.

Ben closed his eyes a bit. "About what?"

"Let's go over there," Vance said, motioning his head to the left. It was away from the activity, away from where anyone could hear them. Vance moved without waiting for him.

Ben looked from him to Reds, who frowned and then turned back to the victim. Ben didn't like what was going on one bit. He followed after Vance. "What the hell is going on, Vance?"

Vance flared his nostrils, and held up a Ziploc bag with a white piece of paper inside. "This was with the body," he said. "It's a message left for you."

Ben looked at him. "For me?"

Vance gave him a nod.

Ben took the bag from his hand. He could feel Vance watching him closely as he flipped it over and read the message.

"What does it mean, Ben?"

Ben heard his partner, but didn't answer. He couldn't. He stood still as his heart began to beat heavily.

"Ben?" Vance said again. "Is there something you want to fill me in on? 'You should have kept your mouth shut?' What does that mean?"

Ben's chest began to tighten. His hands began to shake as he remained silent, his fingers still clamped around the note. *No*, he thought. The notecard, the words on it. A statement. Something said to him a long time ago.

You should have kept your fucking mouth shut, Ben.

"Ben?" Vance reached out and put a hand on his shoulder.

Ben flinched and pulled away.

"What the…? Ben…what the hell is wrong? What does the note mean? Do you know who left it for you?"

Ben remained silent, his throat dry, his chest more constricted than before. He was staring down, seeing not the words on the paper, but instead witnessing a grim, harrowing scene. A moment in time he used to see in his nightmares.

"Ben…what the fuck, man?"

Ben's heart hammered. The trembling in his hands increased. He felt sick to his stomach, his legs grew weak. He shook his head. "N…no," he said. He looked up.

"Ben—" Vance started.

But before he could say anything else, Ben grabbed him by the collar of his leather coat and pushed him back several feet, slamming him against the wall of one of the adjoining buildings.

"Is this a joke?" Ben yelled, holding the notecard up inches away from Vance's face.

Confused and shocked, Vance said, "What the fuck? A joke?"

"Yes!" Ben yelled. "Is this somebody's idea of a fucking joke?"

Vance forced Ben's hands from around his collar and pushed him off of him. "What the fuck is your problem?" he said, his hands balled into fists, prepared in case Ben rushed him again. "What the fuck is the deal with that note? Who left that for you?"

Ben looked at Vance, then down at the note. He shook his head. A joke, he thought. A sick, cruel, twisted joke. Who? Why? He shook his head again as the ground beneath his feet became unsteady. The note began to fade in and out of focus. He shook his head one more time, and then looked up at Vance.

"Talk to me, man," Vance said.

Ben looked at him for a second and then turned his head and looked in the direction of where the victim lay. Reds and Birch were both looking at him. Ben looked at the body. The feet were the only thing he could see.

You should have kept your fucking mouth shut, Ben.

Words said to him a lifetime ago. They reverberated in his ears. He shook his head again, as if that would somehow calm the noise.

Who left the note and why had it been left with the body? What did it mean?

Ben shook his head again, then looked back to his partner, his best friend.

"Talk to me, man," Vance said again, his eyes filled with concern and skepticism.

Ben opened his mouth, paused for momentarily, and then said, "I…I have to go."

"What?" Vance said, an eyebrow raised.

"I need some time to think."

"Think? Think about what? Christ, man…what the hell is going on?"

Ben half shook his head. "I…I can't go into it now."

"What do you mean you can't go into it? We have a killer on the loose and he's left you a note."

"I know," Ben said. "But I just need some time."

"We don't have time, man! If you know who that's from, then you need to talk. Now!" Vance glared at him, his teeth clenched, his hands still balled.

Ben began moving back away from him. He was wrong, he knew, but the note…it was just too much to deal with. He needed time when there was no time. He needed to get away, to be somewhere where no one could see him losing his mind, because that's what was going to happen. He was going to lose it.

He shook his head. "I…I'm sorry, Vance…but I can't do this now. I need some time."

Vance took a step toward him and clamped his hand on his shoulder again. "What the fuck, Ben?" he started. But before he could finish, Ben hit him hard in his midsection, and as Vance dropped down to one knee, he took off toward his car.

Chapter 33

Twenty-six years ago.

Allen was in his basement, thumbing frantically through files. Searching. Twenty-six years ago, something had happened. He'd lied to someone. He'd told someone that they hadn't been responsible for whatever it was that had occurred. That they'd had no control over someone else's actions.

According to Patrick, this is what happened twenty-six years ago. Now Allen was going through old files, while sweat ran down his forehead and the middle of his back, and gathered beneath his arms, trying desperately to find out who the patient had been because his sons' lives depended on it.

If they were still alive.

Allen shook his head. *No.* He couldn't think that way. *They were alive. Patrick had killed another boy. Not his sons.*

His heart had ached when he'd watched the news earlier and had seen that Patrick had done what he said he would do. Allen could have prevented it, or he could have at least tried to. He could have gone to the police. He could have had them ready, waiting to take Patrick down, or kill him if it came down to that. Watching the news report, Allen had trembled. He could have saved that boy's life. But he had to think about his sons. They were alive. They just had to be.

He shook his head again and then pulled down a cardboard box from the top shelf of a metal bookcase. It was the last of five boxes. Twenty-six years ago, Allen had been twenty-five. He'd acquired a true interest in psychology during his freshman year in college, and quickly switched his major from business. The systematic investigation of behavior and the study of the way people responded to different kinds of trauma they endured appealed to him. Particularly in children, whose young, and for the most part unbiased, minds he found extremely fascinating. Working hard, he got in PhD in psychology after an extensive two year program for his Masters and then completed an additional semester working an internship for a private practice, which he ended up working full time for, for a number of years before he opened a practice of his own. Allen enjoyed his job. He enjoyed helping, or at least doing all he could to help children, and twenty-six years ago, that's just what he'd been doing.

He wiped sweat away from his brow, took a breath, and was about to remove the lid of the box when his wife called out his name.

"Allen?"

He laid his hand down on the top of the lid and looked up to see her standing in the middle of the staircase. He'd been so caught up in his search that he hadn't noticed that she'd come down. "Yes?"

"What...what are you doing?"

He looked from her down to the box, and then back up at her. He shook his head. "Nothing. Just going through old paperwork."

His wife nodded, then enveloped herself in her arms and took three steps down. "I...I saw the news," she said softly.

Allen frowned. "Yeah...I did, too."

His wife took two more steps, was at the bottom now. "Did...did you know?" she asked, her voice heavy with anxiety.

Allen closed and opened his eyes slowly. "Did I know what, Amanda?"

Amanda took a step toward him. Her eyes were bloodshot and swollen. Stress lines ran across her forehead and crow's nests traced away from her eyes and mouth that dipped down at the corners. The sight of her broke Allen's heart. She was ten years his junior, but always looked younger than that. Now, instead of looking like a woman in her mid-thirties, she was favoring the late fifties.

She shook her head. "Don't, Allen. Just don't."

Allen sighed as his shoulders dropped. "Yes," he said. "I knew."

"But you didn't go to the police." A statement, not a question.

"We've talked about this already, Amanda."

"We're murderers, Allen."

"Amanda—"

"We could have saved these boys from dying," his wife said, rubbing her arms as though she were trying to stay warm. "But we didn't."

Allen exhaled. He tried speaking again, before she cut him off.

"Murderers, Allen. You and me. Those boys' blood is on our hands. We could have saved them."

Allen slammed his hand down on the top of the box, causing it to dent inward. "Goddammit, Amanda! Our boys…your boys could be alive. What the hell was I supposed to do?"

Tears began falling fast and abundantly from Amanda's eyes. She hugged herself tightly and shook her head. "I…I don't know," she said, her voice breaking up. "I…I just can't…can't do this anymore. I can't! When I wash my hands I see nothing but blood, and no matter how many times I wash or scrub them, the blood never goes away. Oh, God! I can't…I can't take this! I can't handle it!"

Allen dropped his chin to his chest. Her breakdown, her torment…he was feeling it, too. But what could he do? He had blood on his hands but it wasn't his sons.

He looked up at his wife and made a move to step toward her, but stopped when she put up her hand. He took a breath and let it out deliberately. "I…I don't want to lose our boys," he said.

"They're…they're dead," Amanda said.

Allen shook his head. "You don't know that."

Amanda nodded. "Yes. Yes I do. He's a killer, Allen. The things he does…our boys—"

"Are still alive. They are *still* alive, and as long as we don't say anything—"

"Then other boys will die!"

Allen balled his hands into tight fists at his side. Other boys would die, but that didn't have to be the case. He could put a stop to it all somehow.

"Other boys will die," Amanda said again in a whisper.

Allen closed his eyes and dragged his hands down over his face. "Our sons—"

"They're dead, Allen. I just know it. I can feel it."

"You're wrong."

"Who is he, Allen? He's coming to you…he's taken our boys. There has to be a reason why. Who is he?"

"I don't know," Allen said, looking down at the last box.

"You have to know," Amanda insisted.

"I don't."

"So then why you, Allen? Why our boys? If…if you mean nothing…are nothing to him, then why you?"

"Amanda…really…I have no idea."

"Are you keeping things from me, Allen?"

Allen clenched his jaw. "No. Why would you think that?"

"Because I…I just can't believe that his doing this…his choosing you was random. I just can't."

Allen shook his head and opened his mouth.

"Look at me," Amanda said before he could speak.

Allen looked away from the box and reluctantly lifted his head and settled his eyes on hers.

"Are you hiding anything?" she asked.

Allen sighed. "No."

Amanda stared at him as her tears ran. Her gaze was intense and painful, and Allen wanted nothing but to look away. "You…you have to know something," Amanda insisted.

Allen's heart pounded heavily as his chest tightened from the constriction of overwhelming guilt he felt. He hated lying to her, but he couldn't tell her the truth. She was on the edge and he feared that if she knew that a connection, a history of some kind existed between he and Patrick that she would fall over the edge, as he had nearly done. But his boys were alive. He believed that. And so he couldn't fall over. He couldn't crack. And he couldn't let her go over either.

"I don't," he said. "Believe me…I wish I did."

"Then why are you down here, Allen? Why are you going through your files?"

Allen stared at his wife as she watched him, the look in her eyes accusatory and piercing. "I'm just trying to stay busy," he said.

"You haven't touched those files in years."

"Like I said…I'm just trying to keep myself preoccupied."

Amanda watched him.

He did all he could to not look away.

Tense seconds went by.

Amanda rubbed her arms again, then wiped her eyes. "You're lying," she said. "You're lying."

Allen shook his head. "I'm not. I swear."

Amanda looked at him, her eyes unblinking, her tears no longer falling. She shook her head this time, then without a word, turned toward the staircase.

"Amanda…"

She paused, one foot on the bottom step. She didn't turn around.

"Our boys are still alive. You can't say anything."

Amanda took a breath, then released it and put her right hand on the banister. "I can't handle the blood anymore, Allen," she said, her voice barely a whisper, and then walked upstairs.

Allen called out to her again, but she wouldn't stop. When the door at the top of the staircase was slammed shut, he exhaled heavily. *Twenty-six years ago*, he thought. He'd lied to someone. He had to figure out who because time was running out.

He grabbed the lid and removed it, praying the answer he needed lay within one of the green file folders inside.

Chapter 34

Eric opened his eyes to bright, white light. *Dead*, he thought. He was dead. At least he'd made it to heaven. Hell, after everything he'd gone through in his fourteen years, he deserved to be there. Deserved to be with the angels.

Life on the streets had worn out its welcome. He was tired of it. Tired of running and hiding, doing all he could to avoid being caught and put back into the foster system. Tired of searching for safe, warm places to sleep at night. Tired of dealing with the roaches, rats and other insects that scurried around when he did find a place. Tired of stealing food, of robbing people, or when he had to, rummaging through garbage cans to find leftover food to satisfy the rumbling in his stomach.

So, so tired.

But he wouldn't have to worry anymore because he was in heaven now. His old life was behind him. He would no longer have to sleep in cardboard boxes, abandoned cars, abandoned broken down apartment buildings. He would no longer have to deal with people that didn't matter. Of course, no one had ever really mattered anyway. Well, no...that wasn't true. One person mattered. One sometimes annoying, oftentimes bratty little kid. He mattered.

Eric blinked his eyes rapidly, and as he did, the white lights of heaven blurred and then came back into focus to reveal that it wasn't heaven he was in, but someplace entirely different.

White walls with a light, pastel-green trim. A beige loveseat with a small round white table sitting in front of it. A large window with beige blinds pulled open, allowing the sunlight to shine through. These were the first things Eric noticed as his vision cleared. That, followed by the faint sounds of an ESPN broadcast and a soft beeping noise.

A hospital room.

He averted his gaze downward. His legs were covered by a white sheet. Above his legs, against the wall, braced up just below the ceiling was a television—the source of the broadcast.

Eric tried to move, to turn over onto his back, but had to stop immediately as sharp pain rifled through him.

His back.

Where he'd been stabbed on the night the fake cop had taken Brian away.

Eric tried to move again, but gasped as pain and soreness shot through him again. *Brian*, he thought. Eric was supposed to have protected him. He'd told him that he would. But he'd been unable to do anything because he was lying face down, in pain, unable to move, unable to keep his word.

A tear snaked away from the corner of his eyes as he breathed slowly, which hurt to do so. Brian, he thought again. Another tear fell. Then another, and another, until a river began to flow. Brian had been taken by the fake cop the real cop who'd tackled him at the park was looking for.

Eric shed tears as the intensity of the pain coming from the wound on his back increased. His little brother was gone and Eric knew he wasn't going to see him again. He cried and when someone behind him said, "You're awake!" he continued to stay still and let his tears go.

A few hours later, Eric was no longer crying, but was still lying on his side. The pain he had felt before was still there, but wasn't nearly as severe thanks to the morphine the doctor had ordered the nurse to give him for the pain. That's why they thought he'd been crying earlier. But that hadn't been the case at all. Compared to the guilt he felt, the pain had been minimal. Brian had been taken. If only he hadn't gotten out of the car—maybe he could have prevented it from happening. Why did he have to go to the front of the car to relieve himself? Why didn't he just stay beside the door or just hold it until the morning?

Why, why, why? Until the morphine kicked in, the whys wouldn't stop. Now he was on his side, awake, wishing for another dose to put him back to sleep.

His eyes began welling again, and as they did, the door to the room sighed open. He looked up to see a black nurse in green scrubs, along with a black man wearing green scrubs also, but with a white overcoat on, walk into the room. They both looked almost too young to be a doctor or nurse, Eric thought for a fleeting moment.

They approached his bed.

"Hey there," the doctor said, placing his hands on the bedrail. His voice was Barry White deep. "Are you feeling any better?"

Eric looked at the doctor and gave him a nod.

The doctor smiled, then gave the rail a tap. "Good. I'm just going to check your wound, okay?"

Eric gave him another nod, but remained silent.

The doctor tapped his rail one more time and then walked around the bed and stood behind Eric. "Let me know if anything I do causes you too much pain, okay?"

Another nod from Eric.

"By the way, I'm Doctor Reed and that's Angie. She's just going to check your blood pressure."

"Hi," Angie said, smiling at him. She was pretty. Almost looked like Rihanna, only darker with more weight. "Just relax, okay?" she said wrapping a pressure cuff around his arm.

Eric said softly. "Okay."

Behind him, Doctor Reed said, "I'm going to be pulling surgical tape off of your skin. It may hurt a little."

"Okay," Eric replied knowing the pain would be incomparable to the pain he was already feeling.

"So…" the doctor said, beginning the process. "What's your name?"

Eric winced as Doctor Reed pulled tape away from his skin, then reluctantly answered. "Eric."

The tape removed, the doctor moved the bandage away. "Well, Eric… someone was really looking out for you."

Eric winced again as the doctor continued his evaluation. "I guess," he said.

"Oh, there's no guessing. The knife you were stabbed with just missed your lung, and it was left in your back, which minimized the damage done. That, along with the cold air, temporarily helped prevent you from losing an excessive amount of blood. And fortunately for you, the owner of the junk yard you were in came in early to check on the property to make sure everything was okay. He usually has a pit bull there, but the pit had gotten sick and he had to take it to the vet. He saw you on the ground and called 9-1-1 right away. So you see, Eric…there's no guessing…you're definitely on somebody's good list."

Eric shrugged. "I guess," he said again.

"So what happened last night, Eric? Do you know who did this to you?"

Eric's breath caught in his throat as his heart began to beat heavily.

"Eric?" Angie said.

Eric looked up at her. She'd put her hand on his. "Are you all right?"

Eric watched her, but remained silent.

"Eric?" Doctor Reed called out from behind him. "We want to help in any way we can."

"That's right, Eric," Angie said, giving his hand a light reassuring squeeze. "You don't have to be afraid. You can talk to us."

Eric took short breaths, but kept his lips pressed firmly together. He could feel tears threatening to well behind his eyes as thoughts of Brian ran through his mind. *My fault*, he thought. *I let him down.*

"Eric, honey," Angie said. "You can talk to us."

Eric winced as Doctor Reed placed gauze and tape back over his wound. He was supposed to have been dead. Just like Brian.

He opened his mouth, then closed it.

"It's all right, honey," Angie soothed. "Nothing's going to happen to you."

He looked at her. Nothing would happen to him. *That wasn't true*, he thought. If he told them, they would get the police. The police would come and ask him a ton of questions. Three of them he would dread.

What was he doing in the junk yard?

Where were his parents?

Where did he live?

He wouldn't want to answer, but he would have to, and once he did that, once he told them that the junk yard had been his home for the night, that he didn't have any parents or home, the police would call child protective services. And then it would be over. He would be placed back into the foster care system, where bad things happened and mouths stayed glued. He didn't want to go back. He hated the streets and being on them, but they were safer. On the streets he could run and hide if he needed to. There was nowhere to hide in the homes. He didn't want to go back, but he owed it to Brian because he hadn't protected him like he'd promised he would.

He took a slow breath. Slow because of nerves and because he felt pain in his back when he breathed. He exhaled as Angie's soft hand gave his, another gentle squeeze.

"It's all right," she said, her voice soft, reassuring.

"I…I…I saw him…" Eric paused, took another slow breath, exhaled, continued. "I saw him," he said again."

Angie leaned closer toward him. "Saw who, honey?"

"A…a fake cop. That's who did it. And…and he took Brian."

The tears he'd been trying to hold back were running down across his face again. He hadn't meant to say so much, but he couldn't stop talking.

"Who's Brian?" Doctor Reed asked.

"He…he's my brother. The…the real cop said that there were bad things happening to ten-year-old boys. He…he gave me a card, but I…I threw it away. Brian is…was ten and he…he's probably dead now because I left him alone."

Eric stopped talking and cried hard tears. His back hurt as his body shuddered, but not nearly as bad as his heart. He cried, unable to stop.

Angie ran her hand over his forehead and through his hair. "It's okay," she said. "It's okay."

Eric cried and shook his head. *It wasn't,* he thought. It wasn't at all.

He continued to sob and in-between his sobs, he heard Doctor Reed say, "Call the police. I think he's talking about the serial killer they've been talking about on the news."

Chapter 35

Come on, Chris thought. *Come on!*

He was pulling on the chain to Chad's manacle. He had the leverage. He had the determined vigor. But what he didn't have was a set of new hands, and so his 'come ons' were silent pleas for his palms to hang in there just a little while longer. He'd gotten a small separation in the link of his brother's chain, though not nearly as much of an initial separation as he'd had on his, but it was enough. For however long he had, he just had to keep pulling.

But his hands.

His palms were slick with sweat and blood from callouses, which were beyond raw. His fingers ached and were fighting with him, trying to remain loose instead of constricted tightly. The muscles in his hand were cramping, his thumb and middle finger tightening constantly. His hands—they were on their last leg, screaming, crying, begging for the torture to cease.

"Are you close?" Chad asked.

He was still lethargic from the lack of food, but ever since Chris had gotten free from his restraint, the pep had picked up in his voice. For him alone, Chris ignored the incessant cries of his palms, fingers, and muscles, and continued to pull.

"Getting…there," he said, tugging.

"Hurry!" Chad said.

"I'm trying to, Chad."

"What if he comes back? What if he sees you?"

Chris closed his eyes and clenched down. "Chad, will you please shut up? I'm doing the best I can."

He took a breath, held it, pulled on the chain, then eased up, exhaled, took another breath, held it, and pulled again. He pulled the way the super heroes did in the comic books. His fourteen-year-old muscles were rippling, his veins jutting out of the side of his neck.

Come on, he thought again, his hands continuing to cry out for relief.

"Chris…" Chad said, his voice softer, but insistent.

"Be quiet, Chad. I told you I'm working as hard and as fast as I can."

"No," Chad said, his voice panicked. "I…I heard something!"

Chris pulled and then paused. "What?"

"I heard something!"

Chris turned his head toward the door and focused until he heard something too. Faint tapping, growing louder, heavier.

Footsteps!

Chris' heart was already beating heavily from the work he'd been putting in with the chain, but it began to race and pound harder. He took short, rushed breaths. He needed to do something fast. Initially he'd thought of using his chain as a weapon, but it wasn't long enough. Besides, his callouses were burning and throbbing, and at that particular moment, he'd be lucky to get even one good swing out of anything. He wanted to get him and his brother out of there, but he had to be smart about it. He was probably going to get only one shot so whenever he made his move he had to make it count.

His heart beat thunderously.

The sounds of the footsteps grew closer.

He swallowed saliva as sweat trickled down his forehead.

He had seconds to do something.

"Chris!" Chad whispered.

"Be quiet!" Chris said. "And don't say anything. Understand?"

"O..okay."

Chris gently put his brother's chain down, gathered his quickly, but quietly, instructed again, "Don't say anything!" and then made his way back over to his side and did the best he could to connect his link back to the metal faceplate, before laying down on his side.

Literally seconds after he stopped moving, the footsteps stopped just outside of the room.

Chris lay deathly still while beads of sweat trickled and dropped from the bridge of his nose. *Please, Chad,* he thought. *Please keep it together.*

A key was inserted and seconds later the door was pulled open, allowing dim light into the room.

Chris took a slow breath as his heartbeat reverberated in the caverns of his ears. The man hadn't taken another step. Chills crept along Chris' arms as he wondered why. Had the man heard him trying to get Chad free? Despite the darkness, did he notice the separation in link of his chain? Chris wanted to sit up, but instead remained still.

Seconds passed and then the man's voice invaded the silence. "Tonight," he said. "You're both going to die."

And then he slammed the door shut.

Chris remained unmoving, his heartbeat hammering, as the fake cop's footsteps faded away.

Tonight…they were both going to die.

Chad began to whimper. Chris wanted to tell him to be quiet, to remain calm, but how could he, when he was on the verge of tears himself?

Tonight…they were both going to die.

Never had he heard anything so frightening.

"I..I don't wa…want to die…" Chad said tearfully. "Chris…I…I don't want to die."

Chris trembled. "We're not going to die," he said sitting up.

"But…but he…he said—"

"I don't care what he said." Chris unhooked his chain and went over to his brother and clamped his hand down on his shoulder. "We're not going to die, okay. I promise."

Chad sniffled and cried. Chris frowned and for the first time, was glad for the darkness around them. It concealed the tears falling from his eyes as he went back to working on his brother's chain. His hands hurting or not, he had to get his brother free.

Tonight…they were both going to die.

Chris cried silently and pulled on the chain.

Indiana – twenty-six years ago

It was supposed to have been a secret. Their secret. But Ben couldn't take it anymore. The nightmares, the reliving of the torture he dealt with day after day. Every time he closed his eyes he would feel and see it all happening. The hitting; he could feel every blow given all below his neck. The hits were supposed to teach him how to be physically strong. Everything else was to teach him discipline. He could be strong, but could he be disciplined enough to keep his mouth closed?

"This is our secret, Benji. Your mother wouldn't approve of my methods of turning you into a man, but that's because she doesn't understand. She's never been a P.O.W. She doesn't know what it takes. Telling her would be the worst thing for you, Benji. Telling her would be weak and soft. And you're neither of those things right, Benji? You're not weak. You're not soft. Are you?"

No he wasn't.

That's what his answer was each and every time he was asked.

He was a man. He wasn't soft. He could keep their secret.

But it was so hard, so painful, so agonizing. And one day—a cold, windy day—the pain, and the agony became overwhelming. He hadn't meant to say anything but the day before his father's lesson had been vicious. The physical and sexual assault had been at their worst, and as strong as he had tried to be, Ben couldn't ignore the pain, and so when his father had to leave for an emergency call the next night, he did something he had sworn he wouldn't do. He went to his mother and told her all about the lessons of manhood that he'd been learning for the past two years.

The tears his mother had shed when he was finished shocked him. He'd never seen her in so much anguish before. With tears erupting from his own eyes, he hugged her tightly and begged her to forgive him for saying anything, insisting that he never meant to hurt her.

"Please don't cry, mommy! Please. I…I shouldn't have said anything. I wasn't supposed to say anything. I'm sorry!"

Tears falling harder and faster from her eyes, his mother held onto him as though her life depended on it, kissed his forehead, and told him that he had nothing to apologize for.

"Nothing! Do you understand, Benjamin? You have nothing to be sorry about. You didn't do anything wrong!"

"But…but you're crying…"

"I'm crying because I'm angry, honey. I'm angry at your father. He's the one who did wrong, okay? He did. Not you!"

"B…but…"

"No buts, Benjamin. Do you understand?"

"Y…yes," Ben said, nodding and crying at the same time.

His mother continued to hold him, continued to kiss him. She held him throughout the night. She held him into the next morning when the sun rose, the strength of her grasp never lessening.

She held him.

Her son. The blessing she swore to protect from harm at all costs.

She held him tightly against her, rocking him gently until the sound of Ben's father's truck rumbled into the driveway of their home.

Ben raised his chin and looked up at her. She gave him a reassuring smile, kissed him gently on his forehead and lips, then stood up and with sad eyes, told him to lock his bedroom door after she walked out, and to leave it that way until she came back to get him.

Ben wanted to ask her to promise that she would be back for him, but a twisting in his stomach told him that was a promise she may not have been able to keep, so he nodded and said okay with tears in his eyes. His mother gave him a loving smile and walked out of the room and closed the door behind her, and as she did, Ben wanted go behind her, to tell her not to go downstairs, but instead he did as he was told and locked the door and then sat on his bed with his knees to his chest, his back pressed against the wall.

An eternity of seconds passed before a crack went off from downstairs, followed by his mother's voice. "You bastard! You sick bastard!"

Another crack rang out and Ben knew the sound had come from his father's pistol that he kept in their bedroom at the top of their closet. Ben had found it sitting in a shoebox one day while searching for his favorite teddy bear that his father had taken away from him just before the lessons started. He'd touched it many times in the past, always wondering what it would be like to hold, point, and pull its trigger.

"What the hell? Jen…what are you doing?"

"I'm going to kill you for what you did!"

Another crack erupted, followed by the sound of something shattering.

"What are you talking about?"

"You son of a bitch! How could you do that to your own son?"

Another crack of his father's gun.

"Jen…put that fucking gun down or I swear...you're going to regret it."

Ben's mother screamed and as she did, Ben buried his face behind his knees and rocked back and forth slowly as he whispered, "I'm sorry…I'm sorry…I'm sorry…"

Another crack pierced the air.

"I'm going to kill you for what you've done!"

"What I've done? You cunt! What I've done is going to make that boy strong. I'm turning him into a man! Now put the gun down, Jen. I'm not going to tell you again!"

"Go to hell you perverted asshole!"

Another crack, then the sound of Ben's father grunting.

"You bitch! You fucking bitch!"

Ben continued to rock back and forth and whisper softly as tears fell forcefully from his eyes. "I'm sorry…I'm sorry…"

His mother screamed out again. Another crack went off. And then another, this one louder than the others.

Then there was silence.

Ben rocked. "I'm sorry…I'm sorry…"

His whispers were like screams in the silence as the words seemed to bounce off of the walls.

"BEN!"

The sudden explosion of his father's voice yelling his name caused him to sit up rigid.

"BEN...You little piece of shit! You get down here! NOW!"

Ben sat frozen as his heart raced with the force of a jackhammer.

His father called out to him again. "BEN...Get your ass down here or your mother's going to die right now. Do you hear me!"

Ben looked toward his bedroom door. "Mommy," he whispered.

He trembled as he unclasped his hands from around his knees and scooted off of the bed. His father yelled out to him again. Ben's breaths became faster, shorter. His heartbeat increased even more. He moved on rubbery legs to his door. "I'm sorry," he whispered as he unlocked it, turned the knob and pulled it open. "I'm sorry, mommy."

"Get down here, you little pussy!"

Ben moved, his side pressed against the wall from his bedroom door to a flight of stairs leading down to the first level of their bi-level home. The muscles in his legs felt like jelly and several times, he nearly fell.

"Hurry up, Ben!" his father commanded.

Standing at the top of the staircase, Ben paused. He didn't want to go down. He wanted to turn and go back to his room. He wanted to lock the door, open his window, jump down to the hard grass outside, and run until his legs could no longer move.

But he couldn't run, because his mother needed him.

He put his hand on the wooden banister and descended slowly, the beating of his heart increasing with each step. When he reached the bottom, he paused again

"In here, Ben!"

Ben turned to his right and moved deliberately, stepping past a shattered vase and a bullet hole in the wall by the door, and stopped at the threshold of the living room and stared in horror at the sight of his father standing in the middle of the room, holding his mother against him, his left hand gloved and wrapped around her throat, his right hand, gloved also, holding his police issued revolver to her temple.

"I thought you understood, Ben. Strength and discipline. I was teaching you how to be a man. I thought you understood!"

Ben looked at his mother. Blood had colored the middle of her shirt red and had pooled on the carpeting in between her feet. Her mouth hung open, her eyes were half closed as his father choked her.

"You weren't supposed to say anything, Ben. I told you she wouldn't understand."

Ben shook his head slowly. "I…I'm sorry," he said, though it was barely audible. "I…I'm sorry."

"It's too late for apologies, Ben. You should have kept your fucking mouth shut. You should have been a man and kept your fucking mouth SHUT!"

"I'm sorry," Ben said again, his voice stronger, his eyes still on his mother.

She was dying. Right before his very eyes.

"I'm sorry," he said yet again. "Please!"

"I told you it's too late, Ben. Don't you get it? You're weak. You're undisciplined. You'll never be a man!"

"Please…" Ben implored again. "Please…daddy,,,"

His father shook his head. "You shouldn't have told, Ben."

Ben watched as his father's black gloved fingers closed harder around his mother's throat. Weak and near death from the bullet wound to her midsection, his mother gagged, but gave no fight.

"You should have kept your fucking mouth shut," his father said again.

And then from behind Ben, someone yelled, "Drop the gun, Brent and let Jen go!"

Continuing to strangle his wife, Ben's father looked past his shoulder. "He shouldn't have told, Mark!"

Mark, his father's partner. Ben had never heard him come in. "Come on, Brent. Just put the gun down and let Jen go," he said again. "You don't have to do this."

Mark put a hand on Ben's shoulder and attempted to pull him back, but Ben shrugged it off and kept his eyes on his mother.

Mark continued to instruct his father to let his mother go, to put his gun down, but Ben could tell by the way her mouth had been hanging open, that it didn't matter whether he did or not.

His mother was gone and it was all his fault.

"Brent. . .please..." Mark begged. "Just let her go."

Ben's father shook his head. "He shouldn't have told!"

And then, before Mark could react, he pressed the gun against his temple and pulled the trigger. Seconds later, both his and his wife's body crumpled to the ground.

Behind him, Mark said, "Oh Christ! Oh Christ!" and then grabbed Ben, spun him around, and pressed Ben's head against his chest. "Oh Christ," he said again as more police officers came inside.

"Jesus!" said one officer.

"Shit!" said another.

Mark ordered them to check the bodies and began to usher Ben away. As he did, Ben pulled his head back away from his chest and looked back over his shoulder, and leveled his eyes on his mother's dead body.

He would never see her smile again. He had known it upstairs. And it had all been his fault.

Chapter 36

Ben! Ben!"

Vance coughed as his midsection hurt from the unexpected blow Ben had given him. "Shit!" He stood up, held his hand against his stomach and watched as Ben peeled away in his car. He clenched his jaw, said, "Godammit," and then looked down. On the ground was the notecard.

He took a breath and then bent down and picked up the note. He looked at it and shook his head.

You should have kept your fucking mouth shut, Ben.

The message had jarred Ben in a way Vance had only ever seen him shaken once before. Mikey's death. The look in his eyes, the loss of color in his pale skin, the way his body trembled—he'd looked that way after reading the note.

What the hell did it mean?

Vance forced himself to not crumble the evidence he held tightly in-between his fingers. He was angry and frustrated. "Fuck."

He turned and walked back over to where Reds was. He was standing with his arms folded across his chest, a look of concern and curiosity in his eyes. Behind him, the victim lay zipped up in a body bag ready to be transported to the morgue.

"What the fuck just happened over there?" he asked.

Vance frowned. "I don't know."

"Where the hell did Ben run off to?"

"I don't know," Vance said again.

"Did this have to do with the note?"

Vance clamped a hand down behind his neck and pulled. "Yeah. Shit."

"And now he's gone." It was more a statement than a question.

Vance flared his nostrils. "Yeah."

Reds gnawed on his bottom lip and raised his eyebrows. "You remember what T. said right?"

Vance nodded. He remembered all too well.

His cell phone rang suddenly. He grabbed it, hoping it would be Ben. It wasn't. "Newsome."

"Vance…it's Cribbs."

After their initial meeting, Vance had assigned Seth Cribbs along with his partner Derrick Weston, the task of talking to friends, relatives, ex-boyfriends and ex-girlfriends of perps he and Ben had locked away. It was grunt work but they hadn't complained.

Vance turned away from Reds. "What's going on? You and Weston make any headway?"

"A call just came in to the station from a nurse over at Met. General. She said they have a kid there who was stabbed in the back last night and that the kid claims a fake cop was the one who stabbed him and then took his brother away and killed him."

"Killed him?"

"Yeah. She said he was a little hysterical, but that he did say something about a real cop telling him about bad things happening to ten-year-old boys. He says his brother was ten."

Vance's heart skipped a beat. "Did the nurse give you his name?"

"Yeah…Eric. No last name though. And his brother's name was Brian."

The hairs on Vance's arm rose. Yesterday at the park. The kid he'd tackled…the kid he had warned about bad things happening to ten-year-old boys. His name had been Eric, but he hadn't said anything about a Brian. Of course he wouldn't have if he were trying to protect him. He looked over toward the body bag. "Shit," he said.

"They think the fake cop he's talking about could be our guy," Cribbs said.

"You said he's at Met. Gen.?"

"Yeah. Go to the front desk and ask for a Nurse Murphy. Angie Murphy. Either her or a Doctor Craig Reed."

"Okay. Thanks."

"You want Weston and me to meet you and McCallum there?"

"No. You two continue with what you're doing in case nothing pans out."

"All right." Vance ended the called and turned back to Reds. "Shit," he said again.

"What was that about?"

Vance looked from Reds to the body bag. "I think our John Doe might have a name."

Reds raised an eyebrow.

"Kid over at Met Gen may have survived an attack from our sicko. He claims his ten-year-old brother was taken away and killed by a fake cop. I'm going to go and talk to him now. I need a picture of him to take with me."

"You're gonna have to wait an hour. The film has to be developed."

"Developed? Don't you use a digital camera?"

Reds shook his head. "Courts don't always accept digital photographs since there's a chance the images could be altered. Sucks but we have to take them the old fashioned way."

"Shit! I can't wait an hour."

Vance moved to the body. "Birch…unzip the bag."

Birch, who was just about to assist in the transport to the ambulance complied and opened it enough to give Vance a clear view of the victim. He didn't want Eric to have to see what could be his brother this way, dead with a pacifier in his mouth, but he had no choice. He took a photo with the camera on his cell phone.

He looked over the photo to make sure the image was clear and then looked down at the deceased boy. "We're going to find the sonofabitch for you, Brian," he said softly. "I promise."

Vance told Birch he could zip the bag back up and then walked back over to Reds. "Listen," he said, lowering the volume in his voice. "I have something to ask you, man."

Reds looked at him curiously. "Judging from the drop in volume and the look in your eye, I have a feeling this is gonna be a question I won't like."

Vance exhaled. "Reds…I need for you and Birch to keep quiet about this note."

Reds raised an eyebrow and shook his head. "That note's evidence. You know we can't keep quiet about it."

"Just don't say anything about it for a few hours, Reds."

"Are you fucking crazy, Vance?"

"Man, I'm just trying to get this fucking case solved."

"What does that note have to do with, Ben?" Reds asked eyeing him intensely.

Vance frowned. "Shit, man, I don't know. That's why I'm asking for this favor. I just need a few hours to try and find Ben and get this shit figured out."

Reds looked at him, his eyes filled with skepticism. Vance understood the position he was putting Reds in by asking him to let him take the note. If anyone discovered this, Reds could lose his job and so could Vance, as taking the note was essentially tampering with evidence. "I don't know these kids' stories," Reds said, "but whatever they are, they didn't deserve what happened to them. They deserve justice."

"That's what I'm trying to bring them," Vance said.

Reds looked at him, his eyes serious, unblinking. "You need to find out how Ben is involved in all of this," he said.

Vance exhaled. "I know. And that's what I'm going to do."

Reds looked at Vance, while Vance stared back. "You and Ben," Reds said. "You two have some history."

"Yeah."

"You were his kid's Godfather right?"

"Yeah. What are you getting at, Reds?"

"What am I getting at? Dude…you're asking me to look the other way while you take evidence away from a crime scene that clearly links Ben to the case."

Vance sighed, but remained quiet.

Reds looked at him, the skepticism in his expression thicker. "Look...I know how it works, man. Partners cover up for each other all the time."

"I'm not trying to cover anything up," Vance said.

"But you want me to allow you to take evidence away from the scene that your partner is connected to?"

Vance flared his nostril and clenched his jaw. He had to go. He had to get to the hospital. "Reds...I'm just asking for a few hours. I promise you...I'm not trying to cover anything up. Come on, man. You know me."

Reds stared hard at him. "This is a fucked up thing you're asking me, man," he said.

Vance nodded. "I know."

"These kids deserve justice," he reiterated again.

Vance said, "And I told you I am doing everything I can to bring it to them."

"No matter the cost?" Reds asked an eyebrow lifted. "Can you stay behind the shield and do what you have to do, if you have to?"

Vance kept his lips pressed together firmly as he stared back at the light-skinned man with red hair and freckles. He didn't like it, but he understood why Reds was questioning his position between loyalty and duty. He didn't know what the note to Ben meant. What Ben had told or to whom he'd told—it didn't matter. What mattered was that based on the words in the message, the implications of Ben's actions at some point in time, had produced another dead body. Ben was his best friend, his partner. A man he trusted with his life. A man he'd do anything for. Except lie to protect a killer.

"I don't know what Ben may or may not have to do with all of this, but I'm a cop, Reds. I took an oath to do what was right and to bring justice to those who need it. It's as simple as that."

Reds looked at him. "Nothing's ever simple, man."

Vance opened his mouth to reply, but then closed it. Reds was right; nothing was ever simple. He opened his mouth again after a few seconds and said, the volume in his voice low, "Can I take the note or not?"

Reds looked at him.

Vance stared back, pleading with his eyes.

"This is fucked up, Vance."

"A few hours. That's all."

Reds dropped his chin to his chest, blew out a breath of air, then lifted his head, turned and looked to see Birch and the rest moving the body. "Shit," he said. He turned back to Vance. "Take it. I'll talk to Birch. I swear, Vance if this shit fuckin' blows up in my face—"

"I'll take full responsibility."

Reds shook his head. "Shit…a case like this. That might not mean shit."

Vance put his hand on Reds shoulder. "I owe you, man."

Reds shook his head. "Get me a date with T. Then maybe we'll call it even."

"Shit…I said I owe. I didn't say I could do the impossible."

"Before this moment, man, I would have said it was impossible that I'd let someone take something away from my crime scene."

Vance gave him a half smile. "Thanks."

Reds shook his head in disbelief again and then turned and walked away without saying anything else.

Vance took a breath, exhaled slowly, discreetly slid the note into his jacket pocket, and ran to his car. As he did, he called Ben's cell phone. It rang once and then went straight to voice mail.

"Ben…shit…I don't know what the fuck is going on, but we need to talk. I'm on my way to Met. Gen. Call me or meet me there."

He ended the call, 'no commented' his way past reporters, jumped into his car, turned the ignition and sped down the road.

Cribbs had said that the nurse had said something about a fake cop taking Eric's brother. That bothered the hell out of Vance.

Chapter 37

Amanda Kline paused. She had one foot on the first of five concrete steps leading up into the police station. She had to keep going because it was the right thing to do. Innocent boys were dying and she could put a stop to it. Or at least do her part to make the madness end. She was doing the right thing.

But still she paused.

She'd said her boys were dead. That the monster had done to them what he had done to the other boys he'd killed. They were in heaven now watching over her because they were dead. She had to believe that, because if she didn't, she wasn't going to bed able to go up the other four steps. If she didn't commit to them being gone, she wasn't going to do what she knew she needed to.

Another body had been found. Another boy killed by the Pacifier. More blood on her hands. Her heart, already broken, had shattered even more when she'd seen the breaking news report when she'd watched the broadcast in the morning. She hated watching the news, but she had to because she was waiting for the next report to say that two boys had been found dead. When that report came, then and only then would she stop watching. It was a form of self-torture. One she felt she deserved for not doing the right thing like she was now.

She looked up to the front door leading inside. She'd left Allen in the basement, going through his files. Going through old paperwork, he'd said. It was bullshit, she knew. He knew something but wasn't telling her. She heard it in his voice, saw it in his eyes. There was a reason her boys had been taken and he knew why. Damn him. Whatever secret Allen was hiding didn't matter anymore, because her boys were dead.

Dead!

Enough time had passed. There'd been enough death. She couldn't take anymore.

Amanda took a slow breath, then exhaled and walked up the remaining four steps. It was time she and the lead detective on the case, Vance Newsome, had a talk about her husband's most special patient.

Chapter 32

Ben didn't understand. His father's words—words from a moment in time that had shattered him into a thousand pieces that no one had ever seen. Where had they come from? Who had left the note for him? No one had been in the room to hear his father say those words, so how could the note have been left?

Ben sat forward, rested his forehead against his steering wheel and pressed the palms of his hands flat against his ears. His head was aching, throbbing with his father's voice.

You should have kept your fucking mouth shut…
You should have kept your fucking mouth shut…

He squeezed his eyes closed tightly, ground his teeth together, pressed harder with his palms. He was trying to keep the past away. Trying to avoid seeing things he didn't want to see. Trying to keep the silence behind his lips from becoming a scream, trying to ignore his father's cantankerous echo.

You should have kept your fucking mouth shut…
You should have kept your fucking mouth shut…

His fault. It had all been his fault.

His mother dead.

His father dead.

He squeezed his eyes shut tighter, bore down on his teeth harder.

All his fault.

Someone knew that.

All these years. He thought he'd overcome the tragedy. He thought he had survived. But he hadn't. Oh God, he hadn't.

Just like his mother, who'd looked at him with her dying breath. Just like her father who'd cursed him with his. Ben had died, too. Years of therapy...sessions known only to him and a few others...they hadn't helped, because he had died the night he revealed a secret he should have never told. He should have kept his fucking mouth shut. He should have been a man. He'd heard the faint whispering since that awful day. He realized now it had been his conscience from the grave.

Ben shook his head again, and then he fell apart.

Twenty-six years ago

"How are you feeling?"

"Not too good."

"Is it the voice again?"

"Y...yes."

"Do you remember what we spoke about last time? Do you remember the things I said?"

Allen watched his young patient intensely. This had been his third month with Ben McCallum. A ten-year-old boy who had experienced things no child should ever have to experience. Physical and sexual abuse. "Lessons" of manhood from his father, a decorated, well respected, and trusted member of the police force who had killed Ben's mother and then taken his own life right in front of Ben. Allen knew patients with tragic stories such as Ben's were unfortunately far from rare, but he had never actually worked with one. Usually cases such as Ben's went to senior members of the practice, but just a few weeks before Ben's file was brought to him, two of the practices senior members were killed in a head-on collision on their way home from a seminar. The loss put a strain on the practice, and because of that, Allen's inexperience was ignored and he was given Ben McCallum's file.

Initially, getting Ben to open up had proven to be a difficult task. As expected, the boy was withdrawn and refused to give little more than one-word responses. He would sit on the far end of a couch Allen had in his office for his patients to relax on, and be nearly immobile for the hour long sessions, save for the constant open and closing of his hands. But Allen was persistent, and after weeks of careful and cautious dialogue, he was able to get Ben to, first expand his safety zone, and second, to get him to eventually confide in Allen, the ordeal he had gone through.

In the beginning, the recounts of the abuse or "lessons" had to be pulled out of him slowly, with measured caution, but little by little, Allen found himself pulling less and less as Ben opened up more freely.

The details of the abuse jarred Allen. He'd read case study after case study about childhood trauma, but to actually hear it come directly from a child's mouth had been chilling. The doctor in Allen understood clinically that abusers were generally victims themselves and while their actions weren't excused, they could be explained with rational or scientific reasoning. But while the professional side of him could find the reasoning, the emotional side just couldn't come to grips with someone doing the things Ben's father had done.

Ben nodded, but didn't reply.

During their previous session, Ben had revealed that he had been hearing a voice inside of his head telling him that if he had kept his mouth shut, his mother wouldn't have been killed. That everything that had happened had been his fault. The admission hadn't surprised Allen. Victims of abuse, particularly children, when unable to avoid the reality of abuse by dissociation, often times constructed a system of meaning to justify the trauma they'd endured. That construction would, at times, produce "voices" in their heads. Voices that often blamed them for the things that had occurred.

"You have to ignore the voice you hear, Ben," Allen said. "The voice is your conscience. You blame yourself for what happened and I understand why you may feel that way, but Ben, what happened wasn't your fault."

Ben shook his head as his forehead knotted. "It…he…he says that's not true," he said, his voice tight with grief.

"You did the right thing, Ben."

Ben shook his head in disagreement again. "I shouldn't have said anything. I should have just kept the secret."

"No, Ben. No you shouldn't have." Allen wanted to go to him, to hold him the way he would his own son. "Your mother wouldn't have wanted you to keep that a secret."

His fingers closed down, Ben put the palms of his hands against the sides of his head and closed his eyes tightly as he bent forward. He shook his head, then nodded, then shook his head again, whispering inaudibly as he did. Allen watched him agonize with his guilt, his pain. Watched him struggle with the voice inside of his head telling him, insisting that it was right.

"Ben…" he said easily. "Your mother—"

"My mother died because I told!" Ben yelled out, cutting him off.

The sudden outburst caught Allen by surprise. "Ben…please believe me," he said watching the child closely. His demeanor had changed. He'd become more agitated, more tense. "Telling her was the right thing to do."

Ben looked up at him suddenly, his eyes dark. "How…how can you say that?" he asked, the tone in his voice, deeper, edgier, stronger. "My mother was alive until I told. It's his…" he paused, shook his head again. "It's my fault."

Allen stared at his patient with keen eyes. Under extreme conditions of prolonged abuse, some children formed separated personas with their own names, psychological functions, and personality traits. With the change in his body language, and voice, the slip of the word "his" that he'd noticed, Allen watched Ben intently and wondered if he was indeed witnessing the emergence of an alter self.

"It isn't your fault," Allen insisted. "I know it's hard for you to believe that, but the only one to blame, the only one who was at fault was your father. He wasn't well, Ben."

His palms pressing harder against his temples, Ben began to open and close his hands. "He…he was trying to teach him…me how to be a man," he said, "He was trying to teach about strength and discipline, about how to be a man. All he…I had to do was listen!"

Allen's heart began to beat heavily. "Don't listen to your voice, Ben," he said. "Your father wasn't teaching you about manhood. He was abusing you."

Ben shook his head, pressed harder against his temples, clenched his jaws, opened and closed his hands with more vigor. "No….No….No!" he yelled. "You're lying!"

Chills ran along Allen's spine. He was pushing Ben dangerously close to the edge, he knew that and part of him was telling himself to ease up. But as frightening as the transformation he was witnessing was, the fascination of it was even more compelling.

"I'm not lying," he said. "Your father is the one to blame for everything. He should have never touched you."

"He was teaching...He was—"

"He was taking advantage of you."

Ben began to rock back and forth as his hands continued to open and close. "Lies," said, his stare penetrating, hate-filled. "You're lying!"

"You weren't to blame, Ben," Allen said again.

Ben shook his head, rocked back and forth, and then let out a guttural scream, and before Allen realized it was happening, sprang off of the couch and attacked him.

"You're a fucking liar!" Ben raged as he wrapped his fingers around Allen's throat. "You're a fucking liar!"

Allen gagged as he covered Ben's hands with his own and tried to pry the boy's hands from around his neck.

"It was his fault!" Ben screamed, "His fault!"

Allen pulled at his hands, but found it nearly impossible to force his grip to loosen, as Ben squeezed with a strength that didn't seem possible for a ten-year-old.

Allen struggled to breath.

"Lying!" Ben, who wasn't Ben at all yelled out. "You're fucking lying!"

And then as suddenly as he'd attacked him, he was being pulled off by two orderlies they kept on staff for emergency purposes.

"Lying!" Ben screamed. "All he had to do was keep his fucking mouth closed!"

The orderlies wrestled him to the ground, and fought to get him restrained, one pinning his arms behind his back, the other forcing his legs down.

"Get off of me! It's all his fucking fault!"

A nurse rushed into the room, a syringe in her hand. After waiting for the right moment, she jabbed it quickly into his shoulder and depressed the sedative contained inside.

Ben continued to scream, continued to call Allen a liar for a few more seconds before the shot took effect and put him to sleep.

Rubbing his neck and breathing heavily, Allen watched in stunned and frozen silence as the orderlies slipped restraints around Ben's wrists and ankles. One of them hefted him up over his shoulder like a rag doll while the other asked Allen if he were all right.

Allen nodded as he rubbed his neck, but remained silent. Seconds later, the orderlies left, taking Ben with them. That would be their last session.

Twenty-six years ago.

Allen stood with one hand cupped over his mouth, his fingers squeezing his cheeks, as the last file from the last box he had, fell from his other hand and dropped to the ground, its contents scattering at his feet.

He shook his head.

Twenty-six years ago.

He began to tremble.

His legs became weak and he stumbled back against the wall and slid down to the ground.

Ben McCallum. The boy he wanted to help. The boy who'd tried to kill him. He stared at the papers, one in particular. The first page, with Ben's name and date of birth.

Tears ran down Allen's cheeks, and through clouded vision he stared at his patient's full name.

Benjamin Patrick McCallum.

Chapter 39

Ben, I'm at the hospital. Look, man…I don't know what the hell is going on with you, but we need to talk. Whatever it is, man, you can trust me. You know that."

Vance paused and ground his teeth together. He'd called Ben three times during the twenty minutes it had taken him to reach the hospital, each time getting nothing but voice mail. He slammed his hand down on his steering wheel and then said, "Give me a call, Ben. Shit…ASAP."

He ended the call and let out a frustrated breath as he opened his car door. He had an ill feeling churning in the pit of his stomach. The note, Ben's reaction to it, Eric. Puzzle pieces were coming together, and although he couldn't clearly see the picture they were forming just yet, something told him that when the fuzz cleared, the picture revealed was going to be one that he wasn't going to like.

He cursed Ben for not answering his phone, for not being there, and then hoped that his friend was okay and climbed out of his car. It was time to put his focus back on the task at hand; his meeting with Eric. He knew that he wasn't truly responsible for what had happened, but he still couldn't help but feel partly responsible for what had happened to Brian and Eric. He had known Eric was living on the streets. He should have gone a step further and insisted on taking Eric to a shelter. Vance hurried into the hospital, determined to get them the justice he'd told Reds he was sworn to do.

Chapter 40

Sarah McCallum looked at Brandon with a solemn expression as he sat staring out of his driver's side window, his warm breath fogging the glass. His arm was laying on the door panel, his fingers drumming, breaking up the tense silence that existed. "Are you okay?" she asked softly.

Brandon continued his off-rhythm drumming for a few seconds before he turned his head and looked at her. "You're kidding, right?"

Sarah frowned. He had called her earlier in the day telling her that he'd made reservations for dinner, and that he wanted her to wear something special. He had a surprise for her. She was supposed to ask him what the surprise was. He was supposed to laugh and say that he couldn't tell her, while she continued to beg. The conversation was supposed to have ended with Brandon hearing her groan with disappointment.

That was the way conversations about surprises had worked in the past. That was how it was supposed to have been then.

But it wasn't.

Sarah hadn't asked, hadn't escalated to begging. She simply said, "Okay," and then hung up the phone, and when Brandon pulled up in front of her condo in his expensive black Armani suit, crisp white shirt, and polished black, leather shoes, and she had gotten into the car, the sweater and dingy blue jeans she was wearing could hardly be called special.

"I'm sorry," she said, her voice low.

Brandon scoffed again. "Sorry? That's funny."

Sarah's frown deepened. "I didn't mean to hurt you, Brandon."

Brandon looked at her his expression filled with skepticism. "Really? So what did you mean to do?"

Sarah sighed. "Brandon—"

"I called and told you I made reservations. I told you to wear something special. That I had a surprise for you. And what did you do? You let the whole day go by…you let me get my hair cut, shower, shave, put on one of my most expensive suits...you let me stop and buy roses, and then drive in bumper to bumper traffic to get here on time to take you out, only to see you in jeans and a sweatshirt, just so you could tell me that you can't see me anymore."

"Brandon—"

"Why didn't you just spare me, Sarah? Why let the whole goddamned day go on? Why couldn't you just tell me this over the phone?"

"I couldn't do that," she replied.

"Why the hell not?"

"Because it wouldn't have been fair of me to do that to you."

Brandon dragged his hand down over his clean-shaven face. "Fair? What's fair would have been for you to do this over the phone. That would have been fair."

Sarah pressed her lips together. She really was trying to be fair to him. After all that he'd done for her, he deserved more than a phone call. He deserved to be told in person that she was going to try and work things out with the man that she couldn't bring herself to make her ex.

"I'm sorry," she said again. "But I just couldn't do that to you."

Brandon pulled his hand down over his face, then squeezed his slightly jutting chin, before putting his arm back on the door panel and drumming his fingers again. He shook his head and worked his jaw repeatedly. "This is bullshit, Sarah," he said staring out of the fogging window. He turned and looked at her. "You used me."

"I didn't use you, Brandon."

"The hell you didn't! You used me to make Ben beg you not to go through with the divorce, which is what I'm sure happened the day you went to pick up the papers. You never had any intention of being with me.

You just wanted to get him to the point where he would feel like he could really lose you. You know... I had a feeling this was going to happen when you came back into the car that day."

"Brandon," Sarah said, stung by his words. "That's not what I intended at all. How could you even say that?"

"How could I not, Sarah? I mean he signed the papers. All you had to do was sign them and get them to your attorney, and everything would have been a done deal. I thought we had something special. I thought we could move on to the next level, but the truth of the matter is, us moving on was just never in your plans, was it? Jesus...it's just now hitting me that you've never even told me that you loved me. I'm such a fool. I was so caught up in being head over heels for you that I never even noticed or maybe I simply didn't care." He paused momentarily, then continued. "I can't believe this," he said, looking out the window again.

Sarah's shoulder sagged as guilt weighed down on her. She wanted to wholeheartedly deny what he'd said, but sadly, there was a measure of truth there. She may not have consciously set out to use him, but if she were to truly be honest with herself, then she had to admit that, yes, on some level, she had wanted Ben to feel that he had lost her.

Being with Ben was hard. But the more time she'd spent apart from him, the more she began to realize that as tough as it was being with him, as painful a reminder of Mikey's death it had been, the truth was that she loved him. And no matter how good to her Brandon was, no matter how much of himself he had given, or how genuine his feelings were, she was just never going to feel the same or give the same of herself to him. So in essence...yes...she had used him.

She exhaled softly and although she shouldn't have, she reached her hand out and placed it against his cheek. "I'm sorry, Brandon. I really never meant to do this to you."

Brandon turned his head toward her, causing her hand to rest against his lips. He kissed the inside of her palm. "I love you,' he said softly.

Sarah nodded. "I know you do. And although I've never said it...I love you, too. You've been a great friend."

Brandon set his jaw, looked at her with hard eyes and then moved her hand away. "That's definitely not what I wanted to hear."

"I'm sorry," Sarah said.

Brandon pressed his lips together and sucked them in as though he were sucking on something sour. "Yeah," he said after a few seconds. "So am I."

Sarah looked at him, inhaled and exhaled, then leaned over and gave him a gentle kiss on his smooth cheek. "Goodbye, Brandon. And thank you for everything."

Brandon raised his eyebrows. "Ben's a lucky man."

Sarah moved away from him and opened the passenger door. She took a final lasting gaze at the man who had helped her survive, and then got out of the car. Barely a second passed before Brandon pulled off after she closed the door.

She shivered as a cold breeze washed over her. She looked up to the sky. There were no clouds. Just grey. The weather man had said something about there being a chance of snow. Sarah breathed in the cold air, exhaled, and then went inside of her building to run the divorce papers through her shredder.

Chapter 41

I'm looking for Dr. Reed."

Vance was standing at the front desk in the middle of the emergency room at Metropolitan General, his badge flipped open in his hand. On the other side of the desk, sitting in a leather chair that had tears along the arm and head rests, was a box-shaped, light-skinned black woman with a wide forehead and large frightened eyes. Vance read the name on her badge—ShaKita. By the drawn, irritated look spread across her face, it didn't take Vance being a detective to know that she was having a rough morning.

ShaKita looked at Vance's badge, then up at him. Vance gave her a smile that usually disarmed the defenses any woman tried to throw up. Unaffected, ShaKita rolled her eyes, not bothering in the least bit to be discreet, and pointed to her right. Vance turned his head. Standing at the far end of the counter, talking on the phone, was a tall, lanky man. Vance assumed he was Dr., Reed.

He said thank you to ShaKita, not because he'd meant it, but simply because he'd been raised to do so, and then walked over to the doctor and held up his badge.

Doctor Reed looked at him, nodded, held up his index finger and pointed to the phone. Vance took a step back to give him some privacy, but remained close enough do that Reed would feel compelled to end his call quickly.

"Yes, Mrs. Jackson, you do need to finish taking all of the antibiotics I prescribed," Reed said into the phone. "It's already at the lowest milligram available. Are you making sure to eat at least a half hour before you take it? Mmm hmm…yes, that would help with the dizziness and the nausea. Yes…at least a half hour. No…I'm not married. I'm sure your daughter is a lovely woman."

Vance looked at Reed. Reed looked back and him and shook his head.

"Mmmm hmm…perhaps one day if my schedule allows. I rarely have the time to take lunch. Dinner? Well… possibly. I'll let you know when I can."

He looked over at Vance, with an apologetic frown.

Vance pointed to his watch.

Dr. Reed nodded. 'Okay, Mrs. Jackson…I have to get going now. Mmmm hmmm…yes…another emergency. Well, thank you. Make sure to eat at least a half hour, okay? Yes…I'll look at my schedule and let you know if dinner would be possible. Okay, Mrs. Jackson…you take care."

Dr. Reed ended the call with an exhale and then said, "Sorry about that. That was a special patient I treated a couple of days ago. Very sweet woman. Younger than most at eighty."

Vance nodded, He wasn't interested in Mrs. Jackson or how young she was. He said, "I'm Detective Vance Newsome."

The doctor extended his hand. "Craig Reed."

Vance took it. "You made the call about the kid who survived a stabbing?"

Reed nodded. "I had the nurse who was helping me call."

"Was she in the room with you when you did your checkup?"

"Yes."

"Okay. I'm going to need her here, too."

Dr. Reed nodded, then headed over to the front desk, where an attractive black nurse was standing, talking to ShaKita. He pulled the nurse to the side, said something to her and then pointed in Vance's direction. She nodded and seconds later they were both standing in front of him.

"Detective Newsome…this is Angie Murphy."

Vance took her hand. It was warm and soft. Beautiful, with a gentle touch, he thought. He gave it a shake and then let go and looked at the doctor. "So how's he holding up?"

Reed raised his eyebrows and sighed. "Physically, he's going to be all right. The blade just missed his lung and didn't hit anything else that was critical. His attacker left the blade in his back, which was fortunate for him, because had it been pulled out, he may not have been so lucky. Someone was definitely looking out for him. Essentially, what could have taken his life turned out to be nothing more than a flesh wound. So again, physically he'll have only a scar as a reminder.

"Now…as far as the emotional damage goes…" Reed paused and exchanged a glace with Angie. They both frowned. "I'm no therapist, but I'd say it's going to take some therapy for him to get over what he's experienced."

Vance dipped the corners of his mouth slightly also and again thought about how he should have insisted on taking Eric to the shelter, instead of leaving him out on the street. But he always believed that things, both good and bad, happened as they were supposed to happen. It was tragic that another innocent boy's life had been taken, but had Vance taken Eric away from the park, then there would have been no note to Ben, and he wouldn't be standing where he was, a few feet away, possibly on the verge of finding the psychopath.

It was a catch twenty-two.

Either way, there was a loss.

Vance said, "Has anyone come to visit him? Family, friends?"

Angie shook her head. "No. And I've offered to make calls for him, but he said there's no one to call."

Vance nodded again. "Okay. Has someone from social services seen him yet?"

Reed shook his head. "They've been called, but they're backed up and haven't made it down yet."

Vance frowned. "Okay…well I'm going to need for both of you to be present in the room while I talk to him."

Reed and Angie both said, "Okay."

"I'm going to have to ask him some direct questions. Will that be a problem?"

Angie shook her head. "Just don't push him too hard," she said. "He's been through a lot."

Vance smiled. She was protective of him. He appreciated that. "I'll be as subtle as I can, but I have to know everything he knows."

Angie said, "I understand."

Reed leading the way, they walked past four rooms, all occupied, two with patients with horrible coughs, one with a moaner. The last room held a young man who was complaining to a young woman about how his having to get stitches had been her fault.

When they reached the last door on the right, Reed knocked on it, and then pushed it open and walked into the room, Angie and Vance trailing behind.

"Hey Eric," Reed said, walking over to the bed, where Eric lay on his side, his back to the window.

Eric looked up and his eyes widened as Vance stepped into the room.

"This is Detective Newsome," the doctor said. "He has some questions to ask you. Is that all right?"

Vance looked at Eric, while the teen stared back at him, his eyes bloodshot and swollen from crying. Vance's heart went out to him. He wasn't supposed to be in a hospital room recovering from a stab wound. He wasn't supposed to have been living on the street. Where he should have been was at home, talking or texting on his cell phone, or playing video games or on the computer on Facebook. His world should have been filled with warmth, love, and a future full of possibilities. Looking at him, Vance could see in Eric's eyes that it had been a long time since he had experienced anything but cold, dark hopelessness. He'd live a tough life a thousand times over.

Vance gave him a smile. "Hey, Eric."

Eric stared at him silently for a second or two, before he nodded and then look down at the bed sheets.

"I need to ask you some questions, Eric. I also need to show you a picture. Can you handle that?"

Eric looked up at him and then nodded.

Vance gave him a flat-lipped smile, then removed a micro-cassette recorder from his pocket. "I have to tape our conversation too, okay?"

Eric said, "Okay."

Vance stepped closer to him. "I want to show you a picture first. It's a picture of the boy we found this morning. It's going to be hard for you to see, but I need for you to confirm whether or not you know who it is. Can you handle that?"

Eric swallowed, then closed and opened his eyes slowly. "Yes," he said quietly.

Vance removed his cell phone from his pocket and went through the menu and found the picture he'd taken. He expanded it so that it filled his entire screen, then turned the screen toward Eric. *Be strong, kid*, he thought. He said, "Do you know this boy?"

Eric stared at the picture and for seconds didn't speak. He just stared as his eyes began to well and his bottom lip began to quiver.

Angie moved from the door and stepped to Eric's side. She took hold of his hand, gave it a firm but gentle squeeze.

Eric continued to look at Vane's phone as tears fell from his eyes. Vance didn't want to push him, but the clock was ticking and every second was counting. "Do you know him, Eric?"

Angie gave his hand another squeeze. Another couple of seconds went by before Eric finally nodded and said, his voice just above a whisper, "Y…yeah."

Vance let out a breath he hadn't even realized he'd been holding. He'd felt confident about Eric knowing Brian, but until Eric finally confirmed the relationship, a chance still remained for a head-on collision into a brick wall. "What was his name?"

Eric sniffled. "Br…Brian."

"Was he your brother?"

Eric nodded slowly, then said, "N...no. But…he was like my brother. My little brother." Eric sniffled again and then winced as he took the hand Angie wasn't holding on to and wiped at his nose. Angie reached for a tissue and wiped his nose for him.

"Were you with Brian last night?"

Eric acknowledged that he was with a nod.

"Sleeping in the junkyard?"

"Yeah."

Vance frowned. *Had he only insisted*, he thought again. "Is that where you and Brian usually slept?"

Eric shook his head. "No."

"Tell me what happened, Eric. Try to be as detailed as you can be."

Eric nodded while Angie wiped sweat from his forehead. Dr. Reed continued to stand off to the side, his arms folded across his chest, his head bowed.

"Usually, there's a dog there, but it…it wasn't last night. It was so cold, so we hopped the fence to find a car to get into. We got lucky and found the Lincoln. I…" Eric paused as tears began to fall harder. He wiped at them, doing little to deter their flow. "I had to use the bathroom so…so I got up and stepped out. I didn't go far. Just to the front of the car. My… my back was to the car. I was…I was having a hard time getting my zipper down. It was stuck and…and my fingers were stiff and getting numb."

Vance watched the anguish on Eric's face as Eric spoke. His mouth was on autopilot, the words flowing freely while he relived the nightmare he was never going to forget.

"I was finally starting to get my zipper down when I got stabbed." Eric paused again, his thoughts clearly on that moment. "I…I fell right away. I…I never felt pain like that before. They…they don't do it right in the movies. In the movies they move around, but…but in real life…" Eric shook his head. "I couldn't move." He stopped talking and wiped more tears away.

"Where was Brian when this happened?" Vance asked.

Eric sobbed heavily, twice. Angie continued to hold on to his hand, continued to rub his forehead. Reed remained stoic, his head raised this time, his eyes transfixed on Eric.

"He…he was still in the car, sleeping. But…but then I heard…I heard…" He paused again, cried hard tears.

Vance didn't want to, but had to press. "What did you hear, Eric?"

Eric grimaced from emotional pain. "I…I heard crunching."

"Crunching?"

Eric nodded. "Behind me. They were footsteps crunching on the ground. Then I heard the passenger door creak open. I…I tried to move. I tried…but it hurt so bad. It hurt to even breathe. I tried to…to call Brian's name to warn him, but I…I couldn't do anything but whisper." Eric looked up at Vance with eyes that had aged in the minutes since he'd begun talking. "There was this crackling sound next. Like someone being shocked. And then Brian yelled, then he got quiet. I heard the footsteps again, coming closer. I…I thought I was going to be dead then. That whoever had stabbed me was going to finish what they had started. But the footsteps never stopped. They kept going past me. I…I looked up and saw Brian hanging over a guy's shoulders."

"Did you get to see the person's face at all?"

Eric shook his head. "No."

Vance frowned and dropped his eyes to the ground as he clenched his jaws. He had called Beto Aguilar, the department sketch artist, and asked him to be prepared to get to the hospital just in case Eric had gotten to see the killer.

"But I didn't need to see his face though," Eric said continuing.

Vance looked back up at him. "You didn't?"

"No."

"Why not?"

"Because I had already seen it earlier."

"Earlier? Where?" Vance's heart began to race.

"Earlier in the day, me and Brian…we went to McDonald's to eat. I was eating a Big Mac. Brian was playing with his Iron Man toy from his kid's meal. That's when I saw the fake cop watching us."

"You say cop? What makes you think he was a cop, or a fake cop?"

Eric frowned. "I didn't think he was a fake then. I thought he was a real cop because of his eyes."

"His eyes? You got a good look at them?" Vance asked, his heart rate increasing, the beating becoming heavier.

Eric nodded. "Yeah. They were dark and they looked like they didn't trust anyone."

Vance thought about his partner and the dark, accusatory eyes he had. He gave Eric a serious glare. "Do you remember enough of what he looked like to describe him to a sketch artist?"

Eric nodded again. "I'll never forget his face for as long as I live."

Vance worked his jaw, then looked at Reed and said, "I'll be right back."

He walked out of the room and called Beto, who answered on the second ring.

"Beto, man…I need you to get down here ASAP."

"I can be there in twenty minutes."

"Make it ten."

"Shit man…you know how traffic is."

"Run on foot if you have to, man. I need you here."

"All right. I'm on my way."

Vance ended the call, planted his hand on his hip and dropped his chin to his chest. The ill feeling was worsening.

Chapter 42

Eric…this is Beto Aguilar. He's a sketch artist."

Eric looked from Vance to Beto Aguilar, who gave Eric a smile. "What's going on, Eric?"

He was a long, skinny man with slanted eyes, a boxer's nose, pockmarked cheeks and a thick goatee that hung down from his chin. Tucked under his arm was a sketchpad. In his hand he held a putty eraser and three charcoal drawing pencils. Eric used to have pencils and erasers of his own way back when he used to draw. It was a talent he'd gotten from his father. It was the only good thing he had ever gotten from him that mattered.

Eric looked at Beto, but didn't say anything. Vance, the cop from the park was standing behind him. He had left the room for about fifteen minutes, and during that time, Eric had cried an almost unending stream of tears while Angie held his hand and ran her hand through his hair gently. The tears were gone now, but definitely not the pain and guilt.

"I want you to describe the man you saw in McDonald's," Vance said. "Be as detailed as you can, okay?"

Eric nodded. "Okay."

"Good. Dr. Reed, Angie and I are going to leave you guys alone. Beto…" he said looking at the sketch artist.

"As soon as I'm done," Beto said with a nod.

Vance nodded, then with a final glance at Eric, he and Dr. Reed walked out of the room. Angie gave Eric's hand a final squeeze and then followed after them.

When the door closed, Beto hummed a tune Eric didn't recognize and pulled up a chair. "All right, Eric, I want you to relax as much as you can."

Eric nodded. He wanted to adjust himself on the bed, but the wound in his back hurt, so he remained still.

Beto sat down, about three feet away. "You like football?" he asked, flipping open his sketchpad to a clean sheet.

Eric nodded. "Yeah."

"So do I. I'm a big New York Giants fan. You?"

"I like the Cardinals."

Beto nodded. "Cool team. Larry Fitzgerald is a heck of a receiver."

Eric nodded. "Yeah."

"Did your dad like the Cardinals, too?" Beto asked, propping the pad up against his knee.

Eric shook his head. "No," he said, the volume in his voice dropping. He offered nothing more.

Beto looked at him for a lingering second, then grabbed one drawing pencil in his right hand, held the other two in his left and said, "Okay...I want you to tell me everything you can remember about what he looked like. Let's start with eyes first. What shape are they? Round, oval, rectangular?"

Eric took a short breath, wincing as he did, and thought about the cold, dark eyes of the killer who had taken Brian away. "They're rectangular. Kind of like the heroes in the comic books."

Beto nodded and began drawing on the pad. "Are they small or wide?"

"Kind of small. Like he's squinting."

"Would you say they're deep-set? Meaning does his forehead sort of stick out above them."

Eric gave it some thought. "Yeah," he said.

"Okay. Good." Beto moved the pencil furiously. "This might be hard to remember, but can you recall any wrinkles at the corners of his eyes?"

Eric mulled over the question, then shook his head. "I don't know. I don't really remember."

"How old do you think he looked?"

"Mmmm...maybe like forty."

Beto nodded again. "Okay. Good. That helps. What about his eyebrows? Do you remember if they were round, angular, bushy, thin?"

"They're kind of thick and kind of straight. They kind of make him look like he's angry."

"Mmm hmm," Beto said.

He worked his pencil for a sec, then grabbed his putty eraser, fixed a mistake he'd made, and went back to the pencil. "Okay…now what about his nose? Do you remember if it was thin, wide, crooked, beak shaped?"

"I think it was a little long and kind of crooked."

"Like it was broken?"

Eric nodded. "Maybe. Yeah…I guess."

"Was it wide?"

"I don't think so. It was typical, I guess. Kind of like mine with the crookedness."

Beto worked the pencil, nodded, and said enthusiastically, "Good, good. Do you remember what his mouth looked like? Was it wide? Were his lips thick or thin?"

"It wasn't wide. Average, I guess, too. They were kind of thin, but not too thin." Eric paused and sighed. He could see the killer's face, but recalling it was much harder than he thought it was going to be.

Beto looked up at him. "Don't sweat it, Eric. You're doing a great job."

Eric gave a half smile.

Beto smiled back. "Are you thirsty? You want a Coke or something?"

"I can have a Coke?" Eric asked surprised. The nurses had given him nothing but water or apple juice.

Beto closed his sketchpad, leaned it against the leg of his chair and stood up. "You don't tell, I won't tell."

Eric smiled, wider this time. "I won't."

"Cool. Be right back."

Beto walked out of the room, leaving Eric alone. He stared down at the closed pad, wondering what picture Beto was creating from the things he was saying. Would he be close to recreating the man he'd seen? Would he be far off? An eager, yet frightened anticipation ran through him.

A few minutes later, the door opened and Beto re-entered the room, a Coke bottle in his hand. He walked over to Eric, unscrewed the cap and handed it to Eric. "Here you go."

"Thanks."

Eric raised the bottle to his lips, again wincing from the movement.

"You need some help?" Beto asked.

Eric shook his head. "I got it." Despite the pain, he put the bottle against his lips and savored the taste of the Coca Cola hitting his taste buds.

"Coke's my favorite soda," Beto said propping his leg, grabbing his pad and pencils, and opening the pad to the page he was working on.

Eric burped, then said, "Mine, too."

Beto cleared his throat. "Okay…so we have his eyes, nose and mouth down. Let's move on to facial hair. Did he have any? A beard, goatee, moustache?"

Eric took another sip of his soda, wiped some from the corner of his mouth, burped softly again, and then said, "Umm…maybe a little around his mouth and on his face."

"Kind of like he had shaved and it was growing back?"

"Yeah. Kind of like that."

Beto worked the charcoal, then grabbed the eraser again, fixed another mistake. "Do you remember what his chin looked like?"

Eric shook his head. "Not really. I mean it wasn't like sticking out or anything. It was pretty normal."

"Okay. Cool. Do you remember anything about the shape of his face? Like was it round, thin, sort of skeletal, maybe muscular?"

"It…it was kind of square shaped, I think. Kind of like how they would draw it in the comic books."

Beto nodded, worked the pencil. "Do you remember anything about his cheekbones? Did they stick out at all?"

Eric shook his head. "Not really."

"Okay. What about his forehead? Can you remember if it was wide or long?"

Eric shook his head. "Not really."

"Okay. What about his head? Was he bald or did he have hair?"

"He had hair kind of like the way Keanu Reeves had it in the Matrix movies."

Beto nodded. "Cool movie."

"Yeah."

"What color was his hair?"

"Black."

"Any gray?"

Eric thought about it. "I don't think so."

Beto moved his pencil back and forth, side to side and at angles in short, quick strokes. Then he tilted it sideways and used it as though it were a crayon. After that he used his index finger. Eric watched the sketch artist as he worked. Something in his demeanor had seemed to change. His humming had ceased and his jaw seemed tighter, his eyes more focused.

After a few seconds, Beto looked up. "Okay…just a couple of more questions and then we'll be done. Okay?"

Eric nodded. "Okay."

"All right. Do you remember any scars or marks anywhere on his face?"

Eric gnawed down on his bottom lip and squinted his eyes.

"It doesn't matter how insignificant you think it might be," Beto said, his voice lower. "Sometimes the smallest things can make all the difference." He was staring at Eric with an intensity that he hadn't before, making Eric feel uncomfortable.

Eric thought about it. Any scars. Any marks. Anywhere. Seconds worth of thinking passed before he said, "There might have been a scar or something by his eyebrow, but I'm not really sure."

Beto closed his eyes a bit. "Do you remember which eye?"

Eric shook his head. "No."

Beto nodded. "Okay. I'll put one by his right eyebrow." He did a couple of more quick strokes, then put his pencils down and stared at the sketch he'd made.

Eric watched him with curious eyes. Something, he thought. Something didn't seem right. "Is…is it finished?" he asked.

Beto stared at the pad for a few more seconds, then looked up. "It's done," he said. He stood up, looked down at the pad again, clenched his jaw, and then turned the pad so that Eric could see it. "Does this look like the man you saw?" Beto asked.

Eric stared and breathed heavily as his heart began to pound. He was back in McDonald's at the table, staring at the man, the killer he was certain had stabbed him and who had killed Brian.

"Eric?" Beto said. "Do you recognize him?"

Eric opened his mouth, but no words came out. He just stared, as his heart raced.

"Eric?" Beto called again.

He told himself he wasn't going to cry anymore, but staring at the all-too-perfect recreation Beto had created, tears, whether he wanted them to or not, began to fall from his eyes. He nodded his head slowly, looked up at Beto and said, "It…it's him. That's the man from McDonald's. He's the one who killed Brian."

Beto frowned, then nodded. "Good job," he said. He put a hand on Eric's shoulder and gave it a light squeeze. Then he took the pad and walked out of the room.

Good job, Eric thought. He thought about Brian, and the promise he'd made to him. The promise he hadn't been able to keep.

He shook his head as his tears fell. Brian was dead. He hadn't done a good job at all.

Chapter 43

Vance filled his lungs as Beto stepped out of the room, his sketch pad tucked in the crook of his arm, his pencils in hand. He'd been waiting with stress-filled angst as Beto had been in the room drawing what Vance was afraid was going to add exponentially to the confusion he'd been experiencing since he'd read the note left for Ben. The note tucked safely in his pocket.

As Beto walked over to him, his face drawn, his eyes glazed over, Vance feared that nothing was ever going to be the same. It was something he'd been thinking about when he'd waited for Beto to arrive with his back pressed flat against the wall, his head down.

He exhaled slowly as Beto stepped to him to confirm that madness had truly taken over. "Did the picture match his description?"

Beto nodded slowly. "Yeah," he said, his voice low. "It did."

Vance flared his nostrils and clenched his jaw. "Well," he said, putting his hand out. "Let's see what you got."

Beto looked at him for a moment, then looked down at his pad and released a lengthy sigh.

"Something wrong?" Vance asked, watching him, sharing his anxiety.

Beto frowned and then lifted his head. "Dude…this drawing I just did…" He paused, not wanting to say what Vance knew.

"What about it?"

Beto sighed again and slammed his thick eyebrows together. "Nothing. It…it's just that…"

"That what?"

Another disbelieving head shake. Another sigh. "This picture, man... it...it looks just like Ben."

Vance stared at Beto as the lanky Puerto Rican frowned again. He worked his jaw, took a slow breath, exhaled and said, "Let me see it."

Beto raised his thick eyebrows, blew out a breath, removed the pad from beneath his arm and handed it to Vance. "Dude," he said, his voice flat. "If that's not Ben on that pad, then either I've got one hell of a hard on for him, or he's got a twin that no one else knew about. Now I damn sure don't swing on the other side of the fence, and if he does have a twin, then that's the ultimate definition of identical."

Vance looked at him for a moment and then took the pad reluctantly and flipped it over to see the sketch. When he did, whatever air he had left in his lungs rushed out of him as though he'd been punched hard in the stomach again. The last part of Beto's statement resonated in his mind.

The ultimate definition of identical. A twin. Christ, it just had to be, because he knew his partner better than anyone. But staring down at what was practically a charcoal snapshot of the man he trusted with his life on an almost daily basis, a frightening measure of doubt ran through him, making him question whether he had ever truly known Ben McCallum. And that made him sick to his stomach.

Vance stared at the picture, at the eyes. The eyes of the man staring back at him clearly belonged to someone who could do unimaginable things to innocent boys before strangling them to death and then leaving a baby's pacifier with their body to be found. They were cold, calculating, dark. They were killer's eyes.

They weren't Ben's eyes.

The Ben he knew was no cold-blooded psychotic killer. The Ben he knew had become flustered and distraught with confusion at the sight of a sadistic note. The Ben in the drawing was not his partner. It couldn't be.

He looked up at Beto. "Did you tell anyone you were coming?"

Beto shook his head. "No. I just rushed outta there and headed here."

Vance nodded and then ripped the sketch out of the book. "You never drew this," he said as Beto looked at him with his mouth hanging open, his eyes filled with confusion. "Okay?"

"But…"

"You never drew it, Beto."

Beto slammed his eyebrows together again. "Dude…is that Ben?"

Vance looked at him for a long, silent few seconds and then said, "I'm calling in a favor. You owe me. Remember?"

Beto stared at him. Three years prior, evidence had been discovered, implicating Beto's seventeen-year-old brother in the murder of another teen from a rivaling neighborhood. Vance had known Beto since high school and because he didn't want to see his little brother go to jail, he'd made the evidence "disappear" with the promise from Beto that his little brother was going to take full advantage of the second chance he'd been given. Beto's little brother was now in college working toward a degree in Criminal Justice.

Beto nodded. "I remember," he said. "What's up?"

"I need you to stay here and keep an eye on Eric."

"But—"

"I'm not asking you to stay in the room with him. I just need for you to hang around and call me if anyone comes to see him. And I do mean *anyone.* Can you do that?"

Beto said, "Yeah. I got you."

Vance nodded. "Okay. And remember…this drawing doesn't exist, all right?"

Beto looked at him.

Vance stared back.

Beto sighed, said, "Okay."

Vance gave an apologetic smile, then crumpled up the drawing. "I have something to take care of. Keep an eye on Eric and tell no one that you're here, all right?"

"All right."

Vance shook Beto's hand, took a final glance toward Eric's room and then walked out of the hospital. As he stepped outside, his cell phone rang. He looked at it. It was Cribbs. He thought about not answering, but then hit the Talk button. "Yeah."

"Vance…it's Cribbs. We need you here right away."

Vance's heart beat and he wondered if Reds had said something. "What's up?"

"We have a woman here who says she can deliver the Pacifier to us."

Vance stopped in his tracks. "What? How?"

"She says the killer has been meeting with her husband who's a psychiatrist and has been telling him when he was going to kill."

"Christ! And they never said anything."

"She wanted to, but the psycho kidnapped their two sons, one of whom is ten years old, and threatened to kill them, too if they said anything."

"Damn."

"Yeah., tell me about it."

"Are you sure she's legit?"

"She's broken up, man. If she's lying then I'm calling the academy and demanding that she get an Oscar."

"Okay."

"Stubbs wants you and Ben here ASAP before we make any moves."

Vance gritted his teeth.

Nothing was ever going to be the same again.

"I'm on my way," he said. "But Ben's gonna stay here and keep an eye on the kid, Eric."

"Whatever. Just get here pronto. Stubbs wants us to move on this."

Vance frowned. "I'm on my way." He ended the call, and as he did, a cold, biting breeze blew over and around him. Vance closed his eyes, breathed in the sharp air and then exhaled. "Goddammit, Ben," he whispered.

He moved as the wind blew again.

Chapter 44

Amanda Kline pressed tissues to her eyes but it had been for nothing. The tears couldn't be stopped. It had been the same with the words that had spilled out of her mouth when she'd told Detective Cribbs and his partner, Detective Weston all about her knowledge of the man that was murdering ten-year-old boys and leaving pacifiers with their bodies. The flow of her torturing confession couldn't be contained. With a determined stream of tears, she told them all about her sons being taken and their lives being bartered for their silence by a psychotic man whose name was Patrick, who then "confided" to her husband when he was going to kill or that he already had killed. Why Patrick had chosen her family to torment she didn't know, but she was sure her husband knew something. He had to. Why else would he have been scouring through old patient files he hadn't looked at in years? He had to know something. Amanda was sure of it.

Flowing. Her words. Her own confession.

She was a murderer. She'd let other boys die to keep her own alive. But her boys were dead. No, she didn't need to see their bodies to confirm it. They were dead. She had let innocent boys die for nothing. She was going to go to hell for what she'd done. She was sure of that, too. Redemption could not overcome her selfishness. She accepted that, and so she hadn't come to tell her sins seeking any redemption. She just wanted the killings to stop. She wanted the nightmare to end.

Amanda pressed the saturated tissues against her eyes as she pulled new ones from the Kleenex box the detectives had brought for her. She was alone in an interrogation room similar to the ones she'd seen in the cop dramas on television. She sat before a rectangular, grey table in a simple and uncomfortable black chair. Two others just like it sat across from her on the other side of the table. A row of florescent bulbs hung from the ceiling, giving dull lighting to the drab grey walls and black and white checkered flooring.

And of course, there was the one-way mirror. Wide and long against the wall to her right. On the opposite side, the detectives were watching her, going over everything she had told them, questioning whether she was telling the truth or wondering if she was somehow involved with the killer. That's what they did in all of the shows. Soon they would come in to ask her more questions and then probably place her under arrest for her hand in the sad and senseless atrocities that had taken place. Then, they would send someone to her home and to Allen's office. They would surely arrest him, too, but not until they used him to help catch Patrick. Her life would be ruined then. Her boys would be dead. Her marriage would be over. She would be a felon. And she deserved it all.

Amanda blew her nose and shook as the tears continued to fall slowly. She didn't care what happened. She just wanted it all to end. *If only she hadn't waited.* She closed her eyes, bowed her head, let the tears trickle down slowly. *If she had just done something sooner.* She cried, moaned quietly and crumped the tissues in her hand.

"Mrs. Kline?"

Amanda looked up. Standing just inside of the door she had never heard open was the detective from the television. The one who was the lead on the case.

She straightened up in her chair, wiped tears away and cleared her throat. "Y…yes," she said, her throat dry.

"I'm Detective—"

"Vance Newsome," Amanda said. "You're the lead on the case."

Vance nodded and closed the door behind him and approached her. "That's right."

"I've seen you on the news," Amanda said.

Vance gave her a half smile. "Would you like anything to drink? Water, soda, coffee, tea?"

Amanda shook her head. "No, thank you."

Vance pulled out a chair and sat down. As he looked at her, Amanda thought for a brief moment that he was more handsome in person, although his eyes seemed sadder. Undoubtedly from the pressure of the case.

"Thank you for coming in," he said softly. "I know it wasn't easy for you to do this."

Chills ran along her arms as her bottom lip began to quiver. She rubbed her arms as tears welled again, and then grabbed more tissue and patted her eyes.

"I want you to know, Mrs. Kline, that no one blames you for what's happened."

Unable to hold the grief back, Amanda shook as tears cascaded down her cheeks.

"You and your husband were placed in a horrible position," Vance continued. "Your boys—"

"My boys are dead."

Vance shook his head and sucked in his lips. "You don't know that, Mrs. Kline."

Amanda shook her head. "N...no. You're wrong."

"We don't have their bodies, Mrs. Kline. There's still a chance that they are alive."

"No...no," Amanda said, her tears falling harder, faster. "No. There's no chance."

"But, Mrs. Kline—"

"There's no chance! There can't be a chance! Because if...if there is, then that means that...that I shouldn't have come here. He...he said he would kill our boys if we told anyone. I'm here. I've just told everything. My boys have to be dead. They have to be!"

Amanda trembled and sobbed while Vance looked at her sympathetically.

"They have to be dead," she said again, her voice cracking. "They just have to be."

Vance frowned and then reached forward and placed his warm hands over her cold ones.

"They have to be," she whispered again.

"Where's your husband now, Mrs. Kline?"

Amanda took a breath. "I…I don't know. When I left…he was going through his files at home. He…he might be there or he might be at…at his office."

"The office. Is that where Patrick meets him?"

Amanda nodded.

"Have you ever seen him?"

"No."

"Has your husband ever described what he looked like to you?"

Again she shook her head.

"And you haven't told anyone else about what's happened?"

"N…no. I…I couldn't. Not before. But now…" She paused, squeezed her eyes shut tightly, and lifted her shoulders as she forced a scream down. "They have to be dead," she whispered once again.

Vance gave her hand a gentle squeeze. "You're very, very brave, Mrs. Kline. Coming here took a lot of courage and strength."

Amanda closed her eyes as the corners of her mouth dropped. "I'm… my husband...we're…we're murderers." She opened her eyes and stared at Vance. "Boys died because we did and said nothing."

Vance sighed. "Mrs. Kline…I don't have any children of my own, but my girlfriend has a son who I love very much. If I were put in the same position that you and your husband were put in, I can honestly tell you that I would have done the same thing."

"You…you would have?"

Vance nodded. "Yes."

"But isn't that selfish?"

"You love your sons and you would do anything you had to, to protect them. You were doing what you thought was best to keep them safe. Any parent would have done the same."

Amanda sniffled. "But…but those boys' lives could have been spared."

"And your boys could have been killed in their place."

"My…my boys are dead," Amanda insisted.

Vance looked at her, gave her hand another squeeze, then exhaled, let go of her hand, slid his chair back and stood up. He took a quick glance toward the mirror and then looked back at her.

"Are…are you going to arrest me now?" Amanda asked, looking up at him.

Vance looked at her, his expression empathetic . "You're not going to go to jail, Mrs. Kline."

"But…but all those boys."

"Those boys' deaths are not on your hands. And I know you are trying not to believe this, but neither are your sons."

"My…my sons—"

"Haven't been found, which means there is still a chance. Hold on to that."

Amanda looked at Vance.

Still a chance.

Hold on to that.

She shook her head. She couldn't do that. She couldn't hold on. Yet as Vance Newsome gave her a tight-lipped smile and walked out of the room, she was holding on with every fiber of her being.

Chapter 45

Vance let the door of the interrogation room close shut behind him and looked up to the water-stained ceiling tiles above him. He could have asked Amanda more questions. He could have asked her to go into detail again everything that she had told to Cribbs and Weston. But that would have been too insensitive. Amanda was going through enough as it was. Her agony was clearly genuine and to drag her through the emotional wringer again would have been unnecessary.

He exhaled. The tragedy of the situation that was unfolding was becoming overwhelming. He was losing control. He inhaled, exhaled again and looked to a door to his right. It led to another room from which Stubbs, Cribbs, Weston and profiler, Tiana Wilkins had been watching and listening to his conversation with Amanda Kline. They were waiting for him to come in, give his thoughts and his direction for the next move because he was the lead. They would ask him about Ben. His closest friend, his partner.

A killer?

He couldn't believe it. Wouldn't. There had to be an explanation for it all. Ben, the man he knew and worked beside, the man he'd grieved with—he couldn't be do the things that had been done. It just wasn't possible.

Eric's take that the killer looked like a cop, Ben's reaction and sudden disappearance, Beto's reproduction and statement—there had to be a twin. That was the only plausible explanation Vance would allow himself to believe because to believe anything else meant that he'd lost his mind.

Vance dragged his hand down over his face. He had to tell everyone what he knew. He knew that. Yet as he walked to the door, he also knew that he was going to do just as he had before. He was going to lie. He didn't have the whole story yet, and until he did, he was going to protect his partner, because that's what you did for the people you loved. Amanda Kline knew that all too well.

He turned the knob, pushed the door open and stepped into the room. All eyes fell on him. He frowned, looked at Tiana and said, "What do you think?"

Tiana looked back at him with an expression that said, 'Come on now.' "You know what I think because you're thinking the same thing," she said.

Vance sighed. "Yeah. Hell of a position she was put in. Her and her husband."

Stubbs cleared his throat. "She could have spared a lot of lives had she come forward sooner."

Vance looked at him. He knew it was more the chunks of his ass that had been getting chewed off by his superiors and the mayor that he meant could have been spared. Vance wanted to say that, but instead looked away from him and turned to Cribbs and Weston. "You two head over to the Kline's home and see if you get lucky and find Mr. Kline there. I'll head over to his office."

Cribbs and Weston nodded and then left the room.

Stubbs said, "Is Ben still at the hospital with the kid who was stabbed?"

"Yeah."

"What did the kid have to say?"

Vance thought about Eric and the drawing Beto had produced. *Be upfront*, he thought. *It's the right thing to do.*

He shook his head. "Nothing really. He didn't see who stabbed him."

"What about his story about a fake cop, real cop?"

Vance shook his head again. "A cop gave him a warning about being on the streets and kids dying. His mind just kind of ran from there. He was just stabbed, his friend, who was more like his brother, was killed. Paranoia created the scenario that didn't exist."

Stubbs nodded. "Okay…well get Ben off of baby duty and tell him to call me ASAP. I've been trying to reach him, but he's not answering his cell."

"He probably can't get a reception. I'll tell him."

Stubbs nodded and then took his hefty form and left the room. Vance exhaled and looked at Tiana, who was staring at Amanda Kline through the mirror.

"T.," he said. "Do me a favor. Call Dr. Rose and see if she has an hour or two to spare. Mrs. Kline is going to need someone to talk to."

Still staring at Amanda, Tiana, said, "Okay."

Vance looked at her. Her back was straight, her arms folded across her chest. He didn't see them, but he heard the tears in her voice. He was shocked. He'd never known her to get emotional. He said, "Thanks," and then headed out of the room.

Before he reached the door, Tiana. said, "Finish this, Vance. This is a fucking horrible case."

His hand on the knob, Vance clenched his jaws.

Finish this.

There was a finality to that order that made him shiver.

He walked out of the room without a response.

Chapter 46

Patrick had waited long enough. The time had finally come. The years of watching and festering—the time for revenge was here. Ben was finally going to pay for what he had done. He had ruined everything. All because he couldn't keep his fucking mouth closed. That was all he had to do. Stay quiet. Be a goddamned man and take the lessons.

Everything would have been all right then. Patrick's mother would have never died. He would have never been thrown into the foster care system because he'd had no family around that wanted to take him in. He would have never had to deal with sleepless nights and endless days of loneliness. He would have never had to endure hours of therapy sessions listening to lies. Lies exonerating Ben. Lies telling Ben that he hadn't been responsible for what happened. That what had been happening to him had been horrible and that he had done the right thing by telling.

Lies.

Patrick ground his teeth together.

Fucking lies.

Everything had been Ben's fault. Everything! And now he was going to pay with his life because Patrick was tired. Tired of the pain. Tired of seeing his mother die over and over and over. Therapy never made the memories go away for him. Therapy had never changed the fact that his life had been destroyed.

But Ben…

He had moved on. He had gotten a career, a wife, a son. He had forgotten about what he had done. But Patrick never had. And so he had let Ben have his life, while he waited in the background until the time came to pay Ben back for the life he had taken away from him.

Mikey's death.

Ben thought it had just been a senseless act of violence, but the reality was it had made perfect sense.

Patrick clenched his jaws again and then flexed his fingers, the leather around them creaking as he did. Tonight it was all going to be over. But before that moment came, he had to pay one final visit to Allen Kline to tell him about two more boys that he was going to kill, because Allen had to pay for his lies, too. Patrick was going to enjoy the look in Allen's eyes when he did.

Chapter 47

Allen sat in his office, his desk lamp on, the overhead lights off, a photograph of his wife and sons in one hand, a half-empty glass of scotch in the other. He wasn't there to work. He was just there to wait. For either the police or for Patrick. He didn't know who would come first, but he knew that one of them was coming. Possibly even both. Wouldn't that have been something?

He took a sip of the scotch and winced as the liquid burned its way down his chest. He'd never been much of a drinker, but after figuring out why Patrick, or Benjamin as he'd once known him, had chosen him, he figured drinking was appropriate. He lifted the photo and stared at his wife. She was hugging both of their sons, her arms enveloped around them from behind. A carefree and joyous smile was spread wide across her mouth. Her eyes were bright and free of the dark circles he'd become accustomed to. The picture was only six months old, but to look at her now, one would never know it. Patrick and the horror that he was putting them through had sucked the youth and vitality from her soul, leaving her nothing but a shell of her former self.

Allen took another sip of scotch. He knew the last time he'd seen her, that her will and spirit had been broken, and that she was going to go to the police. He could have tried to stop her, to convince her to hold on just a little longer, but his effort would have been useless. In her mind, her boys were dead. There was no sense in trying to believe anything different.

Allen downed the rest of his glass, put it down, grabbed the full bottle he'd just purchased from the corner of his desk, and poured himself another drink. He couldn't blame his wife for going. The truth of the matter was, she had held on far longer than perhaps many others would have.

Allen sighed and looked from Amanda to his boys. They looked so vibrant, so strong. He raised his glass, put it to his lips and stared at them over the rim of the glass as he sent liquid fire down his throat. Tears began to cloud his vision.

His boys.

The last time he'd seen them, he'd been rushing out of the house. He'd had an early morning session and he was going to be late because he'd overslept. Never did he think that the quick, "See you guys," would have possibly been the last words he was ever going to speak to them. He drank down his second round in one hearty gulp, then poured himself another and his body shuddered as he began to sob.

His boys.

Amanda had insisted that they were dead. He'd said that they didn't know that. That as long as Patrick continued coming to him, there was a chance their sons could still be alive.

Allen trembled as he looked at his boys while his tears fell. He shook his head. They couldn't be, he thought. Not his boys. He was supposed to see them grow into men, supposed to see them marry and raise families of their own. They were supposed to outlive him. They couldn't be dead. But as he downed the rest of his scotch, before throwing his glass across the room, sending it shattering against the far wall, he couldn't help but think that perhaps Amanda was right. That their sons were dead.

Still...he wouldn't leave until Patrick or the police arrived.

Chapter 48

He got it!

Just like his own, the link in Chad's chain was wide enough. Chris unhooked his brother's chain and took a deep breath. His hands were raw, burning and throbbing with pain, as his heart beat heavily. Sweat ran down his forehead but his arms were too fatigued to move. He wanted to lie down and close his eyes for just a few minutes. But a few minutes could mean the difference between life and death and with every tug on the chain to Chad's manacle, he'd vowed that he would do everything he could to stay alive. So he had to ignore the pain, had to ignore the exhaustion. Precious seconds were ticking by.

He took another full breath, exhaled and then put his hand on his brother's shoulder and shook him. "Chad. Chad...wake up."

Chad stirred but didn't wake up.

Chris shook him again with more urgency. "Chad! Wake up!" His brother had cried himself to sleep and had snored while Chris worked diligently on the chain. "Wake up, Chad!" he said, shaking him again.

Chad stirred and then said, "Huh?" his voice heavy with sleep.

"I got your chain free," Chris said.

There was an immediate perk in Chad's voice as he bolted upright and said, "You did?"

"Yeah."

The chain around Chad's ankle scraped on the concrete as he moved his leg. "What...what do we do now?"

Chris looked toward the direction of the door. "We have to find a way out of here," he said, standing up after a few seconds. He made his way to the door in the darkness that no longer seemed so dark, and tried the knob. When it didn't turn he wasn't surprised. False hope had accompanied him to the door, but even before his fingers wrapped around the cold knob, he knew the door would be locked.

"Is it open?" Chad asked, his chain making noise as he stood up.

Chris frowned. "No."

Chad came up beside him. "What are we going to do?" he asked, his voice thick with disappointment.

Chris frowned again and then placed his hand back on the doorknob. He fiddled with it again, pleading for the knob to somehow miraculously turn this time. Of course it didn't. He exhaled and said, "We're going to find a way out of here."

"What if he comes back?"

Chris placed his head against the door. *What if he came back?* It was a question he'd been wondering as he'd worked on his little brother's chain. What if he came back? What would they do?

Tonight...they were both going to die.

A promise. Cold and sincere.

Chris moved his head away from the door's hard wood and said, "We're going to get out of here, Chad. No matter what."

Chapter 49

Allen smelled the smoke first. Then heard the voice.

"Have you been waiting for me?"

Allen looked up. Patrick was standing in the doorway, a cigarette in his mouth, the tip glowing a dull orange, smoke wafting into the room. Allen had always hated the stale, bitter scent of cigarette smoke. He hated it even more now.

He took a glance down at the photograph of his family in his hand, and then put it face down on his desktop. "Hello, Benjamin," he said.

Patrick chuckled, then walked into the room and took a seat directly across from Allen, allowing for the first time, Allen to clearly see his face. "I do look like him, don't I?" Patrick said with a sinister smirk.

Allen stared at him, at his dark eyes. "You are him," Allen said.

Patrick smirked again, then took a pull on his cigarette, held the nicotine for a few seconds, and then blew the smoke into Allen's face.

Allen tried not to cough. He didn't want to give Patrick the satisfaction. But he couldn't help it. He coughed while a fleeting thought about secondhand smoke ran through his mind.

"Would you like to see him again?" Patrick asked, staring at him with amusement in his eyes.

Allen coughed again, then cleared his throat, and with the taste of nicotine on his tongue, said, "Yes. I would."

Patrick smirked again. "What do you want to tell him?" Do you want to feed him more bullshit? Tell him more lies?"

Allen shook his head. "I just want to help him."

"He doesn't need your help, Allen."

"Yes he does," Allen countered. "And I think that's why you came to me. I think you want me to help him because you know that what happened to him wasn't really his fault."

Patrick took a pull, released smoke into the air, and then shook ashes onto the desk. "That's bullshit, Allen. And you know it."

"It's not bullshit. Do you hear me, Benjamin?" he asked, closing his eyes a bit, watching the man in front of him closely. "What happened wasn't your fault. Your mother didn't die because of you."

Patrick flared his nostrils and said, "Shut up, Allen."

Allen's heart began to race. What he was doing…the road he was going down…it was dangerous. Perhaps even suicidal. As he sat waiting, watching, he knew that his only hope of getting his boys back—if they were in fact still alive—was to somehow find a way to reach Benjamin McCallum. And so he'd sat and waited and prayed that when the time came, he would have the strength necessary to push his way past Patrick's dominance without getting himself killed in the process. Again, it was part suicide, but he had no choice. The hourglass had been flipped upside down and the sands within were trickling down, leaving the top half nearly empty.

Allen took a breath, opened his mouth to try and reach out to Ben once again, when Patrick suddenly slammed his hand down on the desk, causing the bottle of scotch to fall over, sprang up from his chair, lunged forward across the desk, wrapped his gloved fingers around Allen's throat, and lifted the shell-shocked doctor out of his chair. "I told you to shut the fuck up!" Patrick raged.

Allen wrapped his hands around Patrick's and tried to pry himself free.

Patrick grabbed the index and middle finger of his right hand and bent them back until they broke.

Allen screamed out. Or tried to. Patrick's vice around his throat made it almost impossible for sound to escape. It also made it impossible for air to get in.

"You should have listened to me, Allen. You should have kept your fucking mouth closed just like HE should have!"

Patrick's grip tightened. Allen gagged, tried to take a breath. His eyes watered from the pain of his broken fingers and from the asphyxiation. His head felt light and swollen. He tried again, with his left hand to break Patrick's grip. Patrick grabbed hold of it and twisted until his wrist gave way and snapped.

Allen let out as much of a scream as Patrick's hand around his throat would allow.

"I should kill you, Allen!" Patrick said, his eyes closed to slits, his teeth bared. "I should kill you for continuing with your lies. He was never stronger than me, Allen. NEVER! Who do you think withstood the pain of all of the lessons? Him? That pussy? No, Allen. It was me. It's always been ME! I kept us together! I'm the man that he could never have become!"

Allen's head felt as though it were about to explode. Both hands throbbed with pain. In front of him, Patrick began to fade in and out. He opened his mouth as far as he could and tried to take in whatever amount of air he could. He began to shake, his body fighting and losing at the same time.

"The one time, Allen," Patrick continued. "The one time I let my guard down, the one time I allowed myself to rest, that little shit went and ruined EVERYTHING!"

Patrick let out a growl and then shoved Allen back viciously, sending him toppling backward over his chair. The base of his spin hit the carpeted floor first, which did little to lessen the shockwave of pain that coursed through him, and then the back of his head banged hard against the bottom of his bookshelf. The room began to spin as spots appeared and reappeared before his eyes as he lay on the ground, his leather chair turned over on its side and sprawled across his legs.

"He fucked everything up and YOU tried to make him believe that he didn't!" Patrick said, appearing over him. He kicked Allen in the small of his back. "You told him lie, after lie, after fucking lie!" Patrick yelled, kicking him three times successively.

Tears ran down Allen's cheeks as his head, hands, spine and back all hurt with intense and excruciating pain. He breathed in slowly, quickly, deeply and sparsely all at the same time.

Patrick bent down beside him, vice-gripped his hand around Allen's throat again. "I want to kill you, Allen," he said, his voice deathly low, yet even more menacing. "I want to squeeze the life out of you just like I tried to do years ago. Do you remember that? I was going to kill you that day but you were lucky because we weren't alone."

Allen stared up at a very faded image of Patrick hovering over him. Unconsciousness was moments away. Or perhaps death. He blinked quickly several times as his heart beat hard and slow.

"There's no one to save you, now Allen," Patrick said, bringing his face closer to his.

The scent of cigarette smoke wafted into Allen's nostrils and Allen wondered if he would smell smoke in hell, because surely that's where he was going to go. Soon. In just a few more seconds.

And then Patrick released his grasp and stood up.

Air rushed back into Allen's lungs as instinct took over and he inhaled. He coughed a few times, his throat searing as he did.

"I want to kill you, Allen," Patrick said, standing over him. "But I waited too many years behind the scenes to make you and him suffer."

Allen coughed again as Patrick began to back up. He could breathe, but he still felt Patrick's hands around his neck, still felt as though his airway was being constricted. He tried to move, but a wave of dizziness and nausea came over him, forcing him to remain still. He could feel blood trickling from the back of his head, and he was sure he had a concussion.

"I'm going to kill again, Allen," Patrick said. He was steps away from the door. "Two boys this time. I'm going to show them how to be men and then I'm going to choke them until they have no breath left to make sure they don't tell a soul."

Despite the lightheadedness and the physical agony, Allen pulled his legs slowly from beneath his overturned chair. He had to get up.

"You should have told the truth, Allen. You should have told him that he should have kept his fucking mouth closed."

Ignoring the hurt, Allen scooted back until his back pressed against the edge of his bookshelf, and then slowly pushed himself up with his legs.

The room was reeling as he leaned against the shelf and stared at a very blurred Patrick standing in the doorway. "St…stop…" he said his voice raspy. "Pl…please!"

"I waited twenty-six years for this, Allen. I won't stop until I'm finished."

Allen pushed himself away from the bookshelf, stumbled forward as though walking on the deck of a ship in rough waters. He clipped his hip on the corner of his desk and fell to one knee. He looked up. Patrick had stepped through the doorway now. "Pl…please," he begged forcefully. "Please…don't…"

"I'll see you in hell, Allen," Patrick said. And then he disappeared.

Allen cried out. "NOO!"

He pushed himself up, moved forward, tripped over his own feet, stumbled into the chair Patrick had been sitting in and then fell to the floor, the side of his head crashing to the ground this time. "My boys," he whispered as the room cycloned around him. "Please…Not my boys…"

And then there was nothing but darkness.

Chapter 50

Vance stepped into Allen's office and as his eyes settled on the doctor sprawled out on the floor, the stench of smoke hit his nostrils. It was a smell he was familiar with.

He removed his glock from his holster, held it in stiff-armed, fire-ready position, swiveled his head from side to side, looking around the room, as he made his way over to Allen's unmoving body. "Dr. Kline?" he said, eyeing the blood slowly oozing from the back of the doctor's head.

He knelt down beside Allen, his index finger now lying just beneath the trigger of his glock as he was certain that no one else was with them, and took the index and middle finger of his left hand to check for a pulse. Just before his fingers touched skin, he noticed deep, red marks around Allen's neck. He thought of the slain boys they'd found with bruises around their necks, whispered, "Shit," and then pressed his lips firmly together and placed his fingers against Allen's jugular vein. Seconds later he let out a sigh of relief as Allen's blood pulsed.

He stood up, pulled his cell phone from his pocket, and was about to make a call to get paramedics on the scene, when Allen stirred. Vance paused, his finger about to press the send button, and looked down. His intention had been to come and talk to Allen Kline to get as much information as he could about Patrick. Why had Patrick taken his sons? Allen Kline knew something and Vance needed to know what before anyone else did.

Vance needed to hit the send button and get the medics on the scene. He needed to call Cribbs and Weston and get them to get there as fast as they could. He needed to show them the note and the drawing. He needed to tell them that Ben had disappeared.

So why didn't he do that?

Ben wasn't the killer. That just wasn't possible. So the note was simply a taunt. And the drawing… He'd often heard that everyone in the world had a look-a-like, someone that resembled them so closely that one would think they were related. Beto's drawing was proof that the theory was true, because without a doubt, it couldn't have been a picture of Ben.

There was nothing to hide. So why not make the calls?

Allen stirred and moaned. Vance looked at him, worked his jaw, then cursed, closed his phone, slid it back into his pocket and bent down and hooked his hand beneath Allen's arm. "Dr. Kline?" he said, helping the doctor roll over onto his side.

Allen looked up at him, his eyes glassy and heavy with fear and confusion. He said, "Wh…who…"

Vance removed his wallet and flashed his badge. "I'm Detective Newsome. I just finished talking to your wife, Amanda." Vance saw recognition flash in the doctor's glazed eyes.

Allen said, "He…he's going to…to kill my sons. Please…you've got to….to stop him."

"How long ago did he leave?"

Allen made a pained expression as he closed his eyes. *Stay with me*, Vance thought. *For just a few more question at least.*

A small amount of blood was gathering beneath the doctor's head and Vance knew he should have made the calls. But every second was precious. He said, "Dr. Kline…how long ago did Patrick leave?" Vance asked again, watching the doctor closely. His eyes went to Allen's throat, to the blood collecting on the carpet, then back to Allen's half-closed eyes.

Allen squinted his eyes, took a short breath and shook his head ever so slightly. "I…I don't know…"

Vance frowned. "Do you have any idea where he may have gone?"

Allen shook his head.

Vance could see in his eyes that unconsciousness was coming again. "Dr. Kline…Allen..." he said, his voice louder. "I want to find your boys. I want to save them…but I'm going to need you to stay with me, okay?"

Allen made another pained expression, then gave a half nod.

"Is there anything that you remember, Allen?" Vance said. "Anything at all that you think may help me?"

Allen's eyes closed momentarily and then opened them. Vance gritted his teeth as he took a quick glance at the pool of blood, which had grown larger. *Come on*, he thought again. *Give me something. Anything.*

Allen shook his head and then nodded. "Hi…his…" he started, the volume in his voice diminishing.

Vance stared at him intensely. "What is it, Allen?"

A faint cough escaped from the doctor's lips as his eyes began to roll upward.

No, no! Vance balled his hand into a tight fist. He wanted to shake him, make him speak. "What is it, Allen?" he said again, fighting the urge to do just that. Allen's eyes began to closely. They would stay closed for a while this time, Vance knew. He let out a breath. "Dr. Kline?"

Allen's eyes fluttered open and to Vance's surprise, his eyes settled directly on him. "His…his name," he said.

Vance nodded as his heart began to pound. "Yes?"

"His name…" Allen continued. "It…it's B…Ben…Benjamin Patrick McCallum."

Vance's heart dropped into the pit of his stomach as all of the breath rushed from his lungs.

"Don't….don't let Patrick hurt them…" Allen begged. "Pl…please save my boys." And then his close as his head and body went limp.

Vance watched his chest rise and fall slowly as a long, steady chill fell over him.

Benjamin Patrick McCallum.

Ben…his partner, his friend.

Patrick…the killer.

Vance swallowed saliva, then put a hand on Allen's shoulder as he grabbed his phone and made the call he should have already made to the paramedics. After that he called Cribbs and Weston, instructed them to get a uniformed officer over to Allen's office, and then gave them Ben's address and told them to get over there right away.

When he was finished, he rushed out of Allen Kline's office. Ben's house was five blocks away. He would get there before Cribbs and Weston. He hoped he would find Ben McCallum there and not Patrick. As he raced to his car, Beto's words again ran through his mind.

The ultimate definition of identical.

Chapter 51

Sarah McCallum was smiling. It had been a long time since she'd done that. Smiled. Really smiled.

She was on her way to see Ben. To tell him that he was right. That she still loved him and that she didn't want to end their marriage. She'd smiled when she was with Brandon, but never the way she was now. Never on the inside. Their son was gone, but she and Ben could and would get past the grief. They would make it because their love was real and it would withstand through the tragedy. She realized that now. Running away hadn't been the answer, but it had been necessary for both of them, she believed.

Sarah walked quickly as the wind whipped angrily around her. She was anxious to get back to where she belonged.

Chapter 52

Footsteps.

Chris steeled himself and pressed his hand flat against his brother's chest. They were waiting for the door to open. The plan was to attack as soon as the fake cop stepped inside. Chris would hit him high. Chad would hit him low. If they moved fast enough, hit hard enough, maybe they could buy time to get away. They had to.

Chris' heart beat so heavily he could hear the loud thuds in his eardrums. His palms were sweaty, his open wounds burning from the sweat. But it didn't matter. It was time to go home, and one way or another, he and Chad would get to on their terms, not the fake cop's.

The footsteps drew nearer. Chad shuffled his feet, the end of his chain scraping on the ground. Chris tapped his brother's chest, said, "Shh," softly.

The footsteps grew louder, and then stopped just outside of the door. Chris held his breath as a key was inserted into the lock.

Chapter 53

It was time.

Allen's payback. His punishment for enabling Ben to believe that it had been okay to carry on. Sure there had been others who had tried to do the same thing, but Allen had been the first. And so it had been his voice, his words that Patrick had never forgotten. The ones he heard while he'd waited in the background.

Payback. It was something Patrick vowed to get the day the orderlies kept him from killing Allen. Payback. Twenty-six years in the making. First Allen, and then Ben.

Patrick couldn't wait.

Ben thought he'd known suffering. He thought he had hit bottom with the loss of his son and the ruin of his marriage. But he didn't know shit. Not yet. But he would. Soon. After Allen's sons were gone, Patrick was going to stop and go back behind the curtain and watch as Ben had to deal with the horror. He was going to leave for Ben the memory of the moment Mikey was killed. He was going to leave with Ben the images of the lessons he'd shown each one of the boys before he wrapped his fingers around their little throats and ended their lives.

Patrick was going to watch with satisfaction as Ben recalled every detail of every act, and tried in vain to deny the undeniable. He was a killer. Patrick would watch while Ben felt suffering on a level he never imagined possible.

Twenty-six years in the making.

Patrick would finally have his revenge.

He smiled, turned the key and then pulled the thick, heavy door open. It was time to teach Allen's sons lessons that Allen would never forget.

Chapter 54

Alyssa Taylor put her hand flat against her stomach and smiled. She was going to be a mommy again. Her eyes welled with tears as she looked down at the E.P.T. test that had just confirmed what the missed period and nausea each morning for the past three mornings had already told her.

Pregnant,

It was such a joyous and special confirmation. So different from when she'd found out she was pregnant with DaShawn. She loved her little protector, but she hadn't been ready in the least for the responsibilities when she found out motherhood was coming. Five weeks in, she'd had no clue that there would have been such a major repercussion for a one-night stand that had ended with semen on her breasts. She'd known all about pre-cum, but the statistics on becoming pregnant because of it oozing out had been so low, that never once did the thought cross her mind that she would be one of the "lucky" few. STD's, sure. But pregnancy?

Because she'd had no symptoms and because she'd had irregular periods after she had stopped taking her birth control pills just two months prior because of stomach cramping, she'd had no idea that she was carrying. The only reason she found out was because of a late night trip to the E.R. after she woke with extreme pain in her abdomen that caused a river of tears to fall from her eyes.

Five weeks pregnant is what had been revealed to her hours later. Five weeks with no way to get in contact with the good-looking brotha she'd met at the club.

DaShawn had been punishment for irresponsibility until the first time she felt him kick. After that he became a blessing that she thanked God for every day. Now he was about to become a big brother.

Alyssa smiled and wiped her joy-filled tears away. She didn't know how exactly he was going to react to the news, but because she knew how good of a man Vance Newsome was, she was sure that when she broke the news to him, his reaction was going to be a favorable one. Just as she thanked God for DaShawn's life, she did the same for Vance's existence in hers. He was a godsend, a man sent to complete her. A man she knew was going to be her forever.

She wanted to call him and tell him the news, but he was working hard trying to bring the killer the media had dubbed, The Pacifier, to justice. Four boys dead, all John Doe's. Alyssa couldn't imagine the things that had happened to them, happening to DaShawn. The thought made her shiver.

She said a prayer for Vance and Ben to find the bastard and then she looked down at the E.P.T. test again. She couldn't wait to break the news to the men in her life.

Chapter 55

Allen was on his way to the hospital. That's what Amanda had been told by the police officers who'd come to give her a ride to meet him. He'd been attacked and had suffered a concussion, along with broken fingers and a fractured wrist. They hadn't been able to tell her who had attacked him, but she didn't need for them to.

She knew.

And as she sat in the back of the unmarked cruiser, clutching her purse tightly, she was certain, now more than ever, that she was never going to see her boys again.

Chapter 56

The door opened.

The fake cop took one step inside.

Chris yelled, "NOW!" and moved.

He pushed away from the wall, pivoted to his right and just as he had to Eli Henderson during their fight in gym class earlier in the year, he swung out and connected with a right hook to the side of the fake cop's face. At the same time, Chad hit him in his midsection and kicked at his shin, just as Chris had instructed him to do.

Caught off guard, the fake cop staggered backward.

Chris didn't hesitate. He lunged forward with another punch, this time catching the man in his chest, and then kneed him in his groin.

"RUN!" he yelled as the fake cop fell back another couple of steps and then dropped down to his knee, giving them just enough space to do exactly that.

Stepping into an expanded room with more concrete flooring and grey walls, Chris saw straight ahead, another door, leading to a staircase. "That way!"

He pushed Chad forward and prepared to follow when the fake cop's fingers clamped hard around his ankle. He was pulled down swiftly.

"You little shit!" He began to pull Chris toward him.

Chad screamed out his name.

Chris ordered him to, "RUN!" as he lashed out with his legs and hit the fake cop in his mouth with the heel of his foot. For the briefest of seconds, the fake cop's fingers unclamped from around his ankle. A second was all Chris needed.

He shot up, yelled at Chad, who'd remained frozen by the door, to, "MOVE!"

Chris ran past a metal beam in the middle of the room and headed to the staircase, just steps behind Chad, the fake cop on his heels.

Chris passed a set of crates stacked on top of one another. He grabbed the top one and knocked it down behind him, sending its contents—a hammer, a couple of screwdrivers, some screws and nails, and a roller without the brush—scattering behind him.

Chris heard the fake cop stumble. He yelled for Chad to, "HURRY!"

They scrambled upward on the narrow staircase, their chains clattering loudly.

Chris nearly stepped on the back of Chad's heel. "MOVE, CHAD!" He pushed his brother in the back, sending him reeling upward past the top step.

With room in front of him, Chris took the last four remaining steps in two's, and as he reached the top of the staircase, the fake cop barreled into him, sending him crashing to the floor.

"You little, shit!" the fake cop yelled, hitting him in his back and ribs. "I'm going to kill you!"

The fake cop grabbed a handful of his hair, pulled his head back, and slammed his forehead down onto the tiled floor.

Seconds later, everything began to fade, and just as darkness fell over him, the last thing Chris heard was his brother screaming his name.

Chapter 57

Vance heard a scream over the rush of the wind. A boy's voice. Young. Pleading for his brother to be let go. Vance's heart pounded as he removed his glock from his holster and took the four concrete steps leading to Ben's front door in one leap.

The little boy yelled again for his brother's life. "Please stop! Please... let him go!"

Vance took a breath. He was about to kick the door in and witness something that was going to break his heart. On the other side of the door would be Ben or Patrick as Allen and his wife called him. Patrick, the cold-blooded killer that Vance had to stop at all costs, because that was his job. To find the criminals, the deranged psychos, and bring them to justice. Sometimes the end result for the perpetrator was a cell with room for just a bed, a desk and a toilet. Other times a casket was all that was needed.

Vance exhaled and dreaded the end result he would be faced with as he kicked the door in, pointed his gun and yelled, "Police!"

Chapter 58

Patrick looked up and smiled. The moment had come and it had shaped up better than he could have imagined. He tightened his grip around Allen's oldest son's throat as he held him tight against his body. "Hey, Vance," he said with a smirk.

Vance took a step forward, looked from Patrick to Chris, then to Chad, who was standing in between them. He stood almost petrified, his back straight, his shoulders raised, his arms down and pressed against his sides as tears streaked down his face.

His glock leveled on Patrick, Vance took another step forward and called out to Chad. "Step back, son!"

Chad shook as he sobbed. He didn't respond.

Vance called to him again. "Son…I need for you to step back, okay?"

Patrick watched with in amusement as Chad turned his head and looked at Vance over his shoulder. His heart raced with excitement, with pleasure as Chad nodded and then shuffled his feet.

"If you move anymore, Chad," Patrick said. "I'm going to kill your brother." His eyes had been on Vance when he'd spoken, watching him as Vance stared back.

The confusion, shock and disbelief in Vance's eyes made chills creep up Patrick's arms.

Vance closed his eyes a bit and said, "B…Ben…what the hell?" He turned his head from side to side. "Why are you doing this, man?"

Patrick stared at the creases in Vance's forehead as he struggled to understand and come to grips with what was happening. He continued to hold Chris close to him, his fingers wrapped firmly around the teen's throat, but not so firmly that he would die. He didn't want that to happen. Not yet.

This was so, so much better, he thought. So much more climactic. His final act, his coup de 'grace was shaping up to be pure perfection.

An old memory—one that had haunted him every day for the past twenty-six years—ran through his mind. His father standing in the middle of the living room, choking the life from his mother, while Ben stood like the coward he was, watching, saying and doing nothing. That scene used to terrify Patrick and make the fire-raged hatred inside of him burn hotter.

That scene.

Now recreated with different players gave him one hell of a rush.

Chapter 59

I'm sure you know my name, Vance," Patrick said. "Why don't you fucking use it."

Vance's heartbeat was out of control. Thudding, pounding, stealing his breath away.

Benjamin Patrick McCallum.

Patrick, not Ben standing in front of him, choking another little boy.

The ultimate definition of identical.

Vance stared at the man he'd seen a thousand times and didn't recognize him at all. He clenched his jaw, tensed the muscles in his arms as he kept his gun trained on Patrick. "You don't have to do this, Patrick," he said.

Patrick smiled. It was evil, filled with self-satisfaction. He said, "I do, Vance. I really do."

Hairs rose along the back of Vance's neck. There was such a maliciousness to Patrick's tone. Vance had been in tense predicaments before, but never had they been this frightening.

He flexed his fingers around the butt of his glock. Its weight had increased, its metal had become hotter. He looked from Patrick to Chris. The blood from the wound on his forehead was flowing faster. His eyes were closed, his body limp. Vance could tell that Patrick's grip wasn't tight enough to kill.

Yet.

In front of him, Chris' little brother continued to stand still, sobbing. Vance wanted to grab him. To pull him away from the horror taking place before him. "Why don't you let the boys go, Patrick? They're innocent. They haven't done anything."

Patrick shook his head. "They're not innocent, Vance. None of them were."

"Let them go," Vance implored again.

Patrick said, "I can't do that. I've waited too long to do that."

Vance swallowed dry saliva as sweat ran down his forehead. "Waited too long for what?"

"For payback," Patrick said with a smirk.

Vance slammed his eyebrows together. "Payback? Payback for what?"

Patrick stared at him, and as he did, Vance noticed his fingers around Chris' throat flex.

"Payback for what?" Vance asked again.

"You read the note, Vance. You know why."

The palms of Vance's hand itched as he kept his sights on Patrick's head. He wasn't using Chris as a shield. He was daring him, Vance knew. Daring him to pull the trigger.

Any other time, Vance wouldn't have hesitated. His gun would have been discharged, his target would have been hit. His duty, his vow to protect and to serve would have been kept.

Any. Other. Time.

But this time, this situation was like no other he had ever faced. In front of him, despite the painful and terrifying fact that it wasn't, was still Ben, still his partner, his friend standing before him. And because of that, Vance couldn't dare.

He stood, arm stiff, breath short, praying for time. For Cribbs and Weston to get there, so that one of them could pull the trigger before he did.

Chapter 60

Sarah was still smiling when she stepped out of the taxi cab. The smile hadn't gone away and had only gotten wider the closer she'd gotten to seeing Ben. She'd tried to reach him on his cell, but hadn't got an answer. She knew he was working on the case, trying to find The Pacifier. It was wrong of her to hope for, but Sarah did hope that when Ben and Vance found the bastard, that they would be forced to fire their weapons. Wishing death on someone was a horrible thing to do, but a sick individual like The Pacifier didn't deserve anything but that. He was killing innocent boys. Innocent boys like Mikey had been. Ben would find him and bring back a slice of peace that the son-of-a-bitch had stolen away from the city.

Her smile still wide, Sarah turned away as the cab driver, an African man with clear skin the color of onyx sped away, having already taken on another fare, and looked up at her house, and noticed that the door was opened wide, the edge of it broken.

Then she heard Ben's voice. Loud and angry.

Her smile dropped. "Ben?"

She looked at the busted door. Something was wrong.

Cautiously, yet quickly, she walked up the concrete steps, chipped and faded from use and the weather. "Ben?" she said, stepping over the threshold, past splintered pieces of wood.

And then she paused.

In front of her, his back to her, was Vance, his arms stretched out in front of him, his gun in his hands. In front of Vance was a little boy she didn't recognize, wearing nothing but underwear. In front of the boy, standing at the end of the small hallway leading to the basement she always hated, stood Ben, and in his arms, his fingers clamped around his neck, was another boy in boxer-briefs she didn't recognize. The boy was unconscious, or so she hoped, with blood oozing from a gash on his forehead.

Sarah stood frozen, shocked, confused, terrified. "Ben?" she said, her throat tight.

Ben looked at her with a predatory glint she'd never seen in his eyes before and smiled.

Chapter 61

Vance turned his head.

Sarah. Standing in the doorway. Her mouth open, her eyes wide.

Shit.

He locked eyes with her. Said, "Get out of here now, Sarah!"

He turned back to look at Patrick, who was smiling, his expression reminiscent to the Joker.

"Vance…what…what's happening? Ben….what…"

"Get outside, Sarah!" Vance ordered again, keeping his eyes fixed on Patrick, on his hand around Chris' throat.

"Don't you fucking move, Sarah!" Patrick said. "You were unexpected, but your being here makes the party all the more complete."

Vance flexed his fingers around his gun again. *Pull the trigger*, he thought. But he couldn't. Patrick was standing in front of him, but Ben had to be, too. How could he fire? He said, "Let the boy go, Patrick."

Behind him, Sarah said, "Patrick? Vance—"

"Please, Sarah!" Vance said. "Please get out of here!"

"If you move, he dies, Sarah," Patrick said.

Vance clenched his jaw. "Shut the fuck up, Patrick!"

"Or what, Vance?" Patrick asked defiantly. "You're going to kill me?"

Vance looked at him as sweat trickled, as his heart pounded in his ear drums.

Patrick glared back at him, his eyes dark and burning with hatred. "Do it," he said. "Pull the trigger."

Vance swallowed saliva, took quick breaths as heat encompassed his body. The floor beneath his feet became unsteady. The walls around him began to close in.

"Do it, Vance," Patrick ordered again. "Kill him. He deserves to die. He's a pussy, a coward. Do it!"

Vance swallowed dry saliva again. His throat was raw. The walls came closer. The floor beneath his feet became more unstable. He looked from Patrick to Chris, who was still unconscious, to his little brother who was still sobbing. He looked back to Patrick who was watching with eyes that used to belong to Ben, as his mouth spread into a malevolent, self-satisfied smirk.

"I'm going to kill him, Vance," Patrick said easily. "You better pull the trigger."

Vance shivered, his head throbbing at his temples. Behind him, Sarah cried and said, "Ben…please…please stop!"

Vance took a quick look at her over his shoulder, his gun still on Patrick. Tears were raining down her face as she stood with her hands over her mouth. She looked at him with confusion in her eyes.

Vance turned and looked back to Patrick.

"It's time," Patrick said

Vance watched as Patrick's fingers began to squeeze.

CHAPTER 62

It was time.

Patrick squeezed.

Payback for Allen. Payback for Ben.

Goddamned payback.

He squeezed, looked from Vance to Sarah. Her presence had been a pleasant surprise. Everyone that mattered was there to watch him get what he deserved. It was the perfect ending to the perfect script.

Patrick squeezed his fingers together hard, fast, and as he did, he looked at Chad. Ten years old, like he had been.

Patrick smiled and then stepped back behind the curtain to wait for the final scene to end and the credits to roll.

Chapter 63

Bright light blazed in Ben's eyes. He blinked rapidly, trying to clear away spots. Where was he? He blinked, and as he did, spots and fuzziness disappeared, and he found himself in the hallway of his house. In front of him, a little boy he should have never known, yet knew all too well, stood crying uncontrollably. Behind him was Vance, his gun pointed at him, yelling in slow motion. Behind Vance was Sarah, she too crying, moving slowly. Ben' s eyes rolled downward. "No," he whispered, the sound of his voice a magnified echo.

Mikey, looking up at him with tears, fear, disbelief, and sadness as he pummeled on him. Four boys crying as he forced them to do things, "lessons." Four boys, their mouths opened, their eyes wide with dread, their lives slipping away as his fingers constricted around their throats. Pacifiers left behind. Confessions to a man who had tried to help him get past pain, past self-blame. Confessions and threats.

Ben shook his head.

Four dead boys. Two sons held captive until the right time had come to kill them.

Mikey.

Oh, God...Mikey!

Ben opened his mouth. A scream erupted.

The world sped up, went back to real time.

Something slammed into his forehead, sending him falling backward.

Ben felt two things as darkness consumed light. Dread and satisfaction.

Chapter 64

Vance didn't pull the trigger. He was about to. But something happened that made him pause. There was a scream. It had hadn't been a long one. A second or two at best. And within those short seconds, Vance looked into the eyes of his friend, and in his, and on the crests of his scream, his cry, Vance realized that Patrick was gone, and that Ben had returned and had become painfully aware of all that had happened.

And then a crack exploded from behind Vance, and less than a moment later, a hole appeared in the middle of Ben's forehead and blood and brain matter erupted from the back of his head. A surreal, yet all-too-frighteningly real second later, Vance watched as Chris Kline collapsed, still unconscious to the floor, while Ben fell backward, and before he hit the ground, Vance knew he was dead.

Shock kept Vance from uttering a sound as he turned and looked over his shoulder to see Cribbs standing beside Sarah, his arms outstretched, his gun in his hand, while Weston stood with his arms enveloped around Sarah as she screamed endlessly for Ben, while tears cascaded from her eyes.

As Sarah's cries became soundless, Vance looked back to his friend. Unable to move, he stood with his arms down at his sides, his shoulders sagging, and stared at Ben's lifeless body sprawled out, blood pooling on the ground beneath his head, while Chad ran to his older brother, dropped down to his knees and began shaking him while yelling out his name.

Vance should have moved, too. He'd been trained to act in times of crisis. Hours and hours of intense scenarios had been recreated. Pages and pages of different situations, different cases had been read about and discussed. On the streets as both a uniformed officer and as a plain-clothed detective, all of the time invested had paid off and kept him alive, kept those he had vowed to protect alive as well. Taking a course of action had become instinctive. Like breathing, it was just something he did without thought.

But no amount of hours spent in training, no amount of pages read in books, and no amount of real-time experience—none of it had prepared him for the things that had just unfolded before him. And so he stood immobile, his body tense and knowing what it needed to do, but his mind blank and unable to follow his muscles' lead.

He remained.

While Sarah screamed Ben's name. While Chad called out his brother's.

He remained.

His mouth hung open. His eyes didn't blink. His chest barely expanded to take in breaths of air.

He remained.

Even as Cribbs shook him, called out his name, and then moved and rushed over to the two brothers, Vance still remained fastened to the ground.

Patrick was dead. Patrick had murdered four boys. He had done unforgiveable things to them. He had deserved to die. The world was a better and safer place without him in it.

Yet at the same time…

It wasn't better, it wasn't safer without Ben.

Ben. Who was Patrick.

Vance wanted to move, to check on the boys and on Sarah. He wanted to add his own scream to the noise and confusion taking place around him. Cribbs called his name again. Paramedics rushed by him, their shoulders bumping his as they did.

Vance remained still and stared.

Ben was gone.

Chapter 65

Her boys were alive.

Alive.

That word had new meaning.

Amanda sat beside her oldest and held his hand tightly as her youngest son sat in her lap, his head against her chest, snoring. Tears fell slowly from Amanda's eyes. They had been ever since a uniformed officer had come and told her that her boys had been found alive.

Alive.

A word she'd lost faith in. A word she'd given up hope on.

Her boys were alive. Beside her and in her arms. She squeezed Chris' hand. No longer unconscious from the concussion he'd suffered, he was sleeping now. With the exception of some bruising around his ankle and neck, and a large knot on his forehead, along with a gash that would leave a scar, he had escaped relatively unscathed. So too had Chad, who after crying in her arms, told her and the police all that he and Chris had gone through.

Amanda held her son's hand as he recounted the details of all they had endured. Abduction, chains around their ankles, peanut-butter and jelly sandwiches, tugs on the chain, fights to escape and survive. Amanda's heart broke over and over again as she listened to her son's frightening story. Her boys were never supposed to go through anything like that, and while she knew that it hadn't been her fault, she blamed herself regardless. She was their mother. She had protected them in her womb for nine months and vowed on the day of their births when she'd held each one of them in her arms, to do everything in her power to protect them.

Her sons had been taken. They could have died. No one would convince her that there was nothing she could have done to have prevented what happened, even if that was very much the truth.

When Chad finished disclosing everything he and his brother went through, Amanda held onto him as though his life depended on it, and apologized endlessly for not being there. She did the same to Chad when he finally became conscious and looked at her with a small smile on his face. He had corroborated the same details as Chad, and when he was finished, mental and physical exhaustion overwhelmed him and he fell asleep. Chad followed suit soon after. And now Amanda sat with both of her boys back safely where they belonged.

She smiled, kissed Chad on the top of his head, then leaned over and kissed Chris on his cheek. "Never again," she whispered. "Never again." And then she looked up to see her husband watching them from outside of the room.

Chapter 66

Allen Kline stared at his wife through the opened slats of the horizontal blinds covering the window to their room and exhaled. It was a breath he'd been holding ever since Patrick walked into his office and told him that he'd taken his sons, and that their lives had been dependent on his ability to keep his mouth closed.

He wanted to go to the police, but weakness had kept him from doing the right thing. At the time he thought he was being strong, thought that his not divulging what had been going on had been his sons' only hope. But standing with his head stitched and bandaged, his left wrist encased in a cast, and the index and middle finger of his right hand taped in splints, Allen looked at his wife holding their boys and could only embarrassingly acknowledge that he deserved no credit for his boys being alive.

The walls behind Allen's pupils began to sting as tears began to form. He'd done as he had been instructed to, or rather as he's been scared and threatened into doing, and because of that, innocent boys had died. It was a guilt that would remain for a long time. One that would never go away.

He took a breath and released it slowly. He hadn't seen his sons yet. He'd been conscious for the past half hour, but his shame had kept him away. He hadn't been ready to look his boys in their eyes yet. He hadn't been ready to deal with the scrutiny in Amanda's, which he was sure was what he would see in them. But as he stared at her, he saw not blame and disgust, but compassion. He saw an understanding. While she'd been strong enough to do what had to be done, she understood why he hadn't and she had forgiven him. It was in her eyes.

Amanda gave him a slight but warm smile and then her lips moved. He wasn't a professional lip reader, but he could tell that she'd said, "Come in."

Allen breathed in and out again. Behind the safety and privacy of their walls, he would tell them about a traumatized boy named Benjamin Patrick McCallum.

He gave his wife a nod and then, using his elbow, he got the knob on the door to turn down, and then pushed the door open and walked inside.

Six months later

Vance was on an unpaid suspension for taking the note left for Ben and for concealing the composite sketch Beto had made. It had been a formality really. Protocol. Everyone understood why and how he could have done what he was never supposed to do. The suspension, handed down by Stubbs, was given moreso that he could have time to heal.

He'd watched his best friend, his partner die in front of him. Add to that a tragic backstory and a very hurt and vengeful dual personality born from the events in the story, and Vance simply nodded when he was put on leave. Time was something he needed like the air he breathed. It had all been so much to take in. It was still hard to digest everything he'd found out. Ben had been abused as a child for two years, both physically and sexually by his father, and then at ten years of age, had watched, after revealing to his mother what had been happening to him, his father strangle his mother to death before shooting himself afterward. At some point during the time of the abuse, Ben had developed a dual personality who "helped" Ben deal with everything that had been happening. It was a tragedy that Ben somehow had survived. Or at least that's what he had thought. But what he and no one else for that matter, could have ever known, was that Ben's other personality, Patrick, had been hell bent on paying Ben back for what he'd considered weakness. He also wanted to payback Allen Kline, the first psychiatrist he'd come in contact with, who he considered a liar for telling Ben the truth: that none of what had happened had been Ben's fault.

Twenty-six years was how long Patrick waited. For Ben to move on, to get married, to have a child, and for that child to turn ten years old. And then he put his plan into effect.

It was a sad, tragic tale. One that Vance had been an unwilling character in.

Time. Vance couldn't help but wonder if there was ever going to be enough time to get past it all.

"Hey, baby."

Vance looked up. He'd been staring at a photograph of he and Ben standing beside one another with wide, smiles on their faces. Vance, ever the loner back then, was on Ben's right, while Mikey and Sarah stood on his left. It had been taken at Mikey's favorite spot in the park, the same location where one of the boys had been found. It had been a beautiful, sunny Saturday afternoon. The summer before Mikey's death, when everything had been right in the world.

Vance gave Alyssa a smile as she sat down beside him. "Hey, beautiful." He kissed her gently on her full lips and put his hand on her stomach, where his child was growing. His child. He still couldn't believe it. They say every cloud had a silver lining. Alyssa's news to him had been a silver lining that he had needed desperately.

Alyssa touched the glass covering the framed photo. "I wish I could have gotten to know him better," she said solemnly.

Vance sucked his lips in, nodded, and said, "Yeah…me, too."

Alyssa put her arm around him and pulled his head down to rest against her breast. "Are you okay?"

Vance sighed. "I miss him."

"I know," Alyssa said.

"He was supposed to be the godfather for my kid someday."

Alyssa held him tight and kissed him on his head as she ran her hands through his hair. "Oh, baby," she whispered.

Vance took a breath and let it out slowly. "You know…as sad as I am, I'm happy, too. He's not suffering anymore," Vance said, with an exhale. "He suffered for so long. Shit…more than I or anyone could have ever known. I'm glad he doesn't have to anymore. I've been trying to make sense of it all," Vance said, "and that's the one thing I've come to realize. He's free. Finally."

Alyssa kissed him on his head again. "Finally," she repeated.

Vance clenched his jaw and looked down at the photograph. "I have a name," he said, looking at his partner.

"Really? What is it?"

"Whether it's a boy or a girl, I want the name to be Michael." He rose up and looked at her, waiting for her reaction.

Alyssa was silent for a moment as she looked back at him. Then she smiled and said, "Michael Michelle, if it's a girl. Michael Benjamin if it's a boy."

"Those are nice names," Vance said. He smiled, kissed her on her lips again and then put his hand gently back on her stomach.

Chapter 67

Sarah stood stoically. A light drizzle was falling. April showers. She didn't care about the rain. Didn't really even notice it.

She was standing in front of Mikey's grave, staring at the epitaph on his tombstone made of marble.

Michael "Mikey" Benjamin McCallum.
Beautiful son. Treasured angel. Gone too soon.

"I miss you, my angel," she whispered. "I'll miss you forever."

Her son, gone too soon. It was still hard for Sarah to digest the horrible truth Vance had divulged to her. That the hands that had pummeled her son to death, had belonged to the man that loved him more than life itself. Six months later and it was still almost impossible to accept. That Ben could have killed his own child. But of course it hadn't been Ben. It had been a monster brought to life by a father's sins. A monster that had been intent on getting revenge, which he had gotten in the worst possible way.

She knelt down and placed one of two roses she was holding, on the end of his plot beside several other roses. Then she stood up and looked to the plot directly beside Mikey's. More tears fell as the speed and weight of the raindrops increased.

Ben.

She was supposed to have been moving on with him, both of them getting past the pain and rebuilding a life that had been chipped and cracked, but not yet completely broken. She wasn't supposed to have watched him die.

Sarah futilely wiped more tears away as the rain continued to fall heavily, and tried not to think about the last time she'd seen the man she would love forever. She had spent too much money and had spent too many hours in therapy trying to not go back to that moment of seeing a man she didn't recognize, standing at the end of the hallway, strangling a child just before a bullet pierced his skull and ended his life as he'd screamed out. She wiped more tears away. She couldn't see that.

"I...I don't blame you, Ben," she said, a knot thick in her throat. "I don't blame you."

In all of their years together, she had never seen a sign that someone else had been living inside of him. She couldn't help but wonder if Patrick had been present any time during their most private of moments. It was a scary thought that brought chills.

She bent down and placed the last rose in her hand, down beside others on the end of his plot, and then put her palm flat on the wet grass. As she did, a warm sensation came over her, and she swore she could feel Ben touching her back, his palm against hers. "I love you, Ben," she whispered, tears and rain falling. "Forever and always."

She remained still for a moment, letting the warm, familiar feeling pass through her, and then stood up and looked at the words engraved on his marble tombstone.

Benjamin "Ben" McCallum.
Devoted friend, husband and father.
Keep heaven safe for the rest of us.

Sarah looked from son to father and then turned and walked away. As she did, the rain suddenly stopped falling and the clouds separated, giving way to sunlight.

Epilogue

Eric looked out of the window with a slight smile on his face and stared at the activity going on outside. Little kids were riding their bikes with training wheels. Bigger kids were doing tricks on their dirt-bikes and skateboards. Some adults were standing around chit-chatting while the kids played. Others were washing their cars, trucks and min-vans. Everyone had a carefree expression on their faces. Muscles weren't tense, tension was non-existent. No one was worrying, stressing or afraid.

Life in the suburbs. So different from life on the streets.

Eric watched it all from the window of his new bedroom. Six months ago, he'd been lying in a hospital bed, alone, healing from a knife wound to his back, grieving over the loss of his friend, his adopted brother, Brian, who'd been killed as it turned out, not by a fake cop, but a real one with a dual personality. The story had been all over the internet. Interviews with the cop, Vance, other police officers, and the real cop's wife—well, widow now.

Eric had been part of interviews, too. People wanted to know about the kid who'd survived an attack from The Pacifier. Where had he come from? How had he managed to survive? Eric had to admit, he liked the attention. The fifteen minutes of fame. It made him feel important, necessary. He'd gone from being a kid on the street, a no-name, to being sought after. A kid with a voice that people wanted to hear. CBS, NBC, ABC, CNN—all of the networks came looking for him. It was very cool.

It was also the reason he was living where he was now, with his Mom's cousin, who he hadn't seen since his mother's death. She'd seen him on the television and had recognized him. Apparently she'd been looking for him ever since she found out he had run away from home, and when she saw him on the news, she caught the next flight out of town to get to him. Eric didn't really remember her, having only met her one time, but when he saw her, he knew right away that she was related because she looked like the only picture of his mother that he always kept with him.

After telling her why he had run away and why he would run away again if anyone made him go back home, she hugged him tightly and told him that he wasn't going to have to worry about being sent back, because there was nowhere for him to go back to. His father was dead. During the year he'd been gone, his father had been drunk one night and had gotten into a fight with the wrong man. Relief fell over Eric when she told him the news. For the first time, since he'd run away, he felt safe.

Before he was fully healed, arrangements were made for him to go home with her, where she was living alone with her seventeen-year-old son, Derrick. Now six months later, she was his legal guardian and treated him as though she'd birthed him herself, and Derrick had very much become like an older brother.

Eric smiled as the kids played. Never in a million years did he think his life would have changed so dramatically. A new family, a new environment. Clouds had finally dissipated for him and sunlight was shining through. Life was beautiful.

But it was at times sad, too.

At least when he found himself thinking about Brian. There really wasn't anything Eric could have done to have prevented his death from happening—his therapist helped him understand that. But still…he'd made a promise he hadn't been able to keep it, and fair to himself or not, he would always feel a modicum of responsibility for Brian's death.

Eric watched the kids play and smiled.

He had a home now. A family that treated him the way families were supposed to treat their loved ones. For Brian and the rest of the kids the real cop had killed, Eric would make the most of the gift he'd been given.

Enjoy a sneak peek of the next intense tale of suspense by Dwayne Joseph

Almost Dead

Coming September 2014

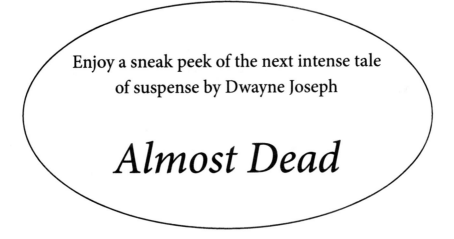

Prologue

1 year ago

"Believe it or not Sean…I've never done anything like this before. I've thought about it. Fleeting thoughts really as I watched movies or read books. I mean who hasn't wondered what it was like? I think most, if not all of us, at one point in time or another have fantasized or daydreamed about how powerful this must be. I'm sure you have right? When you were at your angriest, your most enraged…you've thought about doing it. For a split second or two, or maybe even three, you've thought about letting go. I know you have. Don't look at me like that. You've wanted to kill before."

Sean Scott moaned as the man he'd never seen before stabbed him in his side. This was the fourth time his blood had been drawn.

"Of course you would never actually do it," the man said, continuing with words Sean barely heard. "Because…well…that's just crazy isn't it? Killing…taking someone's life is immoral and insane. Right?" The man slid his hand beneath Sean's chin and raised his head, forcing Sean to look at him. "Do you think I'm crazy, Sean? Do you think I'm insane?"

Sean stared at the man through half-closed eyes. He was shivering from pain, fear and blood-loss. He wanted to scream, to call for help, but his throat was raw from doing too much of that already. Besides, screaming again was pointless as a rag that had been duct-taped into his mouth, prevented sound from going beyond the confines of the room they were in. So Sean just stared. As tears welled in his eyes, as blood seeped out from his right and left sides, his back and left thigh…he stared and thought about his wife and three sons. He was never going to see them again. He knew it. He could see it in the eyes of the stranger glaring back at him with a twisted snarl. He was going to die.

"Believe it or not…I'm not crazy, Sean. I'm not a psycho or some twisted, evil individual who gets off on this. Really, I'm not. But I can see how you would think that of me, because if the shoe were on the other foot, and I was the one tied to a chair, forced to endure incredible pain the way you are, I would think that. There would be no doubt in my mind that you were certifiably fucked in the head."

The man let go of Sean's chin, and took a few steps backward. Sean, weak and half-gone could do nothing but let his chin drop down to his chest. He took a slow pained breath as agony rifled through him. *Why was this happening to him? What had he done?* The last thing he remembered was telling his wife over the phone that he would be home soon before ending the call and opening his car door. The next thing he knew he was tied to a chair, with plastic stretched out beneath him, stuck in a cellar of some sort, being tortured.

What had happened after he told his wife goodbye?

Sean bled and shook as he grew colder with each passing minute. Thoughts of the movie *Saw* came to his mind. Death. Oh God….it was coming for him. He raised his head slowly, and looked through his cloudy, tear-filled vision at the man who was torturing him slowly. He was tall and slender in the way a person who ate only fruits and vegetables was. His head was bald, his nose thin. A thick grey goatee framed his mouth. He wore nothing but a pair of black boxer briefs. Sean wanted to ask who he was. He wanted to ask why he had done this to him. More importantly, he wanted to beg to be let go. But the rag was too thick and the duct tape applied over it, unyielding.

"I'm nowhere close to being crazy, Sean," the man said, running his finger along the edge of the hunting knife, playing with Sean's blood. "In fact, I'm really very rational." He smiled, sending chills along Sean's spine.

Unable to keep his head up any longer, Sean's chin dropped down to his chest again.

"This is really a fascinating experience," the man continued. "It's much more thrilling than I could have ever imagined it would be. This is going to be the only time that I'll ever do something like this, but I can easily see how someone could become addicted to it."

Sean's body shook harder as the man's feet shuffled on the plastic, which had undoubtedly been laid out to gather Sean's blood. *Please God. Please let me be dreaming*, he thought, squeezing his eyes tightly and begging again to just be having the most horrific nightmare imaginable. *Please let me open my eyes and be back in my bed, in my house, next to my wife. Please let me see my kids come running into the room.*

Please!

"I want you to understand something, Sean," the man said standing before him. "I want you to understand that I'm not crazy. I want you to know that what I'm doing is just necessary research." The man placed his hand down on Sean's shoulder.

Sean tried not to, but couldn't help it, and began to whimper as tears fell hard and heavy from his eyes.

"You have to die, Sean and I have to be the one to kill you. I need to know every nuance of this experience, Sean. The sound, the smell, the feel. It's about respecting my craft, my passion. That's why we're here. This isn't about insanity. It's about love."

The man gave Sean's shoulder a firm squeeze, and then reached behind his head and pulled on the duct tape, unwinding it from around Sean's head. The action should have hurt because Sean could feel tufts of his hair being pulled out in the process. But he was beyond pain.

The man removed the rag from Sean's mouth. "Scream for me, Sean," he said, driving the hunting knife deep into Sean's midsection. "This is the final piece of research that I'll need." "Scream for me," he said again. "I need to know what death sounds like."

For a few seconds there was nothing but silence as Sean's mouth hung open. And then air began to sigh out from his lungs. His dying breath. He began to shake violently as his body fought the inevitable.

Sean looked up at the man who'd made him his lab rat. Research he'd said. He tried to think of his wife and three sons. He wanted their smiles to be the last thing he envisioned.

But as the pain from the final stab began to fade away, there was but one thought going through his mind; that the man had been right. He had wondered once or twice what it was like to kill.

Sean screamed.

Chapter One

Present Day

Vance Newsome ground his teeth together. He'd seen a dead body before, but never one like this. What lay before him was brutal in a way that made sense only in the movies when it was done for show. Arms cut off at the elbows. Legs cut at the knees.

Vance stared down at Ryan Reynolds. His eyes were void now, but Vance could still see the horror that had been in them, the absolute dread. There was no sound escaping from his opened mouth, but Vance could hear the scream. Ryan's death had been a painful one. Vance ground his teeth together as sweat gathered on his brow. It was a humid and sticky. He said, "Shit like this makes me consider changing my choice of occupation.

"Shit like this is why I love this job."

Vance raised his eyebrows, shook his head and averted his gaze from Ryan Reynolds' frozen look of terror to a thick, light-skinned black man with red hair, who was squatted down just off to Ryan's side. "You're a sick individual, Reds."

Reds, the lead medical examiner, looked up at Vance. "One man's garbage…" he said.

"I don't see any treasure in this," Vance said. "I don't see anything at all except for a man who was made to suffer."

Reds nodded and as the rest of his forensics team searched the surrounding area for clues, Vance knew they weren't going to find, Reds said, "Well, according to whoever left the note, Ryan was made to suffer for a 'worthy cause'."

Vance worked his jaw again. He'd been at home getting some much needed rest when his cell phone went off. The time had been two in the morning and for the first time in a month, his newborn son, Michael, or Mikey as he called him, had fallen asleep before four A.M. Vance had heard people talk about infants having their days and nights mixed up, but he never imagined it would have been that bad. For three consecutive weeks, he spent hours holding his son, while his wife Alyssa slept, circling his coffee table, sofa and loveseat, begging his son to tell him why he felt the need to cry if his pamper wasn't wet and his belly was full. Although he treasured every moment, it was still a torture Vance had been unprepared for.

Sleep had been so welcomed and so heavy that he hadn't even been dreaming when his cell phone went off. He wanted to ignore the call, but he was a homicide detective, and when his phone rang in the middle of the night, then that meant somewhere there was a body waiting for him.

The call had come from his new partner, Jose Reyes. A fresh from the streets Jr. Detective who'd been promoted for his tenacity. It was a partnership Vance was still getting used to.

Reyes told Vance about two couples walking home after a night out clubbing. They'd cut through an alley they used as a shortcut and found Ryan Reynolds' mutilated body. They called the police right away. The first officer on the scene quickly arrived and found not only Ryan's body, but a note typed in red ink that read:

Here lies the body of Ryan Reynolds. A family man who died not in vain, but rather in the name of research. His was a noble death.

The discovery of the note prompted the call to Stubblefield, or Stubbs as they called him, who then gave the honor of waking Vance to Reyes. Ryan Reynolds was the third victim in as many months that had died nobly.

Vance flexed his jaw again. He was tired of noble deaths. "Timeframe?" he asked Reds, his eyes still on Ryan's. For some reason he found himself unable to look away.

Reds gnawed on his bottom lip, then said, "Based on the rigor that's set in, I'd say eight hours. And although I won't know for sure until I dig deeper, just at first glance I'd say he bled to death."

Vance frowned and surveyed the crime scene ablaze by high-intensity lighting. Other than Ryan's torso and the note, there was nothing else to be found. "Christ," he said. He looked down to Ryan again and shook his head. As he did, his partner appeared behind him. He'd been talking to the two couples.

"Well, as expected, they didn't have much more to tell me than they did the first union the scene."

Vance kept his lips pressed firmly together. He hadn't expected there to be any more details. He took a breath, exhaled and turned and faced Reyes. A Mexican-American, Reyes was a short man built like a gymnast with broad shoulders. He was twenty-five but looked about two years younger, with a bald head and a clean-shaven face, save for a soul patch sitting just beneath his bottom lip.

Reyes cracked knuckles scarred from a youth spent living on the tough streets of LA. "They were out, they danced, had drinks and were on their way home and were taking the alley as a shortcut like they usually do. Next thing they knew they were staring at a dead cut-up body. They backed away. The ladies threw up and the guys called the police. End of story."

"How are they holding up?"

Reyes shrugged. "The ladies are all tears and the fellas are trying to act like they're not fucked up, too."

Vance nodded. The first time he'd come across a dead body had jarred him, too. Now he was just numb. Discoveries like Ryan Reynolds made him wish he could go back to being jarred. "No other witnesses, right?"

Reyes shook his head. "None."

"Okay. Have them taken down to the station for further questioning." Reyes nodded, turned and gave instructions to a uniformed officer to take them down and make them comfortable until they got there. As he did, Vance turned back to what was left of Ryan Reynolds and sighed.

Reyes stepped beside him. "What the fuck kind of freak would do this, man?"

Vance clenched his jaws and continued to stare at the man who'd been killed and tossed like garbage. What kind of freak? he wondered. He had no idea.

"Reds," he said, looking to the M.E. as he spoke to his assistant, Jerry Birch. "Is there anything else here that's useful?"

Reds looked over at him with a 'yeah, right' expression on his face.

Vance nodded. "Give me a shout when the autopsy's done."

Reds said he would and then turned back to Birch. "Let's tag him and bag him," he said.

Vance gave Ryan one last glance, clenched his jaws, and wondered what the man's last minutes must have been like. What thoughts had gone through his mind? Had he thought about his family, his friends? His own mortality? Did he beg and plead for his life to be spared? Is that what the killer wanted?

He shook his head.

"There's got to be a ton of white guys named Ryan Reynolds in this city, man. How the hell are we supposed to get in contact with his family without being able to ID him?" Reyes asked.

Vance raised his eyebrows. "The note said that Ryan was a family man. I'm pretty sure in a few hours his family's going to get in contact with us."

Reyes bobbed his head and said with a frown. "Yeah."

Vance took a breath and wiped sweat away from his forehead as a streak of lightning flashed in the dark sky while thunder rumbled in the distance.

Three bodies in three months. All in the name of research. One female, a Latina named Ines Valdez, killed with a butcher knife. Two males. The first, an African American named Mike Simpson, beaten to death with a lead pipe. And now, family man, Ryan Reynolds, Caucasian, dismembered.

Inez, Mike and Ryan. They all lived in different areas, had different friends, different faiths, listened to different music, earned different levels of income. In no way, shape or form did their lives intersect, yet they all died noble deaths in the name of research.

"Reporters are huddled. Are we giving them anything this time?"

Vance sighed and looked at Reyes. "No comments for now. We need to meet with Stubbs and decide what info we're going to give out first."

Reyes nodded. "Okay."

Vance took a look over and watched as Reds and his team got Ryan Reynolds loaded into a black bodybag. Someone somewhere was worrying, wondering where Ryan was. They were probably calling his cell phone, providing he had one, over and over and over.

Vance shook his head. *Research,* he thought. He frowned and then headed away from the alley. As he walked, raindrops began to fall.

CPSIA information can be obtained at www.ICGtesting.com
Printed in the USA
LVOW10s2135070815

449341LV00001B/80/P

9 781625 173683